WORLDS
APART

WILLIAM L FRAME

Fulton Books, Inc.
Meadville, PA

Published by Fulton Books 2020

ISBN 978-1-64654-353-3 (paperback)
ISBN 978-1-64654-354-0 (digital)

Printed in the United States of America

For Harry

PROLOGUE

The *Fulcrum*

E arth's colonial starship, the *Fulcrum*, sailing under autonomous control through the vast, empty distances of interstellar space, executed an emergency course correction eighty-six years into a one hundred thirty-seven-year voyage. Hibernation pods containing the ship's flight engineers Michael and Kera Collins were automatically activated with the unscheduled course change. Sleeping beside their children's pods, the husband-and-wife team awakened to the projected hologram persona of Cooper, the ship's AI appearing to be standing beside their pods as it waited for a response.

"How long?" Mike asked, groggy from the effects of hibernation.

The AI answered, "Eighty-six years, fifty-six days, twelve hours, fifteen—"

"We got it, Cooper. What's the situation?" Kera asked, interrupting the emotionless AI entity. With ten thousand souls in hibernation, it was their task to maintain the ship's flight systems and verify all course changes that diverged from the original programmed flight path in the event of an emergency.

"My sensors have detected the impact of a rogue planet one hundred eighty-three miles in diameter colliding with an orbiting planetary body with a diameter of one thousand two hundred sixty-one miles. The system is WLF1954, which is aligned with our destination's flight path. The planet was the seventh planet composed of a rocky core covered by a three-thousand-foot layer of methane ice.

The impact was a direct hit, completely destroying both in the event. The system's sun is pulling the debris inward. The *Fulcrum* was to sail through the planetary system, but the highly unlikely and impossible doomsday scenario just happened. I cannot avoid the debris field created by the impact. The debris is expanding outward in all directions as the system's sun pulls it back inward, forming an umbrella of debris. I've altered our course to avoid most of the debris. Our best option is to sail directly into planetary system WLF1954 and orbit the third planet called Planos, which is habitable. I calculate it will take twenty-one hours, fourteen minutes, and thirteen seconds to position the *Fulcrum* behind the planet and use its mass as a shield. The emergency requires my programming to continue transmitting a subspace message to Imperial Command, streaming our shipwide status until the event passes without incident or we are destroyed.

"The planetary survey records list the planet as inhabited by a humanoid species. I've launched a probe to scan the surface and confirm the survey's findings of humanoid life," Cooper informed the pair as they quickly dressed into their ship coveralls.

"How long before we position the ship behind the planet of this system?" Mike asked, zipping up the front of his coveralls.

"Full tactical analysis will be provided on the bridge," Cooper flatly responded to the question.

He glanced at his wife, who was looking worriedly at her sleeping children, when her eyes rose from them to lock with her man's. "They'll be fine," Mike assured his wife.

"Yes, I know, but mother's worry," she said with a smile and then ordered the AI. "Cooper, meet us on the bridge." Kera turned away from the hologram and faced her husband as the hologram disappeared. "Eighty-six years, we're barely two-thirds of the way there and we can't go back to sleep. What are we going to do?"

"I don't know, babe. Let's find out the full extent of what we're facing," he said to her as he reached out for her hand. Quickly they made their way down the corridor to the elevator that would take them up to the ship's flight deck and the bridge.

Once on the bridge, Cooper materialized to stand before them on the right side of the elevator doors. The pair stepped just inside the doors as they stopped and looked at the ship's view screen on the opposite wall. With Cooper's usual efficiency, the view screen depicted the enormity of the calamity threatening the ship. From their current position, Cooper had run multiple simulations showing alternate escape trajectories in dim red lines. All failed, except for one boldly lit green line, indicating their current course toward the planetary systems third planet.

"What's the odds of getting the ship into position before the meteor storm hits the planet?" Mike asked the AI's hologram.

"There is a 65 percent probability of success. We'll have a thirty-seven-minute window once we enter orbit to safely position the ship behind the planet," Cooper flatly answered and waited for a response.

"What's the danger of the other 35 percent?" Mike questioned the AI, wanting to know all possible options and risks involved.

"The 35 percent represents debris mass too small for our sensors to detect. Our shields are designed to protect the ship from small objects in our direct path. However, if caught broadside by a seventeen-thousand-mile-an-hour cosmic debris storm, the ship will be compromised. Worst-case scenario, shipwide decompression seconds before our drive systems explode." Cooper's emotionless statement filled the heavy silence on the bridge and chilled them both to the core of their souls.

"Cooper," Kera asked. "So the planet is habitable?"

"Yes, but while you were on the elevator, the probe has confirmed there are indications of a young dominant humanoid species emerging on this world. Compared to human technological advancement, they are still infants. On Earth, you would refer to them as hunter-gatherers or Stone Age people."

"If we survive this ordeal and the ship is unable to continue, can we colonize this world?" Mike asked, looking at his wife, hoping it wouldn't come to such dire circumstances, but damn the consequences if it did.

"Yes. However, the Imperial Scientific Charter prevents me from releasing colonial equipment. The cargo holds are magnetically locked and completely sealed off from the interior of the ship until we've reached our destination. As you're aware, the charter's bylaws concerning developing life-forms are binding and absolute. Since the probe has detected an intelligent humanoid species living on the planet, even in an emergency. I'm forbidden to provide colonists with a technological advantage over a developing species. You must use your intellect to survive and adapt to this world or perish. I'm only permitted to release life pods. I'm not permitted to take further action."

"If we suffer hull breaches, how much time will we have to evacuate the ship?" Kera asked the computerized image, hating the AI's coldness and lack of humanity.

Cooper's image turned to face her, its frozen motionless blue eyes staring at her as it answered with a response as heartless as the entity itself. "It's impossible to predict the probability or consequences of an astronomical event. You may have only minutes or hours to evacuate. The *Fulcrum's* future depends on the severity of impacts and where on the ship they occur."

"Why do we have to honor the Imperial Charter? We've been asleep for eighty-six years, and with the empire embroiled in a war when we left, our home is probably dead. Why not save the last humans alive in our galaxy and allow us to colonize this one? Who's going to know?" Mike argued, thinking if the ship is damaged and unable to continue, charter or no charter, they will colonize this world regardless of what the AI said.

"Earth is not dead. Over the course of our flight, I have not lost contact. My automatic subspace communications system exchanges data with imperial control on a daily basis. You will be happy to know, the empire lives on with your grandniece Isabella Whitlock guiding the Earth's future as empress. Earth is thriving under the stipulations of the postwar peace treaty.

"Humanity has finally learned to live in peace for the prosperity of all. After the war, the surviving human populations demanded the empire destroy every means of waging war and adopt a highly restricted technological and agrarian trade-based society. Beneficial manufactured goods, crops, and animals are now the bedrock of imperial trade. The empire is working on restoring the Earth after countless generations of mankind's careless stewardship. Every region of Earth contributes to the manning of the imperial spacedocks for the construction of interstellar cargo and colonial starships. Humans are spreading out among the stars of the Milky Way and now reside on three planets outside Earth's solar system.

"There have been seven colonial starships launched since our departure. Two are following our flight path. Therefore, the Imperial Charter and its bylaws remain in authority and cannot be violated," Cooper's emotionless entity responded, making Mike feel he had been talked down to by a machine as if he were still a child, and it pissed him off. Within his mind, he only heard an executioner pronouncing their impending death.

"There seems no option but to go for the planet and take our chances," Kera announced and then ordered the AI sarcastically, "Cooper! I really hate being late to a party. So you better bust your ass and get us there! Course change confirmed."

Mike was still holding on to his wife's hand and felt a little reassured by her confident, calm demeanor as she evaluated the situation and possible outcomes of their predicament. "Let's pray the thirty-seven-minute window is enough time to position the ship without incurring major damage to vital systems," Mike said, giving her hand a gentle squeeze of reassurance.

"Yes, let's pray indeed," Kera quietly responded while wondering if her grandniece regarded them as traitors, outlaws, or cowards for escaping her brother's wrath by kidnapping his heir to the throne, her daughter, Jennifer Hendricks.

CHAPTER 1

The Hunter

The sun slowly rose above the horizon, streaming golden light over the continent's major mountain ranges—ragged snow-capped rocky peaks that effectively separated the continents distinctly different northern and southern landmasses. Light streaming between the ranges towering peaks slowly revealed a panoramic expanse of forests and lush green grasslands stretching southward far in the distance. A hunter stood below the mountain's southern face as the sun's glistening rays began to slowly burn away a chilly blanket of foggy haze from the air. Shivering slightly within his furs, the hunter welcomed the morning's clear light and approaching warmth. He watched intently as the mountain's gloomy shadows slowly began to recede from the grasslands below to reveal what had been hidden in the darkness of night. The hunter smiled as he spotted a large herd of runner beasts grazing on the abundance of long blades of grass that covered the ground in a lush green carpet.

Standing within the trees in the shadow of the mountain, the young hunter scanned his eyes over a herd of runners grazing in the valley and pondered his safest approach. His arrow was held firmly across his bow by strong fingers used to the weapons tension, ready to launch in an instant. His hunt had brought him downwind of the herd peacefully roaming and grazing as they walked on the long grass in the morning light. The herd was still too far out of his bow's range.

So he loosened his finger's tight grip and let his arrow slide slowly back to rest between them.

Staying within the trees, the hunter moved quietly downhill, always keeping his eyes open for danger as he moved cautiously toward his prey. His eyes constantly scanned the area around him because sometimes he was not the only hunter in need of fresh meat. A lone hunter, unfamiliar with what inhabits the terrain around him, could easily find himself one of the hunted, often with a deadly outcome for the unwary hunter.

A few rare times, a hunting party would encounter a kessra pride, the region's deadly six-legged carnivore, twice the weight of most hunters. When encountered on a hunt, hunters often retreated giving the mighty carnivores their space and allowed them to hunt.

Kessras were fearless creatures gifted by the land with a long, tapered snout and a bite that locks while grinding a mouth full of long, sharp teeth. Able to run using all six legs or only the back four gave the kessra an advantage, they could slash and grab at their prey on the run. Their short fur coats were the color of dried grass, which concealed them to near invisibility during the hot moons. They were the ultimate pack hunters. Fearless killers so sleek and swift that when hunting as a coordinated group, it made their deadly strikes seem almost effortless. Kessra prides rarely hunted the day after a successful kill. With their bellies full of meat, kessras preferred to lie in the sun and sleep off their gluttony. To the hunters of his tribe, an encounter with kessras during a hunt was an omen of good fortune, insurance of a safer hunt the next day.

No sound from the hunter's moccasins soft leather soles could be heard as he maneuvered his way through the trees, ever closer to within his bow's striking distance. The runners were still unaware of his presence as he slowly stalked them, keeping himself downwind of the herd's dominant and alert stallion. He was a tall, well-proportioned runner for his breed and bore the scars of many suitors' challenges over the seasons on his rump and shoulders. The tall golden-brown stallion was a stern ruler of his herd, biting or kicking any runner who tried to disobey his commands. The hunter crept closer, admiring the beautiful, fearless, and formidable leader of the herd.

His concealing shelter of trees soon thinned out, giving way to small evergreen shrubs and long green blades of grass, forcing the hunter to conceal himself by lying down on his belly in the damp grass. His leather tunic and trousers absorbed some of the moisture as he crawled ever closer to his target, unmindful of the various insects inhabiting the grass.

His travel rations were nearly depleted; he needed this kill. He would only get one chance to shoot before the herd scattered in panic but only if he was quiet, patient, and quick to act when the time was right. Every so often, he'd raise his eyes above the grass to mark his progress toward the herd. Now sure of being within killing range of his bow, he slowly raised himself up onto a knee, keeping as low to the ground as the long, thick grass would allow.

To the right of his position, he spotted and selected his prey, a young brown colt scampering around his mare with the playfulness of youth. He estimated the colt's age was no more than half a season, just right to provision one man. Sadly, while thinking the colt's short life would end to benefit his own, he drew his arrow back to the bows full tension, stood, and loosed his dart at the unsuspecting animal. The arrow's flight was swift and true striking his intended target through the breast and into its heart. He watched as the shocked colt jumped into the air with the arrow's deadly penetration and fell back to the ground beside its mare, still and lifeless.

The mare immediately sensed her colt was lost and shrilly whinnied her warning, alerting the stallion of danger. Instantly, the stallion ran toward him in defense of his mares. The young hunter stood his ground with another arrow already notched and ready in his bow as the majestic stallion valiantly charged toward him, as the mares obeyed his commands and withdrew.

He drew his weapon back to its fullest extent as the stallion continued to advance. Calming his excitement, he took a few slow deep breaths steadying the arrow poised for instant flight. He watched the stallion race bravely toward his position when suddenly it turned away and swiftly ran up behind his mares. He whinnied as it ran behind them, sounding out his commands, pushing them ever onward, racing away to safety, down across the plain far away from the unexpected death. Leaving in their wake a wide swath of brown churned-up ground, effectively separating the herd from the silent, deadly, and unfamiliar predator that sprang out of the tall grass.

With a sigh of relief and an exuberant whoop of triumph, the young hunter sprang forward and ran toward his life-giving kill. Once the butchering was complete and the meat dried, the colt would provide him with at least a moon's travel rations that could be easily carried in his backpack. Looking around to ensure no other predator was seeking to challenge his claim to the kill, the strong young hunter hefted the dead colt over his shoulders and walked out of the valley toward a cropping of trees and shrubs partially covering a narrow opening to a cave. The cave was large enough to house a small tribe for the winter; he had found it by chance in the waning light two days ago. From the mouth of the cave, the trees' and shrubs' haphazard growth obscured the view of the valley and noisy herd beasts that roamed the grassy plain. The cave's secluded location provided him with a very secure place in which to prepare his kill.

His journey south began at first thaw of winter's freezing grip with his mother's wish of a safe return. He left her carrying a backpack filled with travel rations containing pouches of wild rice, oats, wheat, assorted dried fruit, dried meat, and his favorite snack, stone-baked berry-and-grain honey cakes as well as spare clothes and useful tools. It was now late spring, and it had taken the young adventurer nearly the whole season to cross the mountain's perilous gap without injury or incident worth remembering, except that he had crossed it.

His backpack was much lighter now. His spare clothes, sleeping fur, various lengths of coiled rawhide strips, extra knives, a pair of wooden spoons, two wooden cooking bowls, a few flintknapping tools, two large shards of flint, and an empty water pouch were the extent of his worldly possessions other than his travel rations, which were nearly depleted consisting of two thin strips of dried meat, a single hard cake, and the remains of a grain pouch mixed with the last of the dried fruit.

He had decided not to eat his last hard cake until he made a successful hunt, to savor it as a treat, in order to honor the animal's sacrifice with his mother's specialty snack. The thought of his mother brought a brief smile to the otherwise stern face of the young hunter as he entered the cave and set his burden down beside the wall by the entrance. He then knelt beside the smoldering coals of his morning fire situated near the mouth of the cave and began to blow over the coals, which turned the smoldering embers a bright red with the influx of fresh air. He added small thin twigs until flickers of flame began to dance upon them and then a few larger broken branches for the tiny flames to consume. Within moments, he was warming his hands with the little fire's increasing heat as he added more branches from a pile of sticks resting beside the pit. He set the last of the branches from his pile into the fire. The flames rose in the stone pit, kicking its wavy tendrils higher into the air illuminating the cave around him. The hunter then added a couple of logs as thick as his arms to the flames, increasing its heat to comfortably warm and dry the caves damp, cool air. He checked his store of firewood and figured it would last the night.

The area around his firepit had been prepared the night before in anticipation of a successful hunt. Three sets of upright branches buried deeply into the cave floor for support were strung with the lengths of leather strips from his supplies stored in the backpack. They would serve as drying racks. The fire's smoky heat would dehydrate the meat into hard jerky to be eaten dry as he walked or cooked in a bowl of simmering stew.

The hunter began the arduous task of butchering his kill by carrying the colt back out onto the grass, far enough away from the cave to keep him and his meat safe from predators and scavengers that would soon be attracted by the smell of fresh blood. Working quickly, he gathered up an armful of the long grass and began to weave the tough fibrous blades into a mat large enough and tough enough to hold the butchered strips of meat. His work was quick and efficient, and he soon had a thick tightly woven mat ready to hold the meat. He worked with the sureness of long practice, and before long, a respectful quantity of meat was piled high on the woven mat. He then covered the meat with the colt's inner hide and began to drag the loaded mat back to his cave, leaving the bones and scraps to the scavengers and small predators sure to be drawn to the area by the smell of fresh blood.

It was late in the afternoon before he returned safely inside the warm cave with the meat of his kill. The fire had died down but still had flames flickering on the burning wood, causing the shadows of the empty drying racks to sway across the cavern walls. The hunter added more wood to the fire and began the task of hanging the meat to dry. It was dark outside the cave by the time he had all the meat slung over the three drying racks near his blazing fire, letting the smoke and indirect heat begin the drying process. Rather than throwing out the grass mat, he rolled it up and tossed it into the flames to burn so no animal would be drawn by its smell to his cave, and if one did happen by, his fire and scent would keep it away. Tired from his day's work, he rolled up the colt's hide fur side out and placed it in the back of the cave, intending to scrape off the hide's inner membranes the next day. "It will make a fine sleeping fur," he said to the empty cave as he walked outside in order to relieve himself of a full bladder before lying down to sleep through the chilly night.

CHAPTER 2

Out of the Night's Sky

As the hunter stood outside the cave, letting his stream fall to the ground. He looked upward into the heavens to witness a meteor streaking across the night sky and then another and another. Through his eyes, it appeared the lights were falling out of the heavens in a fiery rain. He believed the mysterious lights within the heavens to be the firepits of his ancestors, and they were falling down all around him. Normally, he enjoyed gazing at the countless lights shining brightly in the night sky, but tonight the view above his head frightened him like never before. Often when growing up, he'd listen to the elders tell their nighttime stories as the tribe gathered around the fire. When they viewed a falling fire in the night sky, the elders would welcome an ancestor's rebirth to the land. A child born under such auspicious circumstances was generally believed to inherit an ancestor's spirit with its first breath of life.

Quickly relieved of his need, the young hunter settled himself, turned, and raced toward the entrance of his cave. Unexpectedly, a bright blinding light burst high in the distant night sky, stopping him in his tracks, as the burst turned the night into day for a fraction of a second and then back into the night, leaving him in total darkness. His night vision slowly returned as his eyes adjusted to the darkness once more, and he looked upward at multiple streaks of fire falling from the sky as one fire high above the land exploded, flaring brightly in the heavens, and then disappeared. Never had he seen fires in the sky fall to the land in mass. Then below the fiery burst, he spotted something different falling from the heavens in the opposite direction of the streaking fires and it appeared to be coming right at his valley, at him, as if to avenge a wrong.

Its approach was swift and horrifying. In utter fear and panic, he dived for the safety of his cave hitting the ground just as the fiery ball violently impacted with the land. Creating in his ears what he could only imagine as the roaring of a thousand beasts calling out in unison. He lay terrified in the dim glow of the fires, paralyzed and in total fear of his life as it churned up the land outside the entrance of his cave. He felt the heat of its passing through the thickness of his clothes as it drove itself deeper into the land until its momentum stopped, and only an utter horrifying silence remained within the eerie darkness of night.

Slowly the incessant chirping and clicking of the night's insects inhabiting the tall grass began to fill the silence with familiar sounds, calming the stricken hunter's nerves. Warily he rose to his feet choking and coughing on the smoke from inside the cave as well as from the outside. The bushes in front of the cave's entrance were burning, so he ran quickly around them in search of fresh air to breathe. Able to get clear of the choking smoke, he stopped with his chest heaving in pain. He fell to his knees, bracing his torso with shaking hands, sucking in lungfuls of clean air as quickly as he could to clear his lungs of the foul smoke. As he was finally able to breathe without pain, his eyes were drawn to the fiery destruction outside his cave.

Moving closer to stand on the crest of a trench made by the objects passing, he turned his head in the direction of the objects fall in time to witness what his mind could only accept. An ancestor had returned in a fiery stone intent on living another life on land. Fear gripped the young hunter as he watched the ancestor stumble from the stone and move slowly away before falling awkwardly to the ground as if wounded.

However, frightening the night had become, compassion for an injured person compelled him into action. He ran toward the figure and knelt beside it but was taken aback by the ancestor's strange garments. Aware of his presence, the ancestor mumbled some incoherent sounds, waved an arm toward the stone it had climbed out, and slipped into darkness. A clear shield covered the head and face, but moisture from its breathing fogged the inner surface. Cautiously, he slapped the side of the strange shield with his fingers, hoping to revive the ancestor. By doing so, he accidentally hit a button, which unlocked a shaped ring of shiny stone around the neck that split into two pieces, separating the head shield from its clothing. He gently slipped it over the prone figures head and set the shield aside, laying the ancestor's head softly in the grass.

Concerned by the ancestor's erratic arm gesture, he stood and looked toward the trench. He walked over to the crest and began climbing down a wall of charred soil. Cautiously approaching the burning wreckage to peer inside the opening, he became aware for the first time that he held no weapon within his grasp. The charred surface covered the entire length of the oblong object, but upon reaching the opening, he realized the object was a made thing. Made by the ancestors of a strange substance that was as hard as the hardest stone. He peered inside and gasped in wonder at the interior of the eerie structure, filled with tiny multicolored lights flashing rapidly in the darkness, making his eyes blink. The brightest of all, a slow pulsing blue orb just bright enough in the gloom to illuminate another ancestor slumped over in an awkward position secured to a strange device. He didn't notice the pebble-sized puncture wound in the shell or through the ancestor's clothing concealing blood still seeping from the fatal wound. It was apparent the land had denied this ancestor another chance at life. Nothing could be done, so he left the body inside the strange shell and returned to the one, which survived its fiery flight down to the land.

As he looked down upon the ancestor, he was surprised to see a young woman's face. She had pale white skin with thin arched eyebrows, slightly slanted eyes, a slender nose, full lips, and a strong chin. Beneath a yellow tight-fitting hood covering her head, he saw a few fiery strands of red hair sticking out in disarray. "She's beautiful," he heard himself say as he stared at her in wonder before picking her up and carrying her to his cave.

He laid her down on his sleeping furs behind the drying racks and began tending to her needs. His first assumption of her being wounded in the fall was correct; her leg was broken. However, her garments trapped her body inside, and he could see no obvious way to remove them. Gently he rolled her onto her side and saw just beneath the shaped ring, a seam running from the ring to the base of her spine with a small tab partially covered by the garment's material. He gave a gentle tug on the tab and let go in shock as he watched the tab slide down the length of the seam separating the material without assistance. Beneath the ring, the material stretched, allowing the ring to be removed from around her neck by slipping it over her head. He rolled her over once more on her back and proceeded to remove the bulky garment as best he could without adding further injury. Not knowing if the garment was needed, he set it aside.

With a clear view of her, he noticed the strange tight-fitting material covering her head also covered her entire body except for her feet and arms. Taking care not to cut her with his bone knife, he pried his fingers between the material and her skin just above the ankle and cut a slit up to her knee, exposing the broken bone jutting up under her skin.

The hunter was relieved the broken bone had not punctured her skin. He carefully examined her wound with his fingers, letting his soft touch guide their way along the length of her broken bone until he knew where to align the break. He couldn't help but notice her thighs and calves were slender, strong, and used to hard work. He then wondered if life was as hard in the heavens as it was on the land?

The hunter shook his head to quell his questioning mind and concentrated on the girl's wound. It would have been easier with another pair of hands to hold her down while he reset the bone, but no one was around to lend him any assistance. So in order to set her leg properly, he'd have to do it the hard way and hope for the best. He then stood to straddle her pelvis and sat down, pinning her to the ground with his weight. He then grabbed her ankle with both hands and slowly pushed his body forward keeping his arms extended, twisting and stretching her leg until he felt the bone snap back into place. He then eased his hold on her leg, letting her stretched-out muscles relax and hold the bone in place. The hunter then went over to the colt's hide in the back of the cave and cut off a sizable portion of the fresh hide. He returned to her side, and keeping the fur next to her skin, he wrapped the broken leg with the moist hide, tying it with multiple strands of leather above and below the break. He knew with the aid of the fire's heat, the wrap would become a hard, stiff splint by morning and would prevent the bone from moving, so it could heal over time. Exhausted by the day's startling events and exertions, the hunter laid himself down onto his fur next to the girl and fell fast asleep.

As was his habit at first light of morning, the hunter awoke from a restless and disturbing night's sleep. He remained motionless, acutely aware of the girl's close proximity, feeling her body heat through his soft-skinned tunic and trousers. During his sleep and throughout the night, he heard her soft moans of discomfort as she slept through the pain her body was feeling. He continued to lie beside her between the sleeping furs they had shared during the chilly night, thinking about what he must do in order to care for her properly.

Aroused by her scent and unfamiliar closeness, he inched himself away from her and slowly slid out from beneath the furs. He left her to sleep as he stood to his full height, keeping a watchful eye on the girl, not wishing to disturb her sleep. He then walked over to the firepit, and with practiced ease, he soon had the smoky embers of the previous night's fire flaming new wood. Resting beside his rock-ringed firepit were his cooking bowls, empty water pouch, and a small pile of clean, smooth palm-sized stones. He took the stones and placed them on a flat stone lying just inside the firepit's ring of rocks to heat. He rummaged through his backpack and removed a spare set of clothes and an empty water pouch to take with him. The hunter grabbed his bow and quiver of arrows, glanced back at the sleeping girl and then left the cave.

During his journey through the mountain's gap, he had followed a stream down the rocky ravines that had eventually widened with the spring thaw into a sizable river following the curvature of the mountain's base on the far side of the valley. With his clothes and empty pouch in his hands along with his bow and arrows slung over his back, the young hunter started walking toward the river on the far side of the valley. Warily, he skirted the crash site, crossing the shallow end of the trench with caution, while hearing multiple menacing snarls and growls from small scavengers drawn to the far end of the site. He paused for a moment and watched the vile creatures repeatedly jumping in and out of the shell, all the while fighting over mouthfuls of the corpse's torn flesh. He knew by nightfall. The scavengers would consume the flesh and move on, leaving behind only bloody shredded fragments of material and the corpses scattered gnawed on bones.

He continued on toward the river, keeping a wary eye on the long grass around him for signs of danger, but he made it to the river's edge without incident. He quickly took off his dirty, bloody tunic and trousers and jumped naked into the shallow chilly water. Scrubbing vigorously, he quickly washed the dried blood from his kill off his skin before returning to the river's edge. He didn't bother to dry himself; instead, he preferred to let the sun's warmth dry his body as he began to wash the blood from his filthy clothes. He was warm and dry by the time his clothes were clean. He dressed quickly into his spare tunic and trousers before slipping on his moccasins. He then knelt beside the river edge and filled the water pouch made from a tough elastic bladder of a midsize grazer. Once filled, he retrieved his belongings and began searching the side of the riverbank for wild orange berries that were slightly tart but very tasty. It wasn't difficult to find a small patch with plenty of ripe, juicy orange berries ready for the picking. Laying his cleaned tunic on the ground, he began picking the fruit, tossing them onto his tunic as he picked. It didn't take long to gather a large pile of the ripe berries. He popped one of the berries into his mouth and savored its tartly, sweet taste before gathering up the corners of his tunic and making his way back to the cave.

CHAPTER 3

The Morning After

Jennifer awoke inside a cave feeling very vulnerable, finding herself dressed in what remained of her cold sleepwear lying between soft, warm animal furs. Her leg was throbbing and pulsating with pain emanating from her broken bone. Raising the top fur, she looked down at her leg. "Oh, gross! Don't puke! Don't puke! Don't puke!" she exclaimed disgustedly, looking at a bloody skin of an animal hide wrapped around her leg. "God, that's really gross." Her leg was obviously set and wrapped in some animals hide and tied into place with leather straps. Although she didn't want to admit it, the wrapped hide was preventing her leg from moving. "What the hell am I doing in a cave?" She asked loudly, wondering if anyone was around and hoping no one was. Someone had tended her injury, that was obvious, she thought, taking in her surroundings while trying to remember something important.

Her view outside was partially obscured by strips of meat drying on crude racks and smoke from the firepit. What she could see above the racks was the top half of the cave's entrance, which appeared to have a series of crudely drilled holes arching over the opening. She glanced at the rock walls of the cave that appeared to be limestone, but she wasn't sure. Her eyes then surveyed the meat drying on the racks around the fire.

"Damn! That's a lot of meat. Who's coming for dinner?" Jennifer quipped as she continued looking around. Tiny beams of light were streaming inside the cave's small opening that passed through the branches and leaves of the shrub from outside. The few blades of grass, weeds, and shrubs growing between the rocks and stones on the hillside above the cave's entrance hid a secret—a small hole penetrated down and through the cave's ceiling. It was approximately a foot in diameter and ten feet inside the cave from the entrance. The naturally formed hole through the stone made a perfect chimney for the fires escaping smoke.

She estimated the cave to be eight to twelve feet in height depending on where you're standing, roughly twenty-five feet wide and forty feet deep. On the left side of the cavern in the back wall was a dark black fissure, she assumed it leads somewhere into the depths of the mountain.

When the hunter returned and entered the cave, he noticed the girl had awakened during his absence. She had removed the tight-fitting cap that had covered her head and hair. He didn't expect her hair to be so long and beautiful as it lay over her shoulders. He thought the long red hair enhanced her natural beauty. During his fitful night's sleep. He dreamed she was a goddess who had fallen from a fire-filled sky with hair as red as the fiery realm she had come from and she filled him with wonder.

She stared at him quietly with curiosity clearly expressed in her eyes. At first, he didn't know what to do as her stare made him feel uncomfortable, except to put his weapons down near the cave entrance in order to show; he meant her no harm. He knelt beside the firepit and poured some water from the pouch he was carrying into two wooden bowls. He then added some sliced strips of fresh meat and the last of his grains and dried fruit to the water. It wasn't enough for two, so with a tinge of regret, he broke the last of his mother's special treat into two pieces and placed each half cake into the bowls. She quietly watched his activity with interest from the sleeping furs as she was famished and savored the thought of a hot meal.

With the aid of his wooden spoons, she saw him deftly retrieve the hot stones from inside the fire and drop them softly into each of the small wooden bowls. Steam hissed with the insertion of the stones, and the water quickly boiled softening the cakes and dried fruit as the water's heat cooked the tiny bits of meat and grains into a crude thick porridge. He knelt beside the fire waiting for the food to fully cook but made no sound as the porridge simmered in the bowls, acutely aware she was watching his every move.

Her curiosity and hunger finally got the better of her, when the sweet smell of the meal prompted Jennifer to say something. And so she whispered, "Hello."

The hunter remained motionless when he heard her speak, as he was still unsettled by her presence. He didn't understand her word but assumed it was a form of greeting. Yet he had to tend to her needs, so he picked up a spoon and stirred the porridge, mixing the ingredients evenly, and tossed in a handful of fresh orange berries on top for added flavor. He then stood, walked around the drying racks, and knelt beside her and handed over the bowl by placing it in her hands. "Thank you," she said to him as she accepted the bowl.

"Your welcome," he replied in his own language seeing her smile in reaction to his voice as she accepted the warm bowl in her hands.

He indicated by signs that he wanted her to hold the bowl securely and then stepped behind her and propped her shoulders up against his knees into a sitting position. Jennifer felt him lift the fur underneath her and slide her gently backward. When he neared the cavern wall, he stepped over her once more and knelt. They were face-to-face and only inches apart, and he smiled in reassurance, then gently lifted her up with his strong hands until she could recline comfortably against the wall; not once did they break eye contact, each fascinated and curious of the other. She winced with pain from the movement but made no other sound, knowing he was only trying to help make her comfortable.

His long auburn hair was tied behind his neck and hung down his back out of the way. His skin color was the most beautiful shade of copper she'd ever seen. His eyes were oval in shape with piercingly bright, inquisitive green eyes. His eyebrows arched nicely over the eyes with three creases on his forehead right above a slender slightly flared nose that accented his face perfectly. His strong, rugged chin was squared off with firm inviting lips, and when he smiled, he revealed a mouth full of beautiful white teeth.

"Oh, that's much better," she said as she took a spoonful of the porridge into her mouth. "This is really good!" she exclaimed with a smile, savoring the wonderfully strange but somehow familiar flavors of the ingredients, before dipping her spoon into the bowl for another bite.

He had no idea what she was saying but guessed from her expressions she was enjoying the food. He stood and pointed at his bowl by the fire while indicating with hand motions that he'd return to sit beside her. She nodded in understanding and watched him retrieve his meal and return. He sat beside her in a cross-legged position against the wall and began to eat in silence, not knowing what else to do.

From the lack of solid food in cold sleep, her stomach filled quickly as her body demanded her long-dormant stomach to begin the digestive processes once again. She felt so stuffed after only eating half of the porridge, but she honestly couldn't take another bite. So she set the bowl down beside her and turned to face her ruggedly handsome savior, determined it was time to make introductions. "Jennifer," she said to him with a smile while pointing a finger at herself and then turned it to point at him.

CHAPTER 4

Taric

"Taric," he replied, tapping his fingers against his shoulder. He then waved his hand toward her and smiled when he spoke her name. "Jenfer."

"Jen-ni-fer," she repeated, pronouncing it slowly so he could hear all the syllables before she repeated his name. "Taric." Pointing to him once again.

Determined to get her name right so as not to offend her, Taric concentrated on the sounds within his mind and repeated what he heard. "Jen-ni-fer," Taric repeated slowly, seeing her clap her hands with glee while beaming him an amazing smile, so he said it again, but only quicker. "Jennifer!"

"Taric!"

"Jennifer!"

"Taric!"

"Jennifer!"

"Taric!"

They then both burst into laughter at their success, laughing hard and long so that they had to stop looking at each other in order to control themselves. If they did make any sort of eye contact, the convulsive fits of laughter took hold once again. It was uncontrollable; they just couldn't help themselves.

"Oh God, I gotta pee!" Jennifer giggled while holding her belly to keep from laughing harder as she really did have to go. She was aware of the condition of her leg and knew she'd need some help, so she tapped him on the shoulder, so he'd look at her and then pantomimed her problem using her fingers and hoped he'd understand.

At her tap, Taric smothered his chuckles as best he could and paid close attention to her hand motions. He watched as she walked her fingers across the ground and then pointed outside the cave entrance. She then made her fingers squat in the dirt and, with her lips, made a soft hissing sound trying her best to imitate a falling stream of water. "Sssssssssssssssssssssh." And then she sighed in relief.

Immediately Taric understood her meaning and admonished himself for not thinking she might need to relieve herself. With an apologetic look on his face, he rose only enough to kneel beside her and wrapped an arm around her back and the other under her legs, while being careful not to jar the improvised splint. He lifted her up to his chest as if she were a feather and encouraged her with a nod to wrap an arm around his neck and shoulder for support and stability before carrying her out of the cave.

As he carried her effortlessly out into the long grass, Jennifer had her first real look at the world her escape pod crashed into. When Taric skirted the shallow depression of the trench, she saw the remains of the escape pod at the far end, it then dawned on her; she had forgotten someone and pointing her hand toward the pod. She screamed out her brother's name, "Peter!"

Taric knew she was screaming the name of the ancestor the land had denied. With tear-filled eyes, she held an anguished expression of guilt on her face as if ashamed to be alive, while she begged the spirits to spare the ancestor called Peter. Sadly, he shook his head from side to side and simply said, "No."

Jennifer heard his reply, it was flat and final by the tone of his voice. She was supposed to watch over him and protect him from danger, she thought as pangs of guilt tore through her breast for not thinking of her brother before this moment.

Then everything came to the forefront of her mind and she relived those final moments in the pod. Her leg had been squeezed and nearly crushed during the pod's impact with the planet. As soon as the pod's momentum stopped, she was the one who reached out and released the hatch. It was too soon. Her action allowed the flames still burning the outer surface of the escape pod to enter their tight confines.

She was unprepared and untrained for the disaster that befell their colonial starship. She and her brother were simply passengers, colonists escaping the terrible wars engulfing the four kingdoms on Earth. She now knew without a doubt that she had panicked when the hot flames entered and swam around her in the air. Adrenaline had surged through her body and she managed to force her leg free, breaking it in her frightening scramble to flee the pod. "Oh, God!" she cried out, sobbing with remorse, condemning herself to hell for it was then when she realized she didn't even think of her brother in her escape. She had left him to die and never looked back, violating their parents' trust in her as they placed them into the escape pod and launched their children into space seconds before the starship exploded. Taric let her cry out her grief for the other ancestor. He wondered what their relationship was? Was he family, friend, mate, or stranger? he asked himself as he walked past the trench while carrying Jennifer to the river?

She heard the loud rushing of water splashing over rocks from the river before she saw it, making her need more urgent. Her heart bled from her grief, saddening her soul. Taric carried her to the crest of the river's embankment and down to the water without stumbling. Before she knew it, Taric had her in the chilly water and swung her onto her back, letting the rivers current lift her as he held on to her arms. The shock of the water drew her quickly out of remorse and almost stopped her need. It was so cold, but she could no longer restrain her bladder and simply let it flow. The relief was apparent on Jennifer's face as she emptied her water into the river. She smiled up at him and pointed a slender arm toward the shore. Taric chuckled as she unconsciously blushed ever so slightly, then swung her back into his arms and easily carried her all the way back to the cave.

Jennifer studied Taric's changing facial expressions on the way back and slowly became aware by the arching of his eyebrows and the shifting of his eyes that something other than her was troubling him. She couldn't imagine the consequences of their encounter on this alien world or the problems of their survival due to her unexpected arrival. Taric's mind was consumed with worry and tried his best to hide it and act normal. But if anything, Jennifer understood worry lines. Her father's face had them when he was in deep thought or when he was angry about something, which was often. Taric's face held the same expression as her father's as it quietly revealed his inner turmoil.

She didn't comprehend how dire their situation really was. Her perspective of him was as if he were a Native American Indian who had been out hunting and that his tribe was no more than a day's walk away. She just assumed Taric's camp in the cave was a temporary shelter for his people when they went out hunting. "Thank you," she said with a smile as Taric set her gently down to rest on the piled furs so she could sit with her back against the wall. All the while she was studying his facial expressions trying desperately to discern what was troubling him, but she didn't have a clue. Was he worrying about her or something else? And if it was something else, then what was it? She silently asked herself as Taric knelt beside her leg. She watched him examine the wet and slightly stiff splint making sure it hadn't slipped from the flow of the river's current but determined Jennifer needed to be closer to the fire for it dry out properly.

Even though the snow and ice moons were still in the distant future, Taric knew they could not leave the valley, and that time would pass all too soon. If he didn't start preparing now for the cold moons, they would not survive.

To Taric's people, the light of day during the warm to hot seasons was for the necessities of life, hunting and gathering a stockpile of dried meat, wild fruits, berries, tubers, and grains to sustain an entire tribe in defense of the snow moon's freezing winds and ice. They also had to collect a large supply of the tough long grasses to weave mats for sitting or sleeping upon and baskets for storing their grains, dried fruits, and dried meat, as well as stacks of firewood to keep them from freezing when the land is covered in a blanket of snow.

His people wasted very little time in their lives. They worked to survive every day. They made every piece of clothing they wore from the skins of their kills. Flint was flaked off into useful sharp shards when struck at the right angle with a hard stone. The shards could then be shaped into a multitude of useful tools from arrowheads, knives for cutting or carving of wood and bone, awls for poking holes, and scrapers for the cleaning of hides. The people made and shared everything, but Jennifer had nothing, not even a practical set of clothes. She only had him and a broken bone that prevented her from traveling. All he had was his skills, a few racks of drying meat, and the contents of his backpack, but everything that he needed the most was not found in the small confines of his backpack.

Fortunately, it was still early spring, and the valley would provide them with water, food, and wood for the cold moons. After Jennifer's leg healed enough to walk on, he hoped she'd be able to assist him with the hunting and gathering of food for the winter, but first, they had to be able to talk, so he sat down beside her, turned to face her, pointed at the fire, and said in his language, "Fire."

He saw understanding in her eyes, and she immediately repeated his words with her words as she pointed at the fire and said, "Fire."

"Fire," Taric repeated, learning the sound of her word and understanding what it meant, knowing she did as well. He rose to his feet unaccustomed to idleness, but he was excited, and he wanted to speak to her. *What was she?* he thought, beginning to rotate the meat on the racks so the strips would dry evenly. Taric began exchanging words with her as he worked. By the time he had finished rearranging the racks of meat, they each had learned a basic means to communicate and could identify items in the cave when spoken in the language of the other. Through hand signs and pantomime, they were slowly able to speak and understand the most immediate and simplest of phrases in the syntax of each other's language. It was a good beginning for each of them to express rudimentary thoughts and needs.

CHAPTER 5

Along the River's Edge

The landscape's appearance changed quickly in their valley from the lush green freshness of spring into the yellowing dry tans of summer. Jennifer calculated it had been forty-four days since her landing and she had seen no one other than Taric the entire time. Today she was going to lose the hard dried out splint on her leg and be done with it. Grateful she would no longer need the pair of crutches Taric had made for her a few days after he set the bone.

She was waiting for him to come outside and called out to him. "Come on, Taric. What's taking you so long?" she said in his language, thinking she said it rather well and smiled.

"Coming. What's the hurry? The river is not going anywhere," she heard him reply in English from just inside the cave entrance.

"Crutches or carry?" he asked Jennifer with a warm smile when he exited the cave, with a bow and a slender bag of arrows slung over his back and another neatly tied bundle over his opposite shoulder.

"You can carry me if you'd like," she replied, knowing he enjoyed the closeness as much as she did. "Taric, where are your people?" she finally asked him, curious about the life he lived in this world.

He took the crutches from her hands and threw them beside the firepit. "You won't need these anymore. Might as well burn them. They'll make good firewood," Taric joked as he swept Jennifer off her feet and into his strong arms.

"My people are on the other side of that mountain range in the north. I was on a journey when you fell to the land," Taric answered, beginning their daily walk to the river's edge, nodding in the direction of the mountains. "What is it like living in the heavens? Are your people up there?" he asked in return, wanting her to be just a girl, but still believing she was one of his people's ancestors come back to life.

"I'll tell you tonight when the stars are out," she answered and then asked. "Do all young hunters take a journey into the wilds alone or are you running from something?"

"I'm not running from anything. I wanted to see the land south of the mountains and meet new people. My tribe is a small one and has more hunters than women to provide mates. There is no future for me in my tribe without a mate. I'm much older than the tribe's oldest girl child. When she comes of age, I'll be too old to be considered as a mate. She'll want a younger hunter in his prime as she will be. Who would want to start a life with an old man as a mate? I wouldn't. So I left the tribe to find my future and I'm not sure where it will lead me," Taric honestly replied, unaware that her modern, jaded, and cynical mind's interpretation of his matter of fact statement meant; she was not worth his consideration as a suitable mate.

"Oh," she replied with a slight frown on her lips and then quickly smiled to hide the pain of her hurt ego and cheerfully quipped. "And then I came along and ruined your whole trip," she said, forcing a slight chuckle out of her throat as she lay her head on his shoulders so he couldn't see her watery eyes. At the embankment of the river, Taric relaxed his hold and lowered her softly to the ground next to the sunning boulder. He steadied Jennifer as she tested her weight on the leg using Taric's body as support by leaning against him. The closeness and scent of him forced her to wave off his willing assistance because she did not trust her ability to restrain herself. *Taric's statement said it all*, she thought as she watched him lay the bulky bundle onto the ground and then leaned his bow and quiver of arrows against the boulder. With practiced ease and easy smile, Taric swooped Jennifer up off her feet and back into his arms. He strode quickly down the embankment nearly to the water's edge.

"No! Don't you dare!" Jennifer screamed out a hopeless plea for mercy. They both began laughing uncontrollably as she twisted and squirmed within his strong arms to escape what was to come.

"Ready," he announced, trying to suppress the laughter convulsing his body. Taric smiled as he held her squirming body firmly in his arms and launched them both into the chilly, quick-flowing, shallow water.

Still laughing at one another with amusement over what had become a morning ritual. They stood up to their waists in the water and stripped down to skin and tossed their clothes onto the shore. The chilly water urged them to wash quickly and return to the river's sandy embankment as soon as they could.

As she washed, Jennifer thought about how their relationship had developed since they began their daily walks to the river in the mornings. It had become her favorite time of day. She was alone with Taric on a personal level, and it was the only time of day he wasn't involved with some other activity. Taric never seemed to rest or simply stop what he was doing and enjoy life, except in the mornings with her.

Every night after eating, he'd go out into the grass and bring armfuls of the stuff back into their cave and weave them into various sizes of tightly woven baskets or large loose ones depending on their intended use. If he wasn't out hunting or drying meat, he was scraping the inner hides of his kills. He was constantly on the move, gathering fruits and wild vegetables was a daily obsession. There were neatly stacked baskets filled with fruits, grains, and dried meat stored in the cool dark inner cave. To Jennifer, it looked like there was enough to feed a tribe. Behind their sleeping furs, Taric also stacked rows of firewood piled high and deep against the entire back wall, and yet every night, he would add more wood and make a few more baskets as they talked to each other in the caves dim firelight.

Jennifer finished washing and limped stiff-legged her way over to a large smooth, comfortable stone by the water's edge. She sat down in the sun to dry and warm her naked body, letting her toes dance above the chilly running water. Before they left the cave, Taric cut the straps securing the splint onto her leg. "Hey, are you going to get this thing off me anytime soon?" Jennifer asked, watching him wade through the water toward her. "I think it's soft enough to pull off," she stated in a matter of fact tone speaking in his natural speech, comfortable with their mutual nakedness, but not with his appealing and desirable masculinity. She was falling for him and she knew it. Yet Taric hadn't shown any signs of being interested in her. He always treated her kindly and would do anything for her, almost in respectful reverence, but he never really opened up or let his guard down around her and she wondered why.

"Let me get this wrap off your leg," Taric said to her cheerfully, grabbing the wrap in his strong hands and with a good pull on the stiff, overlapped hide, he pried it open, allowing Jennifer to slip her leg free. Taric then let the flowing water carry the hide downstream. "Wait here, I have something for you," he said smiling, with his eyes glinting in anticipation. He left her guessing as she dried in the warm sunlight watching him with an expressed interest in her eyes.

Taric quickly ran up the embankment, retrieved the bundle, then turned around in time to see her stand up and face the morning sun. Her radiant red hair was being blown carelessly about her shoulders and breasts by a gentle breeze, accenting her golden tanned skin and slender build. The sight of her standing naked in the morning sun took his breath away as it always did. She was incredibly beautiful and extremely erotic, but living in such close proximity as they were made it extremely difficult for him to express his forbidden feelings of love.

Taric returned and handed the bundle to Jennifer with a smile. He then retrieved his clothes from the shore and slipped them on while watching Jennifer excitedly open the bundle.

"Oh my God! Clothes! Did you make me some clothes? When did you do this? I can't believe it! Oh, thank you, thank you, thank you so much," Jennifer exclaimed with delight, examining the soft moccasins, skin trousers, and a beautiful tunic. She held the light, soft skin tunic in front of her admiring the pretty green, blue, yellow, and red feather adornments he had carefully sewn onto the tunic to hang loose in front of the shoulders and down the gentle slope of her breasts. Taric's estimation of her size was nearly accurate. The beautiful tunic laced together under the arms and up between her breasts fit her slim figure nicely. Her new trousers, consisting of a loincloth and leggings, required a little adjustment for them to fit comfortably. But oh, the moccasins, so soft on the inside fit her feet perfectly, as they could be drawn and tied snugly around her shin's just above the ankles.

"I made them while you slept," he answered, grinning with the success of his surprise. "Sky clothes not good for life on land. You need new ones," he commented, watching her as she admired the new outfit, pleased with her reaction to his gift, wishing once more for her to be just a girl. He loved her, but she was too perfect, too beautiful, and too unique to be a mere girl; she was something else. He witnessed her fall from the dark, mysterious heavens and take her first steps on the land with his own eyes. There was no other explanation within his mind for her presence—she is an ancestor of high rank in her sky tribe and he was not worthy.

The land had blessed her above all others, but Taric was only a lowly unmated hunter without status or rank in his tribe. He had nothing to offer a mating, so why would she choose him? he thought sadly to himself while smiling with her obvious joy, delighted as always to be near her.

Dressed in clothes for the first time since climbing into the hibernation pod aboard her doomed starship, Jennifer felt complete again as she twirled around, and then she stopped suddenly seeing something black and unmoving in the grass. She began to walk along the river's edge toward the spot that had caught her attention.

"What's that over there?" she asked as Taric began to follow her, looking ahead in the direction she was moving.

Taric immediately recognized what she was looking at and reached out a hand, grabbed her arm, and forcefully pulled her back to his side. "Walk backward very slowly, I need my bow," he warned, urging her back with a gentle tug on her arm, never taking his eyes from the spot. "It's a lycur."

They reached the crest of the river's embankment where Taric had left his bow and quiver of arrows, but the animal still didn't move. "Do you think it's dead?" Jennifer asked him, watching the spot for movement as Taric notched an arrow onto his bow.

"If it's dead, I'll throw it into the river. If it's not, I'll still throw it in the river. The body will get tangled up in the roots of some trees downriver and draw the scavengers away from this area," Taric explained, realizing for the first time, Jennifer required a weapon and needed to learn how to shoot a bow. Taric kept Jennifer behind him as they approached the animal's position until it was obvious to him that the beast was dead.

"Why, it looks very similar to a wolf on Earth," Jennifer remarked as she knelt to study the dead animal's wounds.

"It looks as if it was kicked in the head a few times. The lower jaw is broken, probably crushed by a hoof. It's female, and she looks to have recently given birth. She must have a den around here. There might be pups still alive in her den," she informed Taric with an excited smile he did not understand as he kicked the corpse into the water to float downriver.

"So what? If there is a den nearby, leave it to the scavengers. They will find it soon enough," Taric said with indifference and added, "Life is hard on the land."

"No! It doesn't have to be that way. If there are pups in a nearby den, they don't have to die. We may be able to tame and train a couple. That lycur must be a member of this planet's canine species. Wolves were the first wild animals to bond with us. They've proven to be the most loyal, useful, and valuable companion we have enjoyed with another species. Maybe as part of your natural development, your people are supposed to bond with these animals? Maybe, just maybe, no one has thought of it yet? So what's the problem?" Jennifer announced defiantly, then turned away from him as she began to search the area along the riverbank for the animal's den.

Taric was at a loss for words, her reasoning, actions, and astonishing empathy for a dead animal eluded him, but to go in search of a predator's den was just not done. "Leave it," he said again just as they both heard the faint yelp of a pup nearby.

Jennifer followed the sound to its source and found a hole dug into the bank behind some shrubs and between some large stones. She knelt beside it and listened, hearing the cries of a pup calling for its mother inside the dark den. She extended her arm down into the den until she felt a squirming soft little ball of fur begin to nibble at her fingertips and pulled it out. "Well, look at you. It's a girl!" she exclaimed with an exuberant smile, holding a black puppy in her arms next to her breasts. "You're such a cutie," she whispered softly, smiling down at the pup.

"Jennifer, what are you doing? That is a lycur, a predator, an unpredictable killer! Put it back!" Taric ordered sternly, dumb-founded by her actions and attitude toward the little beast.

"I will not!" he heard Jennifer reply defiantly, holding the puppy in one of her hands, letting the creature nibble on her fingers as she stroked its tiny head and body with her other hand. "I'm keeping her!" Jennifer announced as if that was the end of their discussion as she wondered how he could be so callous toward a little puppy.

"It will grow into a killer. You can't keep it. People will not understand. I don't understand, and I've grown to know you," Taric tried to explain but was cut short by a tart angry reply with fire blaz-ing in her eyes.

"What people? Look around, Taric! There's no one here but us!"

Taric, was at a loss for words as he heard Jennifer's stern forceful voice lash out at him and then turn soothingly soft to say. "She's just a little puppy. I promise you, she will not grow into a killer, but she will become our friend. She'll grow to become our partner and pro-tector when we're out hunting. All it takes is a little love and a bit of training. What's wrong with that?"

To Taric, Jennifer's statement of the creature's future was impos-sible to believe because people can't and don't command animals, but to hear her speak, it sounded as if she knew what she was talking about. Just by looking at her, he knew she would not change her mind, and as crazy as it seemed, he best accept the idea.

"Fine, keep it," Taric angrily said to her, knowing he'd lost the argument. But within a heartbeat, she rewarded him with the most beautiful smile he'd ever seen that instantly washed away his irritation.

CHAPTER 6

Under the Stars

The warm air from the day's hot sun slowly cooled with a slight breeze flowing over the mountain peaks and on down the valley, adding a touch of dampness to the air. Jennifer was sitting on some furs spread over the ground just outside the cave. She was gazing up at the distant twinkling starlight in the night sky while with a tender hand she stroked the soft fur of the little black puppy sleeping comfortably on her lap.

Taric came out of the cave, nibbling on some berries piled high in a small woven grass basket. He noticed the little lycur beast Jennifer called a puppy was sleeping in her lap and found the sight of the two together very unsettling. It was unnatural, almost magical, as he watched her interact with the lycur. He sat down next to Jennifer and placed the bowl he was carrying between them.

"I don't know what you believe when you look up at the night sky," Jennifer said to him quietly. "You asked me, what is it like living in the heavens and where are my people? I'm not sure you'd believe me. We're so different, you and me. We're the opposite of each other's culture and worlds apart in our technology and way of thinking. I'm not sure where to begin."

"Just talk and I will listen," Taric suggested with a kind smile encouraging her to begin as he knew it would cause her some sadness in the telling. "Your beginning will happen."

"Yes, the beginning, I'll try, but first, tell me what you see in the night sky," she asked curiously. "It might help me to explain things better and give me a starting point."

"When I look up at the night sky. I see the firepits of all who have lived before me. Our people believe there is life after death. We believe another life begins when our spirit is taken from the land. If I live a good life and I am found worthy, my spirit will ascend into the dark sky to be reunited with my ancestors.

"Some spirits are doomed to forever wander within the shadows of darkness. Lives can be very short due to sickness, famine, or unexpected tragedy. Tragic events inflicted on or suffered through in a person's life can attack a person's spirit and bind it to the land after their death. When an unusual death occurs, our healers gather and perform a ceremony to break any bond with the land the spirit may have so it can rise into the night sky in peace and not be doomed to forever wander in the darkness," he answered quietly revealing to her the simple faith of Taric's people.

Taric's truthful telling of his belief gave Jennifer a beginning she thought he could understand and possibly accept. "Taric, I need you to open your mind and really listen to what I'm going to say. Over countless generations, my people's curiosity made us a very resourceful and intelligent species. Our weapons gradually became so much more advanced than a simple bow and arrow that we almost destroyed ourselves. Your land makes me feel as if I've traveled back in time. Way back to when Earth, my home, was as wild and bountiful with life as your home is now."

"What do you mean by traveled back in time?" Taric asked, interrupting her with a question.

Jennifer realized she'd have to explain herself more simply. It wasn't because Taric was a stupid savage; he was highly intelligent for his world and way of life. His people didn't have the luxury of idle time to think about abstract thoughts. So she tried to answer him as simply as she could and hoped he'd understand.

"Traveling back in time is a human expression of speech. It's a twist of words we sometimes use in our stories. Time travel is not possible, but the idea is like this.

"Imagine, you're here on this spot at this time of day. Then a magical healer walks into your camp and offers you a way to witness the moment of your birth in exchange for shelter and food. You agree and then poof! You're standing beside your mother as she's giving birth to a baby and the baby is you. A child she names Taric. That's the simplest way of explaining the idea. Do you understand?" Jennifer asked him, seeing dim shadows of the firelight play with the gorgeous features of his handsome face.

"I think I understand your idea," Taric answered a little confused but smiled as her concern for him was the foremost expression revealed on her beautiful face. He placed his hand in hers and gave it a gentle squeeze. "I saw you fall from the sky. I will listen and try to understand and believe what you have to say. How can I not?" he answered, giving her hand a gentle squeeze for encouragement.

"Okay. Well, as the saying goes," Jennifer replied with a grin. "A very, very, very long time ago, my people lived their lives much like you and your people do now. Generation upon countless generations of lives spent in the pursuit of a better life for our children, our numbers spread across the land, we tamed the wilds and made ourselves masters of our world.

"Our history began when our ancient ancestors drew pictures of different types of animals and the men hunting them on cave walls. The primitive drawings eventually led to writing—the beginning of conveying our ideas and questions beyond our death. Writing made it possible to record our spiritual beliefs, history, and science.

"Humans have always been a curious species. We have a desire to know the truth of our observations. We ask countless questions and then search for ways to answer them. Through observation and experimentation, we learned to distinguish the difference between fact and fiction. We recorded our discoveries, but for every discovery, there were always more questions to be answered. Our boundless imagination and insatiable curiosity within our souls fuels our mind's quest for knowledge. It never stops. We ask questions we cannot answer in the hope that future generations will discover the answer and expand our knowledge even further.

"Throughout time, we continued asking hard questions because we had to know why things are as they are and how we came to be on our land. Those basic questions made it possible for us to overcome our fear of the unknown. Our accumulated knowledge from one generation to the next grew so vast that over time it made impossible ideas possible and opened up incredible opportunities, including the ability to change our life's reality, which brings me to this point in my life." Jennifer explained with a grin as she continued to stroke the little puppy.

"Now it's time for some hard truth. Everyone living on the land right now is ignorant of what really exists in the sky above us, except me.

"The only commonality between your culture and mine is our awareness of our mortality, and for that, I'm thankful, because it's a beginning. You live to survive each day, your past is only what you can remember, and your tomorrow is the scary unknown. The story of your species on this world is just beginning to unfold and the outcome of your history far into the future will forever be a mystery to you. Your people are a very young species in an eternal cosmic quest to extend life wherever it can.

"The lights you see in the sky are not the firepits of your ancestors as you've been told to believe. They are stars, massive globes of unimaginable power scattered throughout our galaxy we call the Milky Way. A galaxy is a vast collection of countless stars, and there are more galaxies in the universe than the stars you can see in the night sky.

"Every star is just like the sun that rises in your sky each morning. Your star is the source of energy for all life on this world. Without its endless light and heat, nothing would live and this land would be a frozen barren rock.

"The stars are so far away, it takes countless cycles of seasons for their light to travel here. Every sun has a varying number of worlds circling around them and some of those far away worlds are favorable to life. My people learned how to travel in starships from one world to another across the vast distances of space. We've discovered three-star systems with worlds suitable to support human life and ready to

42

colonize." Jennifer paused to gather her thoughts, wondering how much of her narrative Taric was understanding and asked him, "Do you understand what I'm telling you?"

"I am listening. What are starships?" Taric asked, thinking it was a made thing like the hollow stone she had used to fall to the land in.

"Starships are enormous machines able to sail across the vast distances of our galaxy. We discovered a way to put ourselves into a deep sleep for many cycles of seasons without waking or aging during the long journey. My starship, the *Fulcrum*, left Earth in the year 2554 and was traveling to another world, much like this one, but no one like us lives there. It's called Opalla, a world full of natural resources and animal life we can use to create a new home. Our flight was to last one hundred thirty-seven of your seasonal cycles we call years. I don't know how long I slept to get to this world. I must have been in hypersleep for at least seventy-five years.

"My parents were the senior flight engineers on the starship, it was their task to program the ship's course and to certify the propulsion systems were ready for the long voyage. Our ship carried ten thousand souls and it seems I'm the only one left alive. I don't know what happened, but something went horribly wrong. Whatever it was, it caused my parents to abandon their duties and awaken Peter and me. They stuffed us into spacesuits and pushed us into an escape pod before we were fully awake. As my father was closing the escape pod, he told me to watch over my brother, Peter. He promised me, he and mom would be following in another escape pod. It was the last words he spoke to me before launching the pod.

"The ship is dead, and I can't expect a rescue. I'm what we'd say in my world, a castaway. A person marooned on a deserted isle with no way to get back home. For better or for worse, this world is my home for the rest of my life and all I know about it is what I can see from our cave. You saved my life, and now I'm afraid to face the life fate has given me," Taric heard her say sadly as she leaned heavily against his side, still stroking the puppy's soft fur with her fingers as it lay sleeping in her warm lap.

Then as he pondered what she had told him, a spark of hope entered into his thoughts. "You say the lights are stars and not firepits of my ancestors," Taric repeated and then went on to reason within his mind to accept her words as truth instead of the legends of his people. Therefore, this incredibly amazing girl who fell out of the sky was not an ancestor of his people at all. She was just a lonely girl accustomed to a different way of life on a world forever out of her reach.

"When you fell from the sky, I believed you were an ancestor granted another life on the land. You and I are so alike yet so different. What you say about the sky above us, I believe. Your parents gave you a chance to live by sending you here and I was here to find you. Welcome to my land, Jennifer. I am Taric and I was on a journey seeking out my destiny. I believe my destiny found me when you fell from the sky. I have fallen under your spell and my heart tells me to love you," he said softly, letting her see into the depths of his soul as he leaned over and kissed her gently on the lips.

Their lips parted slowly from their long, lingering kiss while staring deeply into the depths of the other's eyes. Mesmerized by Jennifer's piercing emerald-green eyes, Taric whispered very softly once again, "I love you."

Jennifer's heart swelled, feeling the rhythmic beating stop within her chest and sputter to a pulsating, pounding beat as Taric whispered those words. Did he really fall in love with her? she asked herself, unwilling to believe him. She's been nothing but a burden and yet he did everything, everything for her. He could have run away from the crash in fear and left her to die, but he didn't. Why? Would anyone else in this land have helped a stranger who fell from the sky? She didn't know, but he had willingly taken on her care and never once complained.

"Why do you love me?" Jennifer asked, not daring to trust the sincerity in his voice. She knew without a doubt Taric had spoken from the depths of his soul because he was a kind, respectful, and honorable man, but she had to know. The time spent in such close proximity together as her leg healed, day after day, enabled her to accept this unexpected development of her life, but she didn't expect to fall in love.

"Why is it such a mystery to you?" Taric asked with a full smile radiating from his handsome face as he reached out a hand to scratch the little beast behind the ears with a couple of his fingers, accepting it and her.

"I would never have tried to save the life of this little predator, but you did and made it seem as natural as if tossing a stone into water. You tell me this animal can be taught to help us hunt and become a friend. I'm not sure if it's possible, but you act like you know this animal's future and what it will grow into, whereas I still see a wild predator.

"You're unpredictable, exciting, and beautiful. The things you say and do are beyond my understanding most times, but I believe you. Now that I know you, I can't imagine my life without you in it. I feel you in my heart," Taric said softly, tapping his chest with a finger.

She then responded to Taric's loving decree by setting the sleeping puppy down onto the furs, rolled over on top of him, and began to kiss Taric lovingly and passionately, letting his hands explore her body as she melted within his strong embrace. As they gave in to their mutual pent-up desires under the starlight, Jennifer promised herself, while gasping for air between their kisses, to love Taric for the rest of her life.

CHAPTER 7

Last Days of Summer

Jennifer walked out of the river's chilly water and onto the dry, sandy bank only to be eagerly greeted by the playful puppy she had named Jaxx. "Down," she commanded her rambunctious companion while also indicating with a sharp snap of her fingers for Jaxx to sit beside her. Although the sun was high in the sky, goose bumps covered her cold flesh as Jaxx sat down and watched her. She felt the sun's heat couldn't warm her chilled body fast enough, so instead of walking up the bank and around the flat rock where she assumed Taric already lay basking in the sunlight, she reached up to the top edge of the rock and grabbed one of the soft leather hides they used to dry off after bathing. She then noticed Taric's head poking over the edge of their sunning rock. He must have rolled over onto his belly when she grabbed the hide and was watching her every move.

"There you are," she said, as his eyes roamed ceaselessly over her slim muscular frame, clearly enamored by her natural beauty and graceful movements. "What are you thinking about?" she asked him with a teasing smile, enjoying the way his eyes followed her every move. Jaxx was looking up at Taric and whined. "Oh, go on," she said to Jaxx, letting her scamper on ahead to join Taric on the rock.

"I was thinking it's time to hunt something large," he suggested with an excited smile as Jaxx poked her head over the edge next to Taric's grinning face. Together the eyes of human and beast looked down at her as she dried herself off. Without conscious thought,

Taric reached out a hand and gave the playful puppy a gentle scratch behind her ears.

"Oh really! You're such a liar," she laughingly exclaimed with a wide smile, knowing full well what he was really thinking. Jennifer then surprised Taric by saying. "When I was a child, Peter and I rarely saw our parents because they worked in space. My parents were freighters and pilots of interplanetary cargo ships within our star system. Peter and I were raised on our grandparents' ranch. My grandmother had this huge fenced-in garden behind her house and rabbits would dig under the fence during the night to get at the vegetables. Rabbits are small harmless burrow dwelling animals and they can destroy a garden very quickly when the veggies are ripe. So I'd wake up before daybreak and sneak out to the garden with my bow and shoot any rabbit I found in the garden. Rabbits are fast runners and I became pretty good at tracking and shooting them on the run. Sometimes we'd roast one over a fire for our meal, but most times the rabbits were fed to the dogs. My grandma was happy about that because their food was free," she happily exclaimed, but suddenly as if caught off guard, her lovely animated smile slowly faded into the saddest of frowns.

Looking at Jennifer's frozen, glassy-eyed expression, Taric realized it was the first time she had mentioned her lost family. "I'm sure the spirits of your family are doing well in their afterlife. By your absence in the heavens, they know you survived the fall and are still among the living. Do not frown or dwell on the sadness of your loss, be happy to be alive. Show their spirits you're safe and doing well in this world," he said, hoping his words might soothe the pain of loss in her grieving heart. Just by her lack of a response, Taric knew his words went unheard, so he changed the subject and asked, "What's a ranch?"

Jennifer had indeed failed to comprehend what Taric had been saying as she remembered a favorite memory of her grandmother while absently rubbing the soft hide up and down her legs.

"What's a ranch?" Taric repeated a little louder than before without yelling.

"Wha-what?" she stammered, suddenly drawn out of her melancholy by his unexpected question.

"What's a ranch?" Taric repeated. "Is it a place in one of your cities?"

"No, no, a ranch would not be in a city," she answered as she finished drying herself off and began to dress, much to the chagrin of Taric as he watched and listened.

"Cities back home were once a sprawling mass of humanity. But now, because of the war, they have become ugly, nightmarish places. When we left the Earth, most major cities have been destroyed and are littered with the rubble of war. My world is drowning in human blood and there's nothing that can be done to stop it.

"My parents surrendered all our wealth to pay for our passage to a new world. We were fortunate to escape the insanity and horror on Earth. Our starship was the sixth to launch in six years, ten ships were scheduled each a year apart, but the insane wars raging on the planet were getting worse, and I fear the seventh ship may not have launched. The Earth could be a dead world for all I know; I have no idea how long I was asleep before being thrust into a pod and awakening in your cave.

"Anyway, we expected to awaken from our journey a hundred and thirty-seven years later orbiting a world with an outpost on the surface already established. We were planning on being pioneers like in the days of the old West of ancient Earth. We were going to travel across the land just like they did in covered wagons pulled by oxen. We would have all the equipment and livestock we required to search out a place to call home and build a new life for ourselves. At least that was the plan," Jennifer explained, continuing on with her conversation as she walked up the river's bank.

"I did not expect to end up on a world like yours. There's so much for me to learn and adjust to in order to survive here on this land. I'm a stranger in this world, Taric. I can't hide it. I have pale white skin and red hair, while your skin is a natural copper-bronze color. The only physical trait we have in common is our green eyes. Other than that, I'll stand out wherever I travel. I don't know how your people will react when they first see me? Taric, with you I feel accepted, protected, and loved.

"However, people react differently to strangers, and sometimes it creates unpredictable situations, and that little unknown fact haunts my sleep," Jennifer explained worriedly, letting Taric hear her inner turmoil and worries. "I'm too different. I might not be accepted when we eventually encounter other people."

"Jennifer, no harm will come to you. Lay your uncertainty to rest, there is nothing to fear from my people." Taric assured her as he stood up with his clothes clutched in his hands and began to dress.

Jennifer nodded in understanding, held her tongue, and kept her misgivings to herself. Taric was biased and had initially believed she was an ancestor come back to the land, a spirit granted another chance at life. It was only after he got to know her and the truth of her origins, did he finally accept her as a person and not an ancestor.

"Let me show you how well I can shoot," Jennifer said with a smile, changing the subject of their conversation as she walked up to Taric and a busy Jaxx running around their legs eager to be off on an adventure with her pack.

"But what's a ranch?"

"A ranch? I told you, didn't I?"

"No. You didn't say anything about a ranch," Taric laughingly answered then added with a big grin on his face. "I don't know why."

Jennifer chuckled and then whispered to herself, "God, I'm turning into my grandmother."

"A ranch, yes," Jennifer repeated, giving herself time to get over her case of the prattles, as her grandmother often said. "If you stand in front of our cave and look at the plain below us as a reference point. Imagine a herd of large meaty animals living in the open with no predators around to hunt them. One such animal is what we call a cow. We've bred them over countless generations, they've become docile and easily led because they're so dependent on humans for their food and welfare.

What you see below us is our ranch, except here, some of the animals still see us as food. Satisfied?" she asked, flashing him a radiant smile as she placed her hand in his.

They left the rock hand in hand as Jaxx playfully romped ahead a short distance before turning back around to join them as they strolled lazily toward the cave. Jennifer stopped at the crest of the long depression of soil scarred by the escape pods passage. Every day as she and Taric crossed the trench, she never once glanced at the pod, but today she stopped and stood in thoughtful silence staring down the length of the trench at the pod.

Jennifer then came to a decision. Before her life in this world with Taric can begin, she had to forever lock away her other life deep down in her heart. Everyone she knew or loved was forever lost. Fate had decreed she take a different path on her journey of life, and she had no choice but to accept it.

Jennifer turned toward Taric, who followed her gaze down to the end of the trench with his eyes. "What is troubling you?" he asked.

"I have to bury Peter's remains. I can't leave him like that," she said quietly, knowing she'll never forgive herself for Peter's death. She allowed her fear to take control of her senses and it cost Peter his life. She had to lay his bones in a proper grave; she owed him that much.

"I will help with whatever you wish," Taric assured her with a gentle squeeze of his hand. They approached the pod in respectful silence, except for Jaxx's playful yelps, busily scouring the area with her sensitive snout for small rodents.

"I'll climb inside and hand the bones out to you." Thinking it would be less emotional for Jennifer if he did the task, Taric suggested but was stopped by her fingers softly resting on his lips.

"Thank you for offering to help. But this is something I have to do," she said sadly, slowly withdrawing her hand from his lips as tears began streaming from her eyes and on down her face.

With a heart beating wildly within her chest and a damp drying hide clutched tightly in her hand, Jennifer approached the opening and climbed inside the pod. Other than sunlight streaming in from outside, the only other source was from a small pulsing dim blue light still drawing power from the pod's energy pack. Jennifer was unaware the light indicated an active emergency beacon.

Looking around the interior, Jennifer took in the full extent of carnage done by the scavengers and immediately realized her brother's skull was not among the scattered remains. From outside, Taric heard a remorseful guttural cry break from Jennifer's soul as her quivering lips cried out. "Oh, Peter! Please forgive me!" she cried to his spirit with a hope he would hear her pleas. Her hands shook as she began placing the few remains one by one onto the leather hide. She was careful not to damage the gnawed bones more than they were. It made her sick to her stomach imagining Peter's body being devoured by scavengers, one gut-wrenching bite at a time. Tears flowed down her cheeks as she placed the bones on the hide until certain she had them all. She folded the hide over the small pile and lifted the bundle out of the open hatch for Taric to grab.

Before climbing out, Jennifer searched the pod's interior, hoping it contained some emergency medical supplies, thinking some clean bandages and antibacterial ointments could come in handy. She found a small appropriately labeled panel roughly a foot square and opened the tiny compartments latch. Inside she found a med kit as expected but also found a clear plastic box containing a fishing kit and a steel knife with an eight-inch blade. The shaft was bound in leather with the blade safely inside a thick leather sheath that could be tied to her waist. She also found a few days' worth of synthetic food packets, which were high in energy but low in taste. Jennifer decided to leave the food packets in the pod and opened them for the scavengers to dispose of.

The compartment also held something she didn't expect, a hard metal black lockbox with a three-letter-coded locking mechanism bound by security tape. Once opened, the box could only be closed and locked with a code of her choice. She knew before opening, from listening to her parents talk about the ship and the life pods, the box contained a newly manufactured copy of an ancient .45-caliber pistol with a full eight-shot magazine and a twenty-count box of bullets.

She didn't want it, but the gun was too dangerous to leave behind in the pod. Jennifer selected a three-letter locking code and shut the lid tightly, having no option but to take the box. She wasn't thrilled about introducing the concept of a gun to this world and hoped she could rid herself of it soon. Jennifer handed Taric the items that could be useful to them, knowing he would examine every item with interest. Lastly, along with some misgivings, she handed Taric the black box before climbing out of the pod's confines.

Taric looked at the hard dark made thing while turning it over in his hands curiously, wondering its purpose and asked, "What is this?"

Jennifer looked at his curious eyes and sighed heavily. "It's a lockbox."

"What does it do?"

"It holds dangerous things safely. I think for the sake of your world, I should throw it into the river and let the whole thing rust away to dust. Believe me, Taric, your world is better off without it."

"What does it hold?"

"You're better off not knowing!" Jennifer exclaimed, vocalizing her statement a little louder than intended, stunning the normally soft-spoken Taric into silence.

The confused hurtful look he gave her saddened her heart, and so she softened her voice and apologized. "I'm sorry. I didn't mean to shout, but you must understand, the only purpose of what's inside this box is to kill. I know what's best for us and the thing inside isn't one of them. Taric, please trust me. I can't let anything from my world contaminate this one. I have to destroy it."

Taric nodded, giving in to her will because he trusted her. "So be it."

"Really?" she asked, shocked by his casual response.

Taric leaned over and kissed her and let the kiss linger, savoring the taste of her lips before he slowly pulled away and answered with a sad frown fixed upon his face. "Yes. From what you've told me about Earth's history and science, I don't think I want to know any more than I already do. Why? Because it frightens me.

"Before we met, the ability to sail through the stars belonged only to the spirits. Now, I know it's possible. However, to sail through the stars, your people's way of life slowly killed your world. How heavy it must weigh on your heart, knowing the land of your birth is dead because of your people's endless curiosity.

"I wonder if my people will someday do the same to this land. I hope not. You tell me whatever is in the box is dangerous and that it doesn't belong here. You tell me I'd be better off not knowing about it. You know what? I believe you and everything you've told me about your people to be the truth. So if the thing inside is that dangerous to me or my world, I'll not give it another thought. I'll trust you to find a way to destroy it."

Humbled by his honest insight into the ugliness of what her world had become, Jennifer could only whisper, "Thank you."

CHAPTER 8

Attacked

Fragmented and distorted images of Peter's burial flashed within Taric's subconscious mind making his attempt for some restful and much-needed sleep nearly impossible. During the night, he had lain awake within the furs listening to Jennifer's smooth rhythmic breathing and the heavy silence of the cave ringing loudly in his ears. His conscious mind was struggling to understand the unsettling, confusing and fragmented images within his dream while trying to make sense of Jennifer's sudden and unexpected demand.

Before the onset of night, they buried Peter's bones downwind of their cave within the golden speckled light of the forest canopy of amber leaves swaying and rustling softly on the breeze. They placed Peter's bones near the edge of the grasslands among the twisting roots of an old gnarled tree with a trunk that stretched upward only to vanish in the twisted maze of the canopy's branches. The view from the base of the tree revealed the entire grassy plain. Jennifer was pleased with the view. She marveled at the wonderful sights of the animals roaming the grasslands. She hoped her brother would find peace in the spot she had selected for his grave.

She was searching the area for a stone to use as a marker. She soon found a large gray stone with its surface speckled with red and green bits of sparkling crystal ore. The sight of the pretty crystals embedded within the stone's pale-gray rock reminded her of a mosaic sculpture made of tiny rubies and emeralds. It took both of them to move the stone and set it to rest above her brother's grave. Jennifer knelt beside the stone and smoothed the loose soil around it with her hands. She knew with a little passage of time, the stone would appear as if it had lain there since the valley was carved out by glaciers of ice and stone. She then quietly began to cry, sobbing out her remorse for his death in long mournful wails of a lost and grieving soul.

Taric stood patiently by her side, touching her shoulder with a gentle hand as Jennifer cried. When she finally gained her composure, he heard her quietly whisper a simple prayer to her God. "Dear Lord, please welcome my brother into your loving embrace and grant him an eternity of peace and happiness. Peter was my friend, companion, and confidant of all my childhood secrets. He was a brother who charmed everyone he met with a kind smile and a little laughter. His loving heart and kind actions revealed a soul truly touched by your grace. Bless him, dear Lord, and tell him, I'll love him all the days of my life. Amen." Without saying another word, Jennifer rose slowly to her feet and, without looking back, walked away in the direction of their cave.

Sensing her friend's distress and sadness, Jaxx trotted up beside her and every so often would jump in the air to nudge Jennifer's hand with her damp nose as if to reassure her. Taric watched them go, respectfully letting Jennifer settle her grief according to her beliefs and customs. He understood the significance of her prayer and what it meant for her.

As the odd pair disappeared into the trees, Taric gazed down at the stone and made a promise to Peter's spirit. "Rest easy, young brother. I hope your spirit finds peace with your god and may he find your spirit worthy for another life on the land." He then started walking back to the cave, and after a few paces, he stopped, turned back around, and called to Peter's spirit one last time by saying, "Goodbye, my brother."

Jennifer was sitting beside the fire idly, poking the glowing embers with a stick while waiting for Taric's return. It wasn't long before Jaxx hearing his approach ran out of the cave to greet him and escort Taric the rest of the way home. Jennifer smiled as she heard Taric's hearty laughter in response to the little puppy's energetic playfulness. A moment later, Taric entered the cave and sat down on the furs beside her. Jaxx squeezed, wiggled, and nudged herself in between her packmate's legs for a comfortable, warm spot to lay and garner their soothing affection.

Mindful of Jennifer's grieving heart and unsure of what to say, Taric waited beside her in silence. He watched her brows flex up and down on her forehead as she thought, while absentmindedly continuing to drag the stick back and forth through the hot embers. It was interesting watching her think, trying to formulate her thoughts. After a few more quiet moments sitting side by side, patiently waiting for her to break the heavy silence, she abruptly announced with an unexpected underlying tone of desperation and fear in her voice. "It's only a matter of time before we meet other people. Don't tell them I fell from the sky!"

"My love, have I not told you my people are kind and loving? I don't understand why you're telling me not to say anything? I've assured you many times, no one will harm you here. There is nothing to be afraid of!" Taric replied once again in an effort to soothe her fears.

"Do you really want to hear why I don't want you to say where I'm from? Do you really want to know the truth! There are some aspects of the human species, you won't like!" Jennifer loudly stated, almost to the point of yelling. Suddenly angry with him for being so damn condescending toward her when they talked about his people.

"That's something," Taric calmly answered and then asked her with a benign glint reflecting the firelight in his eyes. "Then tell me this truth you fear so much."

"Okay, here goes and don't say you're sorry when I'm done," Jennifer said, pausing to make sure he understood.

"Humans are by nature aggressively violent creatures. We had to be aggressive to survive the countless perils in our world, and I'm not talking about Earth's wild animals. I'm talking about humans. We're a predatory species by nature. Humans are selfish, greedy, and often violent, even among our families. Cruelty and violence of our past have made my species distrustful. It's a basic human instinct to be wary of strangers, but a stranger from another world? No, that can't be known. No one can know the truth!

"Although our body's physical structure and appearance may be similar, were not of the same species. I'm human, my difference in appearance and my origins may be too much for some of your people to accept. It only takes a wild imagination combined with an irrational fear to incite a group of people into a state of uncontrolled panic. We call it mob mentality because sometimes people driven by fear or revenge will actively seek out and kill the focal point of their fear. You're the only one who knows the truth about me.

"If we're to share our lives in this world, I must be accepted as a native of this world. The differences in my appearance can be explained as defects from a complicated birth. You must keep my secret!" Jennifer demanded in a low-pitched, authoritative voice that momentarily sent shivers up and down his spine.

He saw for the first time within the depths of her human eyes, a glimpse of her true strength. Within that brief glimpse, Taric saw a strong-willed woman staring back at him, who was decisive in her actions and reasoning.

Although he believed Jennifer's fears of discovery were unwarranted, he offered her a plausible story to appease her. "We can say you look like everyone else of your tribe, but unfortunately all but you were tragically killed when your cave collapsed during a landslide. We met each other afterward, when our paths crossed while we were hunting in the grasslands."

"That might work," Jennifer said thoughtfully with a slight nod. "Yes, that will work just fine." Then in a softly spoken voice, she changed the subject of their conversation with a question. "What animal are we hunting tomorrow?"

"Gorocs," Taric answered and then spent the remainder of their evening until they lay down to sleep, explaining his technique for hunting a goroc.

Goroc hunting required a stout heart and a fearless approach when armed with long, sharp, bone-tipped laces and sharp stone-tipped arrows for their bows. The goroc herd ruled the open plains with impunity, claiming the best grasses and shrubs for themselves in return for their protection from predators. Gorocs relied on numbers and brute force to defend the herds on the grasslands. Gorocs were the only animals living on the grasslands capable of repelling a kessra pride's coordinated attacks.

A goroc was a wide burly and mean-tempered beast that roamed on the outskirts of the grassland in small family groups. Gorocs had a dense warm underlayer of fine fur next to their skin and an outer layer of long coarse strands of matted dark brown hair that dragged on the ground as they walked. When grazing, goroc heads could be extended outward toward the ground, but when threatened, it could be drawn into its chest by their strong elastic and muscular necks located between the animal's wide shoulders. When fully grown, their head and shoulders stood as high as a man's chest on thick, stocky, short legs that supported their heavy bodies.

Above their heavy brows, a stone-hard plate of thick bone grew to crown the top of their skulls. On each side of the bony plate, gorocs were armed with a pair of curved horns, which made them extremely deadly in a fight. Below the plate, black eyes peered out from flat-nosed faces of wrinkled and hairy jowls that sagged below their chins with a slow, steady flow of spittle spilling out from each side of their mouths as they chewed on the dry grass.

Tired of thinking about his dreams and her fears and fed up with trying to sleep, Taric decided to get dressed and scout the gorocs' location before Jennifer awakened. He quietly slipped out of the furs they shared in the night and dressed quickly in the cave's dim fire-light. Jaxx awakened by his movement was lying on the edge of the furs near Jennifer's feet. The dog, as she called it, raised her head and watched him curiously, but Taric motioned with one of Jennifer's hand signals for Jaxx to stay where she lay. As always, he was astonished to see the lycur obey and lay its head back down on the furs with her eyes following his every move about the cave.

Using the cover of darkness, a pride of hungry kessras climbed down from their mountain lair to the rocky base and stepped onto the river's sandy embankment, lured by their hunger and the strong scents of goroc musk and urine drifting in the wind. The lead kessra's bronze eyes and ears were fixated on the opposite shore, listening intently to the varied animal noises created by the herds as they grazed on the dry summer grass in the early morning darkness. Sniffing the enticing aromas of their diverse prey, the lead kessra urged his pride toward the water. With a low rumbling growl, the pride's alpha male and leader stepped into the swiftly flowing water and began to swim across the narrow river.

Once on the opposite shore, heavy impressions of their wide clawed padded feet sank deep in the soft sand were the only signs of their passage until they reached the long grass crowning the sandy embankment. There they split into two groups and instantly vanished in the tall grass. One group moved silently northward around the herds to position themselves for a three-directional rushing attack. They were to drive the herds south and distract the formidable goroc bulls that would rush toward the source of danger in defense of the herds.

The pride's leader moved easily through the dry grass near the outskirts of the herds. Moving silently into position, the three kessras waited anxiously for their packmates to initiate the hunt. The leader knew the hunt would begin when it heard the grassy plain erupt with the combined noises of frightened beasts stampeding toward them. The pride's alpha male lowered its sleek body even closer to the ground as the anticipation of tasting warm, sweet bloody meat grew within its consciousness. When the hunt began, they would wait as a team for the bulk of the swiftly moving mass of animals to pass them by, as they preferred to ambush the stragglers too slow or weak to keep pace with the thundering mass.

Taric added more wood to the fire to deter any small scavengers from entering the cave and warm the cool air inside. Assured, Jaxx would remain with Jennifer and not follow him outside the cave. Taric grabbed his weapons and left the warm confines of their comfortable little cave. He moved cautiously southward in the darkness, barely able to see the solid trunks of the forest trees growing on the hillside around him. Taric silently moved through the trees to the edge of the grasslands leaving a faint scent of his passage in the loose soil under his feet as he advanced closer to the herds.

Slightly south of the cave moving slowly within the trees toward the grassy plain, a prideless kessra stood, sniffing the scents drifting in the air. It was too old and weak to hunt effectively and was verging on the cusp of starvation when it smelled a familiar scent of a favored prey. Instinctively, the old kessra turned to follow the intriguing scent toward its source.

Taric wasn't the only hunter creeping slowly through the tall dry grass, making sure to stay downwind of the roaming herds. Sniffing the strong savory scents of their prey floating in the air, the kessras moved cautiously through the grass, stopping in instinctive intervals to raise their heads above the tall grass. The stealthy predator's keen eyesight and sensitive noses immediately located the huge goroc bulls grazing on the outskirts of the amassed herds. Once again, the kessras, with their senses heightened by the pungent odor of goroc musk, silently vanished back into the cover of tall grass. Each kessra, so accustomed to hunting as a coordinated pride, moved invisibly toward their assigned spots with practiced ease.

Taric felt a slight breeze of cold air on his skin and shivered just as the first rays of sunlight crested the mountain peaks to slowly lift the night's veil of darkness. The sight of wide swaths of trampled grass and brown soil stretching down the northern plain were sure signs that most of the smaller animals would soon begin their long migration to the warm southern flatlands for the duration of the north's bitterly cold moons.

Once Taric located the gorocs in the morning light, he decided to return to the cave in time to make Jennifer her morning meal. He slowly began crawling away from his vantage point on his hands and knees, keeping his eyes and ears alert for danger. Once he was safely back within the trees, Taric relaxed his guard and turned for home, quickly disappearing within the forests' dark shadows, unaware that his quickened pace and familiarity of the area gave away his presence to three pairs of alert eyes. One pair of eyes turned to follow as Taric moved through the forest, thinking about the bounty a goroc kill would provide them. The hide and fur were ideal for making body wraps, leggings, snow boots, and other necessary items to keep warm despite the regions freezing temperatures.

Asleep under the warm furs of her bed, Jennifer heard a low rumbling puppy growl issuing from Jaxx's clenched teeth. The warning snapped Jennifer instantly awake. "Jaxx, stay!" she commanded sternly in a low whisper while reaching out with a hand to grab her collar as she felt Jaxx's slight body weight lean against her hip and stiffen as if to bolt.

Although Jaxx was not full-grown, she was still a wild animal of the grasslands and driven by her natural instinct to survive. If she could not escape to safety, she would face her adversary and fight fearlessly to the end. But Jennifer knew now was not the time for her to be brave and held on to Jaxx's collar with her fingers.

Within the early morning songs of birds fluttering in the trees and over Jaxx's low growling, Jennifer heard barely perceptible clicks and clacks of long, thick claws striking stone from multiple footsteps of something big pacing the rocks above the opening that led to the interior of her cave.

She looked around for a weapon other than her knife and saw the pair of lances Taric had made for their hunt, but she realized they were too long to be of use in the cave's crowded confines. Despite her size and tender age, Jaxx managed to wiggle loose and jumped to her feet in brave defiance to stand her ground beside Jennifer with her little puppy hairs bristling up along her spine in response to the unseen intruder.

Jennifer reached down and once again got her fingers curled around the collar of the squirming and excited lycur puppy. She lifted her furry bundle of fury up into the safety of her arms and held her. She then remembered the lockbox with the gun and, with Jaxx held firmly to her chest, scrambled over to where she had stashed the box in order to keep it out of the way and out of sight. She pulled the box out from under a mound of soft animal furs next to the firewood along the back wall a few paces above their sleeping furs. Her fingers trembled over the lock as she heard a thump of something heavy landing in the dirt outside the cave as Jaxx's defiant puppy growls grew increasingly louder.

Jennifer was alone and afraid, but Jaxx's brave defiance actually calmed her nerves to make her trembling fingers enter the correct code for the lock to open the box. Once open, she pulled the gun out of the foam lining, slapped the loaded magazine inside the stock, then quickly pulled the slide back to load a bullet into the chamber.

Jaxx's persistent growling suddenly turned into a frightening howl when the light in the cave noticeably dimmed behind her, followed by a deep wheezy rumbling noise. The menacing rumble instantly terrified her, and as she turned around, she saw a kessra no more than fifteen paces away standing at the cave entrance blocking the morning sunlight.

Driven by an insatiable hunger that would not be suppressed, the animal ignored its instinctive fear of fire and stepped into the cave with its eyes fixated beyond the flames. The old kessra could not endure the agonizing pain of hunger anymore and committed its reserve strength to its four hind legs. It leaped upward emitting a deafening and terrifying roar that reverberated off the walls. Outside the cave's confines, the roar alerted the unwary herds of danger.

The kessra propelled itself over the flames in a graceful arc, while stretching and reaching forward with a pair of thick clawed forelegs poised to grab its prey. Bravely in spite of her terror, Jennifer managed to raise the gun just as the kessra was at the crest of its terrifying leap and instinctively fired three shots at point-blank range into the animal's head in rapid succession.

Blam! Blam! Blam! The deafening gunshots sounded from inside the cave, allowing the reverberating echoes to escape and prematurely initiate the mountain pride's attack on the alert herds by panicking them into a massive and uncontrollable stampede. Blindly the animals ran across the trampled and muddy grasslands away from the kessra roar and the unfamiliar noise of Jennifer's gun.

Unable to avoid the full weight and extended claws of the old kessra, Jennifer braced herself as it landed on top of her with dead unresponsive limbs. The forceful impact against her body pressed the breath out of her lungs. Terrified and suddenly struggling to fill her lungs with air, Jennifer frantically began pushing, kicking, and squirming her way out from beneath the dead weight of the beast.

Once she had herself free, Jennifer sucked in, heaving deep breaths of air filling her lungs and easing the pain in her chest.

Shivering from her fright, she looked at the animal that attacked her. The kessra's distorted, bullet-riddled head was bleeding out odd copper-colored blood onto the dirt while two of the hind legs began to sizzle in the fire. After what seemed like an eternity, Jennifer managed a trembling smile and provided a gentle, soothing touch for her brave little companion's timely warning. "You're a good girl, Jaxx. I'm so proud of you." Hearing her words only between her ears, Jennifer cried, grateful for the tiny puppy that saved her life.

Her heart was pounding in her chest as she lay naked on the cave's cold dirt floor half out of her sleeping furs. Her body was still shaking from the ordeal but lifted the growling puppy up to her face and kissed its tiny face over and over again. "It's dead. It can't hurt us anymore," she said softly, letting Jaxx hear her voice even if she could not hear herself speak.

When the kessra roared and leaped over the fire at them, she recalled seeing the animal's wild eyes and deadly claws reaching out for her and thought death had come. Instead, she was amazed to be alive and without injury all because of her brave little lycur.

CHAPTER 9

Aftermath

While running quietly through the trees toward the rocks and open trail that ran along the base of the mountain, Taric heard the chilling roar of a kessra followed by a frightening thunderous noise in rapid succession coming from the direction of their cave. Hearing the roar and strange noise slowed Taric's quick pace to a slow, careful walk. He stopped beside a tree and looked ahead in the morning light, aware a kessra could be hiding in the shrubs somewhere between him and the cave.

Reacting to the roar and gunshots, frightened animals all across the grassy plain suddenly bolted en masse, instinctively fleeing in the opposite direction of their perceived source of danger. The herds stormed down the high grasslands with confused goroc bulls mixed in among the panicked animals. The herds were so tightly packed as they ran, some of the smaller animals were tripped up in their flight and trampled to death by hard hooves of the larger animals running blindly down the plain. The massive herd of animals vanished from the northern grassland so quickly that only a few adolescent goroc bulls remained behind, standing in confused disarray among the varied herd's many frightened and abandoned young.

Suddenly, three kessras appeared leaping high in the air from their concealment in the tall grass toward their prey as another pair running swiftly down the plain ran ahead of the startled stragglers, then turned around and ran back toward the frightened animals, effectively blocking their path of escape, turning the unfortunate ones into the charging claws and teeth of their packmates.

A few adolescent gorocs abandoned in the confusion of the sudden stampede were too young and inexperienced to mount a defense against the pride of skilled predators. The adolescent gorocs were the first to bolt and charge after the stampeding herds, following a freshly trampled trail of churned-up dirt mixed with scattered clumps of dry grass. Instinct prompted many of the young to run, but in the instant they attempted to flee, some of the abandoned young fell as victims of a kessra's swift attack. Most of the young animals survived the swift slaughter and ran for the safety of the herds, leaving the kessras to greedily gorge themselves on the warm sweet copper-colored blood and flesh of their many kills.

Taric left his crouching spot by the tree and was moving slowly toward the cave when suddenly a twig snapped loudly behind him. Taric stopped instantly and stood motionless amidst the shrubs and trees. Turning his head in the direction of the sound, he saw a kessra's head rise above the shrubs with eyes intently fixated on its intended prey—him. Seeing the deadly predator so near to his position, actively hunting him, scared Taric half out of his mind. He could use his bow, but if he missed, he'd die horribly, screaming for the mercy of death to release his soul into oblivion. He had no desire to experience a kessra's sharp claws digging into his flesh while pulling him back into its open jaws of sharp teeth.

If he wanted to continue living, he had to make a run for the safety of the rocks at the mountain base. He knew of a fissure in the rocks that was just wide enough for him to slip through the cracks, but not the kessra and hopefully deep enough for him to hide. It was his only chance, and so, keeping his ears alert for the rapid footfalls of pursuit, Taric took off running as fast as his legs would carry him over the ground and never looked back, his eyes focused on his destination. Losing the advantage of stealth, the kessra charged after its fleeing prey and easily began to close the distance between them with each powerful stride.

Inside the cave, the repeated echoes of gunshots ringing inside Jennifer's ears slowly faded, allowing her to hear the raucous commotion of frightened animals, amid multiple angry roars of a kessra pride hunting in the area. Her mind, still shaken from the ordeal, was slow to process the sounds she heard coming from outside the cave, but as her awareness returned, her fright did too.

"Taric!" she screamed, knowing he was out on the grasslands and, without thinking, ran naked out of the cave armed with a pistol in one hand, and Jaxx held firmly to her chest with the other.

Thinking Taric might have been caught unawares by a hunting pride and unsure of the direction she should take. Jennifer helplessly strained her ears to hear the most insignificant sound amid the frightening commotion of the kessra's hunting prowess. She listened for anything that may give her some indication of his whereabouts but to no avail. Then suddenly, Jennifer heard him crying out nearby in alarm, followed by a very loud roar of a kessra just inside the forest.

She turned around just as Taric broke free of the trees and made a dash for the rocks and disappeared into them as if by magic. An angry kessra was only a half step behind him and was reaching out for Taric's flesh, when she heard him scream from inside the rocks just as the creature slammed its weight against the rocks, roaring angrily at its elusive prey when it could not press its shoulders inside the narrow fissure. It twisted and turned its body repeatedly over the narrow opening, trying to fit inside and only managed to stretch a forepaw into the fissure's shadowy depths.

Snarling in frustration, the kessra pressed its slim head in between the rocks while anchoring the stocky mass of its body over the fissure with five long-clawed limbs gripping the hard stone. Angry eyes blazed with deadly intent inside the crack at Taric, who crouched as low as he could in the rocky crevice to avoid the slashing forepaws sharp claws. The snarling beast's attention was so consumed by the nearness of its prey, it did not notice Jennifer's approach. It continued to repeatedly swipe a long-clawed forepaw at Taric and was finally rewarded when claws sliced into soft flesh.

"Ahhhh! Ahhhh!" Jennifer heard Taric's frightful scream as the enraged creature's sharp claws slashed and pulled at the flesh hiding within the rocks.

"Hey, you son of a bitch! Leave him alone!" Jennifer shouted loudly before firing her pistol two times at the awful beast trying to kill and eat Taric. Her first shot missed to ricochet off the rocks, but her second shot struck the kessra midbody just slightly below the middle shoulder. The force of the bullet's impact knocked the beast off its rocky footing to fall heavily onto the ground.

A furious animal, unaccustomed to sudden searing pain, rose shakily to its feet, bleeding profusely from the gunshot wound. It turned toward Jennifer, snarling menacingly and fearlessly displayed a mouth full of long, sharp teeth within its narrow-headed snout. Jennifer calmly approached the deadly beast, seeing the whole scene play out before her eyes as if in slow motion, as she fired the pistol with all the fury of hell she could muster. Two rapidly fired bullets struck the enraged beast in the neck and through the abdomen, knocking it back onto the ground, unable to move but still very much alive. Jennifer walked up to stand near the kessra, seeing it painfully wheeze out the last few breaths of life. Her anger was impatient for death and refused to simply stand idly by and wait. So she hastened the creature's demise with a final shot to the head.

Hearing a little yelp from Jaxx, Jennifer sadly realized she had held her little friend in her arms throughout the entire ordeal. She set Jaxx on the ground with a little pat and rub behind the ears. "Stay," she ordered with a gentle stroke of her hand over Jaxx's brow and down her spine, but Jaxx was true to her natural instincts and bravely rushed the dead kessra. Jaxx naturally attacked the corpse by targeting the neck in a leap, sinking her tiny teeth onto loose flesh. The tiny lycur fiercely shook its head from side to side, making sure the kessra was dead. Jennifer could only smile, seeing her brave attack on the dead beast.

"Taric! Taric?" Jennifer nervously called out into the rocks. Fearing the worst, but hoping for the best, she looked inside the opening and saw a terrified Taric crouched low, way down in the crack with an arm held above his head and afraid to look up. Jennifer could hardly believe he managed to squeeze himself so quickly into the dark narrow fissure and escape certain death.

"Taric? It's me, Jennifer," she soothingly cried into the opening as tears welled in the corners of her eyes. "It's all over. Look at me? The kessra is dead! Do you hear me? The kessra is dead! It can't hurt you anymore," she cried loudly seeing the claw wounds on his arm bleeding profusely, hoping he could break free of his shock and respond to her voice.

Taric was slow to recognize Jennifer's voice, but when he did, he lifted his head to see her above him, sobbing and reaching out to him with her hand. Ignoring the pain from his wounds as best he could, Taric weakly grabbed onto Jennifer's outstretched arm and pushed slowly with his legs. Taric lifted himself free of the fissure's tight confines and allowed Jennifer's strength to pull him gently toward her. Taric's first step out of the rocks faltered, and he began to stumble forward but was quickly caught and supported by Jennifer as she held him to her side.

Watery eyes and blurred vision made it difficult for Jennifer to accurately gauge the depth and severity of the wounds to his right forearm and hip. "I've got you. Let's get back to the cave and get you fixed up," she said with an encouraging smile while wrapping his good arm around her shoulders and slowly guided him home. Jaxx, with her snout smeared with blood calmly, scampered a few steps ahead in the direction of their cave.

The smell of burnt hair and flesh reminded Jennifer of the kessra she had left inside the cave when they reached the opening, but she paid it no mind. She guided Taric inside, laid him onto their sleeping furs, and set the gun into the lockbox but left it unlocked. She then rose to her feet and walked back around the firepit to where the kessra lay half out of the pit. She grabbed onto a leg with her strong hands and pulled the corpse free of the smoldering embers.

Jennifer then went to the firepit and quickly added small twigs and sticks on top of the few hot embers smoldering inside the blackened pit. Bending low over the smoky coals, she gently blew a couple of breaths of fresh air, getting them to eventually flare up into flame and ignite the small sticks and twigs. When the fire began to grow with small flickering flames stretching into the air above her pile of sticks and twigs, she added larger and thicker pieces of wood to the flames. Fortunately, the cooking stones had been set into the pit the night before and were still fire hot and serviceable.

Jennifer hastily filled a cooking bowl with clean water and, using a pair of sticks flattened at one end, lifted four hot stones out of the pit and into the bowl. Steam rose from the bubbling bowl as the stones quickly heated the water. Jennifer then found the pod's first aid kit and began examining the contents, gauze, scissors, tape, antibacterial ointments, and an assortment of small to large new skin bandages. It was obvious Taric needed stitches to close his wounds, but the kit didn't contain a needle or thread. She was trying desperately to think clearly, fully aware Taric's wounds were serious and could become infected if not treated properly. Frantically, she searched the cave's interior for something she could use to stitch up his wounds when her eyes spotted the fishing kit and knife.

"Yes!" she exclaimed thankfully, reaching out she took the knife and then grabbed the simple fishing kit containing line, hook, and sinker weight. She then gathered her supplies and returned to Taric's side to see a slight smile radiating from his face as tears rolled from his eyes when he saw the dead kessra.

"Hey, don't worry about that," she said softly as she knelt beside him. "I know you're hurting, but you've been injured pretty badly. I'm not a healer where I'm from, but I know enough first aid to treat your wounds, but it's going to hurt a little bit."

Taric sadly cried watching Jennifer scramble about the cave selecting various items she needed to treat his wounds. "My love. No one survives a kessra clawing. Even if you escape, sickness and death always follow," he said flatly, having accepted his eventual death with an overwhelming sense of lost hope inside the fissure.

"Always? A sickness? Really? You mean to tell me no one has ever survived an attack! Well, that's bullshit! Do you hear me, Taric! Bullshit! You're not going to die! So you fucking better get used to the idea of living!" she shouted angrily, her green eyes blazing with fury at his calm acceptance of his impending death.

"It's true. I've seen what happens to a hunter who's been clawed. Death always takes the hunter because kessra wounds will not heal."

Taric sadly responded, accepting his fate with the hopelessness of a doomed soul.

"Taric! Just shut the fuck up! It sounds like an infection. What do your healers do?" she snidely asked, not caring if he answered her or not. She then rambled on by saying. "They probably cover the wound with a poultice of muddy roots and herbs, while performing sacred rites imploring your ancestors to judge the hunter worthy of life and heal his fucking wounds! Well, I'll have you know, that shit didn't work on Earth and it won't work any better here!" Jennifer sarcastically exclaimed, clearly upset with him.

There were four bloody gashes running across his hip, roughly two to five inches in length, but Taric's arm was a patchwork of sliced flesh. She began by placing some gauze pads over the claw marks on his arm. "Hold down firmly. It will slow the bleeding," Jennifer said as she took Taric's free hand to hold the gauze pad over the wound. She then turned her attention to the ugly wounds on his body and did so, none too kindly.

Jennifer slowly began to clean the claw marks on his hip, using a soft cleaning hide soaked in warm water. She carefully cleaned each slash mark separating the torn flesh to wash away dirt and clotted blood from the wounds. Once the wounds were clean of foreign debris and blood, Jennifer tied the line to the hook with a simple twisting fishing knot and cut the ten-foot line in half with the knife.

Taric looked at her but said nothing, somewhat abashed by her harsh and angry words to him. He watched curiously as Jennifer threaded the curved hook for the first time through his flesh, pulling the skin together and tying it securely with a knot. He flinched when she cut the line with her knife. He saw her begin to repeat the process a fingers width down the cut when Taric realized it might be best not to watch, but he was curious and couldn't bring himself to look away.

"I don't think the damage is too great. The claws didn't get enough of you to do serious harm. I'm sorry if this hurts, but look on the bright side of things. You'll have a cool set of scars to brag about," Jennifer said softly in a calmer voice, trying to reassure him with a smile and a little humor as she diligently performed her task of stitching his torn skin back together.

It was midday by the time Jennifer finished stitching his wounds. She used another clean damp bathing hide to gently wash away tiny droplets of blood that formed along the length of her stitched seams. The arm looked horrible, but she knew it would heal as she applied a liberal amount of the antibacterial ointments over the wounds and covered them with a new skin bandage to complete the task.

Jennifer had talked the entire time with such an aura of confidence, he could do nothing but believe her. He endured her creative ministrations in quiet agony as she treated his wounds. He was exhausted from the ordeal, but a glimmer of hopeful belief slowly returned to Taric's soul. She said he would live with such an assuredness of conviction, it allowed him to quietly slip into a deep recuperative sleep.

Seeing him asleep with Jaxx curled up by his head and resting her chin on his shoulder, Jennifer finally relaxed and began to tidy up the area. She began the task by removing the dead corpse from the cave. As she dragged the dead beast into one of the furthest firepits they used for drying meat outside their cave, she heard the pride of kessras snarling and roaring as they filled their bellies with the meat of their kills. She added plenty of wood to cover the beast in the pit and left it.

A slight breeze of cool air flowed over her skin as she walked back toward the cave. With a shiver, Jennifer finally noticed her nudity and her pale skin smeared with Taric's copper-colored blood. She needed to bathe in the river, but hearing the beasts on the plain made the crossing to the river a dangerous undertaking. The thought of them so near infuriated and propelled her into taking decisive action.

Back inside the cave, she bundled up some clean clothes and grabbed the gun and the box of bullets before striding purposefully from the cave. She paused by the entrance long enough to load her empty gun with new bullets. Once loaded, Jennifer deliberately advanced toward the open plain and the feeding kessra pride.

From Taric's lessons of kessra habits, she knew they tended to become dimwitted and lethargic when their bellies were full of fresh warm meat. Besides having a gun to her advantage, knowing those two aspects of kessra lore gave her an advantage of time, a few precious seconds in which to achieve her goal. She counted five as she stepped into view and approached, but they were distracted by the taste of meat and the smell of warm blood as they ate. She walked within twenty paces of the nearest one before it noticed her. Without hesitation, Jennifer aimed for the head and fired. The bullet entered the brain through the right eye and exited through the back of the beast's skull.

Startled by the sudden noise and Jennifer's intrusive appearance, the kessras were slow in reacting to her presence. They rose from their kills, confused by the strange intruder within their midst. They began to snarl threateningly at her while standing over their kills. Jennifer just smiled and welcomed the clear targets they presented to her. Without thinking, she repeatedly aimed and fired her gun at the bloody beasts. Two fell dead with bullet wounds instantly appearing in their chests; another was struck twice in the neck and quickly bled out with a severed spinal column.

Of the remaining two, she struck one in the hindquarter knocking it onto the ground, and before it could rise, she killed it with another bullet aimed at its heart. The last kessra turned and ran from its kill. Jennifer took careful aim as she tracked the fleeing kessra and fired her last shot. She held a grim, satisfied smile on her face seeing it suddenly jump midstride into the air roaring out in pain as her bullet pierced its side. The wounded beast fell heavily to the ground writhing in agony, unable to rise onto its feet and run.

Jennifer quickly reloaded her gun as she calmly surveyed the carnage around her. Armed once again with a loaded gun in her hand, Jennifer let the box with her four remaining bullets fall to the ground. She strode casually toward the wounded kessra, taking her time reveling in its suffering. When she was within a few paces of the stricken animal, Jennifer pointed the weapon and fired.

Standing among the dead kessras, Jennifer counted fourteen animals of varied species and sizes dispatched by the five kessras. The number of dead animals did not belie the efficiency of their hunting skills or appetites. Seven of the animals were nearly consumed with their bloody corpses shredded to pieces and scattered around the area as the kessras feasted on their flesh. When the shock of what she had done hit her conscious mind, Jennifer fell weakly to her knees. Her eyes fell to her naked lap with the gun resting in her hands, and she began to cry.

Jennifer didn't notice the passage of time as she cried over the day's frightening events until the warmth of the sun began to dim as the day slowly began transitioning into the darkness of night. She could hear the sound of flowing water splashing over rocks in the river nearby. Still needing to bathe, she slowly rose off the ground from her knees to stand on wobbly legs. Jennifer tiredly retraced her steps and retrieved her nearly empty box of bullets and bundle of clothes before slowly walking off as if in a dream toward the bathing spot she and Taric shared.

CHAPTER 10

First Snow

Three consecutive sunrises of bright warm autumn days came and went with Taric confined to the bedding of their cave. Jennifer knew he was restless and allowed him to rise from their sleeping furs on the morning of the fourth day. Cold air mixed with misty rain carried on a mild, but steady breeze greeted Taric as he exited the cave. The misty drizzle held within it a faint scent of an approaching snowstorm. The hazy, misty rain shrouding the valley obscured his view of the landscape as Taric stood in the elements for the first time since the attack. He was wrapped in a warm hide with the fur against his skin. He stood stoutly beside the entrance of their cave, straining his eyes to see through the trees and across the valley in the hazy mist.

He closed his eyes, listening intently to the ceaseless commotion of the animals living on the grasslands. Occasionally, he'd hear a mating call of a rutting goroc bull bellowing out his call above the din of the restless herds. Hearing the animals continue their normal lives once again with no sense of the past, stirred within Taric's soul an overwhelming sense of joy for the new life he'd been given. He felt reborn and gifted with an enlightened perception of the world he lived in.

"Jennifer!" Taric said happily, leaning inside the entrance so she could hear him. "I need a swim. I stink!"

"I know. Why do you think I let you go outside?" He heard Jennifer respond from inside the cave, followed with a cheerful laugh.

She smiled sweetly at him a moment later as she walked out to stand beside him, holding rolled-up sleeping furs under one arm and clean clothes for the both of them under the other. She set the clothes on the ground just inside the entrance and walked over to the drying racks next to the outside firepits. She hung their bedding with the fur exposed to the misty rain and commented. "These should be rinsed off by the time we get back, and then I can hang them on the racks inside the cave to dry."

Taric just simply smiled at her, mesmerized by the fluid movements of the incredible woman who held his heart in hers. His wounds still hurt him a little, but he felt less pain and discomfort as the wounds healed with each passing day. Taric picked up their clothes and walked over to join her and asked in the softest timber of his voice. "How do I say thank you for saving my life?"

"A kiss would be nice," she replied happily and leaned into him for a kiss. Taric eagerly granted her wish, anticipating the soft sweet taste of her quivering lips and the feel of her body wrapped within his arms.

"Thank you," he whispered to her, holding her to his chest, reluctant to end their embrace, fully aware that each of them was wanting more from the other than just a simple kiss.

Together they began walking side by side down the familiar path to their bathing spot at the river's edge. The path led them near the herds slowly grazing off the area of tall grass. The animals noticed their presence as they stepped out of the trees and into the open grass.

Taric noticed a goroc bull kept a wary eye on them when they reached the depression made by the pod's fall. When Jennifer went to step over the crest, she tripped and stumbled over the short incline to fall awkwardly into the wet grass blanketing the depression. Giggling with mirth as she got back onto her feet and seeing a surprised expression on Taric's face, she laughingly exclaimed, "Wow! Didn't see that coming."

"Are you all right?" Taric asked, laughing with her after hearing her funny remark.

"Yes, I'm fine. Just a bit clumsy this morning is all," she said before they continued walking hand in hand toward the river. Jennifer glanced down the length of the depression and saw the remains of the partially buried pod had disappeared, obscured by the abundant growth of grass and weeds around it. Taric decided to lead the way to the crest of the river's embankment and gallantly held out his arm to assist Jennifer down the sandy slope to the water's edge.

Jennifer immediately stripped off her clothes and dived head-first into the river, disappearing under the swift-flowing icy water. She shivered as she surfaced and slowly began rubbing her body clean, resisting an overpowering urge to hurry. When finished, she walked out of the river with goose bumps covering her slim, graceful body. Shivering from the cold, she gratefully accepted a drying hide from Taric's outstretched hand as his lustful eyes watched her every move. Feeling refreshed and clean once more, she dried her skin with the soft hide and quickly began to dress in her clean clothes.

"Okay, stinky boy, strip!" Jennifer commanded with an amused chuckle but added as a warning while pointing at the water. "Your bandages have to stay dry, so don't you dare jump in."

As much as he wanted to jump into the water, Taric obeyed and stood naked before her shivering in the cold. He then saw a big smile forming on Jennifer's face as she dipped a washing hide into the water. Rivulets of water streamed from the folds in the hide as she placed the icy wad below his chin and began to scrub, working her way quickly down the extremities of his body. Taric felt the heat of his inner body pulled out of him everywhere the cold hide was rubbed. He watched in nervous anticipation as Jennifer dipped the hide into the river and said. "Turn around."

"No! My back is fine. I'm clean enough," he cowardly announced, shivering constantly as he stood in the cold drizzle. "No!" he pleaded while adamantly shaking his head from side to side, trying not to laugh and failing.

"Come on, don't be a baby. Turn around, the sooner I'm done, the sooner you get dressed. And just so you know, your clothes are getting wetter by the minute," Jennifer ordered, emphasizing her warning while holding a cold, wet hide with a mischievous smile lingering on her face.

"You're enjoying this, aren't you?" he asked her as he reluctantly turned around and braced himself for the bitter cold bite of icy water.

"Yes. Yes, I am!" Jennifer laughingly exclaimed while dipping the hide back into the water and then, in one fluid motion, slapped the soaking wet hide across his entire back. She laughed as Taric tried to squirm and jump away, but she held him firmly and scrubbed until he was clean. When she was done, Jennifer laughingly dipped the hide once again in the water and then tossed it to Taric with a grin. "You can finish the rest," she announced, pointing a finger to indicate without saying what and where he needed to wash.

She was rewarded with the saddest but cutest little frown she'd ever seen expressed on his face, but she sternly responded as a healer and not his lover. "Don't give me that. I'll not risk you ripping out your stitches, just because you're in the mood," she teased, seeing the obvious disappointment on his face and liking it.

With a heavy sigh, Taric gave up and resigned to endure his enforced celibacy, but he didn't have to like it. "That sucks!" he exclaimed, using a phrase of Earth slang she had taught him. Showing her his disapproval with a pouting grin that caused both of them to burst into spontaneous uncontrollable laughter.

Once Taric was dressed, they started walking back to the cave when he noticed Jaxx's absence. "Where's Jaxx?" he asked, looking around for her, trying to remember if she followed them out of the cave or not.

"She's home. I told her to stay and wait for us to return," Jennifer answered, confident the dog was safe without them around.

He looked at her in wonder and said, "You have such strange and fascinating talents. I saw you encourage a wild animal to befriend you? Jaxx listens and reacts to your voice as if it knows what you're saying. Who would've imagined a predator could become a friend?"

"Jaxx is your friend too. She's bonded to both of us because we're raising her with kindness and affection. It's a lifelong companionship based on trust and love. I've seen how you play with her and how you enjoy having her around. Now, try to imagine a day without her in your mind. It's hard to do because she's a member of our family.

"Jaxx's life will be short compared to ours, but it will be full of playful excitement and devoted love. Her life is determined by an unknown allotment of time, just like ours is. But on the day this animal dies, our eyes will shed tears, and our hearts will feel the pain of her absence," Jennifer replied, letting him know how influential he is in taming the animal and liking the fact that he cared enough to notice and ask about Jaxx's absence.

"It's not just Jaxx. It's everything I've experienced since you've come. When all others die from the sickness after a kessra clawing, you called it an infection and knew how to prevent the sickness from setting in and helped my body heal itself from a wound. No one before me has ever survived.

"Why are impossible things, so possible for you? I think it's because I can see the vast chasm of knowledge that divides your people and mine. I must have appeared to you as nothing more than an ignorant savage, yet you kindly accepted me for who I am more than how I live.

"You've taught me to see the truth of our ignorance in many ways. You've opened something inside of me that's wondrous and frightening at the same time. Now, I think I understand why you're so afraid to meet other people. How can anyone know so much and not be seen as an ancestor with magical powers?"

"No. No, Taric, you're mistaken. I find you extremely intelligent and knowledgeable of the world around us. My people without our technology would die here. They would need someone like you to show them how to survive. Our knowledge base is so vast, we specialize in separate areas of expertise, but living off the land and having to make everything you own is not one of them. Knowledge like that comes from a lifetime of experience, passed down from generation to generation. It's your people's common knowledge.

"When you explain the habits of the animals and how to hunt them, I listen because you're the expert here. I'm your student when it comes to learning about your land.

"I would've died if you had not found and cared for me. You knew how to reset my leg. You know how to make tools from stone, bone, wood, and leather. You know where, when, and how to stock a cave with enough supplies to last an entire winter. That's knowledge, so don't ever think you're ignorant, because you're not. Knowledge has many sources and levels," she answered kindly as they walked beside each other, letting him know of her faith in him. Trusting in his ability to teach her how to survive the rigors of living in this new world of hers.

Taric was gratified that she didn't think of him as an ignorant savage but remarked as they walked across trampled soil and grass toward the trees near their cave. "You didn't care for the wrapped hide around your leg when you woke up after your fall from the sky. I could tell by the disgusted look you had on your face. What's the word you used?"

"Gross."

"Yes, gross, that's the word," Taric confirmed with an amused smile.

"Well, yes, it was a bit disgusting and gross looking, but I don't fault you for it. It was the shock of seeing it for the first time. But I knew it was the right thing to do. You improvised using what you had available to make a serviceable splint for my leg. It was disgusting and awful looking, but it was also a creative solution for the need. The hide dried out perfectly and prevented me from moving my leg. Even though it looked horrible on the outside, it was soft against my skin on the inside and comfortable to endure," Jennifer admitted as Taric stopped suddenly and looked back at the herds.

"What's wrong?" Jennifer asked a little concerned, wondering what he was looking at.

"Oh, ah, nothing's wrong. I was just thinking, it's too bad the kessras didn't get a couple of gorocs in their hunt. We could have used some of the meat, but the hides would have made excellent sleeping furs and a couple of wraps to keep us warmer in the middle of the cold moons." Taric lamented over the lost opportunity to take advantage of the dead pride's prowess.

"Why not go and get a couple?" Jennifer asked him as they reached their cave. "There's a full magazine of bullets. I could use the gun," she said to him before walking inside the cave. Jaxx was curled up in a ball, wide awake with her tiny eyes happily watching Jennifer's approach, while wagging its tail and waiting to be called.

Jennifer knelt and called her by name. "Jaxx, come on, girl." The pup instantly bounded over to her and began to lick one her of her hands, while the other hand's fingers, lightly scratched her soft furry back, up and down its spine.

"Good girl," she cooed, praising her playful puppy while waiting for Taric's response to her question.

Taric hadn't seen her use the strange weapon on the morning of the attack; he only heard it's thunderous and frightening noise as it killed. She kept it safely locked away in the box and out of sight in the back of the cave. All he knew was Jennifer used it to kill the entire kessra pride. It was another amazing feat he never imagined to be possible, and yet although the weapons use saved both of their lives, she disliked having it around and he wondered why.

Taric's bow was resting against the stone wall of the cave by their sleeping furs. He walked around the furs and picked up the bow and started to pull the string back when he heard Jennifer politely chide him. "Don't! Put it down. It's too soon to be thinking of using a bow. Please wait until the stitches are removed to test your arm strength. I don't have any more fishing line to redo your stitches."

Jennifer then took a cured hide, cut off a small piece, and rolled the hide tightly around a small twig before tying the roll with thin strips of leather at the ends and in the middle. "Here, use this to slowly squeeze and relax your hand. The exercise will help stretch and loosen up the muscles in your forearm. When your hand gets tired, give it a rest, but try to exercise the muscles three or four times a day," she said, handing him the roll while thinking she should've had him start rehabbing the day before.

"No. You have to get close to gorocs. It's too dangerous I can't ask you to try and kill a goroc without assistance," Taric said, alarmed by her proposal while accepting the roll from Jennifer and spinning it loosely in his palms, before giving the roll a slight testing squeeze. He could feel underneath the bandage as he squeezed, the muscles of his forearm sorely stretching his wounded skin. Liking the sensation, he clenched his hand tighter around the roll before slowly relaxing his grip.

"Look, with a gun, I don't need to get close or have a backup to kill one. It'll be like target practice and be over in a few seconds. However, I think I'll need your help with skinning and butchering the beast after its dead," Jennifer confidently countered his argument, while watching with approval as Taric began to slowly tighten and relax his grip on the roll before adding, "Besides, once the bullets are used, the gun will be harmless, and I can throw it into the river and be done with the awful thing."

"All right, we'll go out together. But tell me, why do you dislike the thing that saved our lives?" Taric replied, reluctantly agreeing with her but a little curious nonetheless.

"This was not the first time a gun has saved my life. Throughout our time on Earth, humans have always been violent creatures. We have killed our fellow man over an endless variety of reasons. Our history is a long tale of death and destruction. We're very efficient when it comes to killing. Guns were invented to kill men in battle. It was faster and easier than a lance, knife, or arrow.

"But our normal way of life vanished within the ravages of our idiotic wars. Our society broke down as our cities burned and nation's warred, destroying almost every precious thing we had created or accomplished over the centuries. People fled the ruined bombed-out cities scavenging and stealing whatever they felt like taking, including young defenseless girls. Our world was already in the midst of this horrible self-destruction when I was born. Under my grandparents' strict tutelage, guidance, and insistence, I learned to use a gun by the age of seven. I liked it, learning to shoot at paper targets was fun. I got really good at hitting what I aimed at by the time I became a teenager.

"I grew accustomed to having a gun with me when I went out riding horses, but that all changed one day. I just turned fourteen and was riding my horse alone on the range. During the ride, my horse was spooked by something and threw me off its back before running off.

"There were three men crossing our land, and they spotted me running after my wayward horse. Rather than help me, they chased me down and surrounded me, intending to rape me. I had no choice but to defend myself and so I killed them. You never get over something like that when you're a child. The sights and sounds of killing someone will stay within your memory forever. I learned that little tidbit of information when I climbed into my bed at night and went to sleep. I'd see in my nightmares the shock on their dirty leering ugly faces as the bullets struck them and exploded out the back of their skulls."

Hearing her explain her reasoning saddened and angered him at the same time, but when she finished, "I'm sorry" was all the response he managed to say of Jennifer's tragic story.

Jennifer went to the back of the cave and retrieved the box and opened it. Taric got his first look at the mysterious and powerful weapon and noticed the odd shape and confusing manufacture of it. Jennifer started to explain how it worked as she pulled the magazine out of the handgrip. She removed a bullet from the box and slipped it into the bottom of the magazine. To Taric, the magazine appeared to be a hard shell holding short polished sticks with gray stones stuck on the ends inside it. He watched with interest as she slipped the magazine back into the handgrip, hearing an audible click as it locked into place.

"Have you ever thrown a stone with a sling?" she asked, seeing him quietly nod in response before continuing. "A gun is like a sling, but it throws a bullet, so far and so fast your eyes can't follow its flight through the air."

Jennifer grabbed a bullet from the box and showed him the bottom. It was flat with a lighter piece of something shiny pressed in the center. "The dot in the center is refined flint. When flint is struck by steel, it creates a spark. The spark ignites a tiny mixture of sulfur, charcoal, and potassium nitrate packed inside the casing, which explodes inside the gun, propelling the bullet out of the muzzle toward the object you aimed at," she explained while placing the last two bullets in the lockbox and closed it.

Jennifer stood up and felt Jaxx jumping up at her leg excitedly. "Oh, you poor thing. We're not leaving you this time," she said softly as she stooped over and picked her up. "It's okay. you're coming with us," she cooed softly while snuggling with the puppy under her chin before setting her back down onto the ground to dance around them.

With a knife strapped to her waist, Jennifer lifted one of the poles lying against the cave wall and turned toward Taric and asked, "Can you carry the other pole? We can use them for a travois."

"Sure," he replied, picking up the pole with his good arm and followed Jennifer out of the cave with Jaxx scampering along beside her eager for an adventure.

It wasn't long before they reached the edge of the grassland and surveyed the milling herds. The big goroc bulls were the first to notice them and moved closer to their position in order to keep a wary eye on them but kept their distance.

"Remember, goroc hearts are in the body cavity between the shoulder bones where the lower half of the neck joins the body," Taric instructed, curious to see how she would hunt with the gun.

"We can leave the poles here," Jennifer said, jamming the sharpened end of her pole into the soft ground as Taric did the same with his. Together, they disappeared back into the trees, skirting the herd while staying downwind searching for a vulnerable target. The bulls watching them relaxed their guard when they disappeared in the trees. Jennifer was the first to see an adolescent bull with a young female beside it grazing on the grass on the outskirts of the herd.

"How about those two?" Jennifer asked, seeing the excitement in his sparkling eyes and curiosity on his confused face.

"Two!" he exclaimed with disbelief. "I'd be happy with one."

"Can you keep Jaxx with you?" she asked him and then softly whistled for the rambunctious dog. Jaxx heard her call, stopped sniffing whatever it was chasing in the grass, and quickly ran back to them. Taric picked her up and stroked the neck of the puppy, noticing she was getting bigger and putting on weight.

"Watch this!" Jennifer said and walked out of the trees to the edge of the grass, roughly forty paces away from the pair. It happened so quickly as Jennifer aimed and fired three shots into the bull's neck, then three more into the female. Both fell to the ground bleeding internally from punctured hearts and dying before the echoes of the gunshots faded.

Once again, Taric watched the herds fleeing down the plain in a frightened panic. Away from the thunderous noise and sudden death of the pair of gorocs, leaving the hunters alone on the grass. Light snowflakes began to fall from the cloudy sky as they stood beside the goroc pair. At a distance, they didn't appear to Jennifer to be as large as they were but, standing next to them as they lay on their sides, were as tall as Taric's shoulders.

"We have to hurry," Taric announced, indicating the snow falling around them while drawing his knife to begin the arduous task of skinning the animals.

"I'll get the poles," Jennifer said, walking back to the trees to retrieve them.

The snow had begun to fall in thick white flakes by the time the goroc skins were removed. Jennifer tied one of the hides securely to the poles and then started piling a few large portions of bloody meat onto her travois that Taric had quickly separated from one of the carcasses. The fresh, clean white snow around the pair of beasts was soon tarnished with the bright copper-colored blood of the dead animals.

With the travois loaded with meat and second hide, they began to pull their bounty back to the cave. Suddenly, a goroc bull that had run in the opposite direction of the herds burst angrily out of the trees and charged at them. Jennifer barely had time to raise the gun and fired the weapon repeatedly until the bullets were spent. Her heart was pounding in her chest and was ready to run when the animal slowed and staggered to a stop no more than ten paces in front of her. Breathing heavily and spitting blood from its mouth, the beast gasped with its last breaths of life. It struggled to advance toward them on shaky legs but didn't have the strength to move more than a step or two as its vital organs started shutting down. Sadly, they watched the bull's final moments fade as the last of the animal's strength left it and fell dead to the ground.

"Well, that's that?" Jennifer remarked, referring to the spent weapon.

Taric walked up beside the beast and drew his knife to claim the hide. He cut swiftly down the inside of the legs, up the middle and around the base of the neck, pulling the skin away from the underlying tissues as he worked. Together they removed the hide and loaded it onto the travois, leaving the three carcasses to the scavengers that would respond to the smell of fresh meat in the night.

"Well, only two bullets left," Jennifer sadly said, holding the gun in her hand.

Taric knew from this point forward, hunting gorocs would never again be as easy as it was this day, amazed by the creative and frightening ingenuity of Jennifer's people. It wasn't long before the pair with Jaxx riding on the travois returned to the cave and pulled their burden inside its chilly confines, fully aware that winter had come to their valley.

CHAPTER 11

An Unexpected Surprise

Jennifer stood next to the cave's drying racks, busily plucking the preserved meat from her goroc hunt off the cords and dropping thin, dry strips into a basket at her feet. She worked quickly moving around the three drying racks inside their cave, choosing some for the basket and turning others around on the cord to dry a little longer in the fires smoky heat. When she was done, her basket was full, and the remaining strips of meat occupied a single rack.

She felt the cold air from outside blowing through the gaps between the pegs mounted in the stone and a temporary thin hide they used to cover the entrance of their cave. She hadn't appreciated how effective the hanging strips of meat were in blocking some of the chilly air that seeped into their cozy cave, amazed at how much it helped in keeping the back half of their cave a little warmer, until now.

"Taric, please tell me the goroc hide is ready. If the wind gets any stronger, the hide may be ripped to shreds, and then we're going to freeze. It doesn't look like it's going to hold," Jennifer warned, watching the rawhide skin stretch and bow inward against the wind.

She had been watching Taric closely, studying his tools and curing process. He let her examine a palm-size rectangular-shaped piece of flint he used for the task. The tool, he used for scraping the inner membranes from the hides had a sharp V-shaped cutting edge running along the length. Opposite the sharp edge, the tool had been ground repeatedly against a flat coarse grinding stone that wore off tiny granules of flint to form a comfortable grip.

In long downward strokes, Taric slowly scraped off layer by layer the inner membranes and fatty tissues that once held the skin to the goroc's body. It was extremely hard, repetitive work to clean and preserve a goroc's thick, heavy hide.

"I should be done with it soon," he answered tiredly, as he worked washing the inner side of the hide with heated urine collected for the task, vigorously rubbing it into the skin to preserve and keep the hide from rotting.

"You know, I understand the use of urine in preserving the hide, but do you have to cook it? It smells terrible," Jennifer asked him with a wrinkled expression on her face as he dipped his scrubbing hide into the warm yellow liquid.

"Sorry, I know it stinks. Normally, this task is done outside in the warm sunshine with the hide stretched and pegged into the ground. Working the hide vertically in a frame is very difficult. I'm constantly tightening the laces that are holding the skin onto the frame," Taric said as he smeared the liquid over the hide, making sure every inch was saturated until it could hold no more and drip down the length of the hide.

"What's next?" Jennifer asked him, wanting to know the next step in the process as she walked with her loaded basket into the small inner cave they used to store their food.

"Well, when it's nearly dry, I'll begin scrubbing it down with sand and water to clean and soften the leather. Once it dries, I'll brush off the sand, trim it away from the frame and then fit the hide to the pegs surrounding the entrance," Taric informed her with an easy proud smile of accomplishment as she stepped back into the main cave.

"Well, let's hope it's heavy enough to block the cold air from seeping inside, I'm getting chills down my spine," Jennifer responded gratefully and then asked, "The furry side will be on the outside correct?"

"Yes. Trust me, the thick fur will block the outside air and keep the heat of our fire from escaping," Taric confidently responded with the assurance of warmer nights ahead.

Jennifer had given up trying to keep Taric from exerting himself. Despite his injuries, he was a man who could not sit idle when there was something that needed to be done. She watched him work and knew he was getting tired. She could see his movements slowing as he continued to saturate the goroc flesh with the urine.

"Hey, why don't you take a break and eat something? You've been at it for most of the day, why don't you wash and sit down and eat dinner?" Jennifer suggested and then added under her breath in a low whisper as she spooned some stew into bowls. "Maybe if I can get you to sit down long enough, I can remove your stitches."

Jaxx had been lying in her bedding near the wall, watching and listening to her packmates with little interest as they talked and moved about the cave until Jennifer spooned some food into the bowls. Immediately aware food was at hand, Jaxx stood in her furs, arching her back, relaxed, and leaned backward stretching out her front legs. With a slight shiver, Jaxx leaned forward stretching out her hind legs as far as they could stretch. She finished limbering up with a hearty shake of her little body to fluff out the hairs of her fur.

"Well, look who's awake," Taric remarked, seeing Jaxx stretch in her bedding as he washed his hands in clean hot water over a large wooden bowl. Taric let out a soft chuckle, when Jaxx sat upright in her furs and followed Jennifer's every move with her little black eyes, patiently waiting for her bowl.

"Do you think she's hungry?" Taric asked while chuckling, amused by Jaxx's expressively curious eyes as she waited in anticipation of her nightly meal.

"Oh, yeah! She's always hungry, the little glutton," Jennifer responded happily as she placed Jaxx's bowl on the ground before handing Taric his dinner bowl. She then grabbed her bowl and sat down beside him on their furs.

Once she was settled comfortably next to Taric, Jennifer pointed to Jaxx's bowl of food with an extended index finger, giving her lycur permission to come and eat. As was Jaxx's custom, when she finished eating and licking her bowl to a spotless appearance of clean. Jaxx sat upright in front of them and waited for the scraps of meat and gravy sure to be left in her packmates bowls.

"There's something I want to show you in the back cave," Jennifer said between bites of the rich goroc stew.

"What is it?"

"Do you remember seeing a small hole in the back wall of the inner cave? Well, when I was getting vegetables for our stew this morning, I could have sworn I heard running water on the other side of the wall. I was wondering if you had noticed it before?" Jennifer asked him, spooning another bite of food into her mouth.

"I didn't know there was a hole!" Taric answered, surprised by the information as it could let pests into their stores of food, and asked, "Was there any sign of our food being eaten?"

"No, but I think we should check our supplies after we finish eating. I'm pretty sure if something was feeding on our food, Jaxx would have sniffed it out. She's in and out of the back cave all the time. I've even caught her a couple of times, trying to sneak a piece of dried meat from the baskets," Jennifer stated, informing Taric of Jaxx's sneaky little tendency of pilfering food in the middle of the night.

"Well, she is growing," Taric said, defending the charming creature, unconcerned with their lycur's clandestine nighttime activities. He finished eating, leaving a few scraps in his bowl, and set it on the ground in front of Jaxx. He gave her head a gentle stroke with his hand and pointed. With her tail wagging swiftly from side to side, Jaxx eagerly devoured the remaining pieces of meat before lapping up the remaining broth in his bowl.

After dinner, Jennifer and Taric walked into the back cave, followed by a curious and restless Jaxx. Jennifer went to the back of the cave and moved a couple of full baskets out of the way. She motioned to Taric as she leaned her ear close to the small rough-edged hole and said, "I can hear water running behind this wall. Come over here and listen, see if you can hear it."

Taric moved in as Jennifer made room and leaned in and quietly listened with his ear pressed over the hole. Stepping back, a surprised Taric exclaimed, "I think your right! There's flowing water behind this wall!"

Poking his finger through the jagged hole, Taric measured the thickness of the stone and added, "You know what? I think when the baskets were stacked, one of them must have hit the wall and made the hole. The wall is not very thick in this area. It might be possible to break our way through."

Elated and excited over the prospect of freshwater, Jennifer began moving and restacking their food stores. She quickly cleared a space to the right and left sides of the hole wide enough for a person to pass through as if a larger opening was already there. "I think you're right. Our cave is made of limestone, and it's soft compared to other types of rock." Jennifer said while dragging a stick in a circle around the hole.

Taric just smiled as Jennifer dragged the tip of her stick across the cave wall in a circular arc leaving an impression in its wake as tiny granules of sand fell away.

"Imagine, having fresh water at our disposal without leaving the warmth of our cave," Jennifer said with glee in her voice.

"Well," Taric replied with a grinning smile. "It will have to wait until tomorrow. Tonight, I need to finish the hide and get it fitted over the entrance."

"Well, after I clean our bowls and you finish curing the hide, Jaxx and I can open the hole a little more using your hammerstone. I really want to see what's on the other side!" Jennifer exclaimed, eager to get started on the project, as she pulled on Taric's arm.

"Let's get busy then," Jennifer added with a teasing grin, seeing Taric's smile in the near darkness, knowing he was feeling refreshed with renewed energy and led him back into the main cave.

Taric vigorously scoured the hide with wet sand while listening to repeated impacts of the hammer stone striking the caves back wall. Taric was nearly finished scouring the cured hide when he heard, Jaxx barking at the unmistakable sound of stone cracking and breaking inside the cave. After another hard impact with the hammerstone, he heard Jennifer exclaiming excitedly, "I'm through!"

When the stone gave and broke, Jennifer had produced a hole in the wall the width of her hand, and within the darkness on the other side, flowing water could be clearly heard. Making sure Jaxx was safely out of the way, Jennifer repeatedly struck the hammer against the wall below, above and around the small opening. Her endeavor quickly paid off and earned her a larger hole. Jennifer continued her process of striking around the hole's circumference, chipping away at the limestone wall in bits and pieces. She soon had an opening wider than her body but still too small to climb through.

Undaunted by her task, she hit the wall equal to her head height and was rewarded with a vertical crack that began a couple of feet above her head and snaked all the way down to the hole. Elated with excitement, Jennifer called out, sticking her arm through, trying to judge where and if the stone thickens. "Hey! come and see this! The wall is barely an inch thick in this area."

Taric walked into the inner cave in time to see Jennifer strike the hammerstone against the wall above her head and see it crumble and fall to the ground with the impact. "Wow!" was all Taric could say as the wall crumbled to the floor. He walked up beside Jennifer and kissed her, hearing the wonderful sound of water splashing against stone from inside the opening.

"I wonder how close the water is? I can't see in the darkness. Can you make a torch or candle so we can see in there?" Jennifer asked Taric while wiping an arm across her sweaty forehead smearing small droplets of sweat. She was too excited to stop and felt the wall's interior surface for moisture with a hand below her waist.

"I can make a torch. I'll be right back," Taric answered and walked away, leaving Jennifer with her task.

Jennifer hit the stone repeatedly until the lower portion of the wall broke away and fell to the ground. She continued hitting the edges of the opening, knocking off the jagged edges, smoothing out the outline of the opening. When Taric came back into the inner cave, he held a flaming torch in his right hand and another unlit torch held firmly in his left hand. He handed Jennifer a torch made of fat tallow and strips of scrap rawhide tied securely onto a branch of firewood.

"This is your discovery, after you," he said, igniting her torch with his and then waited for her to walk into the dark interior of their watery cave.

With a tinge of excited apprehension, Jennifer stepped through. She stood on the right side of the opening, waiting as Taric stepped into their new cave and stood to the left of her. The additional light from his torch clearly illuminated the interior in front of the new doorway as they held their torches above their heads.

To their surprise, they stood on a smooth limestone ledge with scattered rocks of various sizes covered in fine granules of sand. The ledge overlooked a drop-off, no more than ten paces from the wall, where an underground stream flowed swiftly between their ledge and another on the opposite side. Jennifer knelt down to a knee and scooped up some of the fine sand into her hand, feeling the texture of it with her fingers as she stood up and said. "At one point in time, this cavern was the passageway of an underground river that had much more water than it has now. The sand and rocks had to have come from somewhere upstream and was carried downstream to be deposited here as the river water flowed over the floor."

Looking up, while stretching her arm with the torch held high above her head, Jennifer could see the ceiling was only a few feet above the torches flickering flames. Judging by their torches light reflecting off the cavern's white walls, the cave appeared to be roughly twenty to thirty feet in width. But where they stood in front of the new passageway, the cavern's length could not be determined in the darkness outside their torchlight.

Jennifer turned to the right and began walking along the sandy ledge, feeling the smoothly rippled wall with her hand as the ledge sloped gradually downward. As she walked, the ledge narrowed until she stood upon its narrowest point. At her feet, the edge of the ledge was barely two feet in front of her. In the light of her torch, she could see the other ledge on the opposite side of the cavern roughly three feet away.

A waterworn chasm separated the two ledges as swift water flowed violently between them a couple of feet below her feet. With her eyes, Jennifer followed the path of the water between the walls of the naturally eroded chasm. She noticed that where the cave walls came together, the water flowed out of the cavern through a tunnel. By the sound of the water splashing loudly over the lip, Jennifer could tell the water fell heavily and far as it disappeared from her sight in the darkness of the tunnel.

"This is amazing!" Jennifer happily exclaimed as she walked back to rejoin Taric, who still stood by the doorway with a curious expression on his face.

"Is it me or does the cavern feel warmer to you?" Taric asked her as he repeatedly stepped in and out of the cavern through the new opening.

"You know, now that you've mentioned it, it does feel warmer in here," Jennifer responded, thinking she must have been too excited to notice the difference in temperature when she entered the cavern.

"Shall we walk the ledge and see how big this cavern is?" Taric asked her while peering into the darkness on the left side of the opening.

Together they walked up a gradual incline, noticing the ceiling rising steadily higher above their heads. As they walked up the incline, they could hear water splashing ahead of them in the darkness. The ledge slowly widened out to a large oval-shaped flat area. Taric paced off the area and determined the ledge was about seventy paces long and thirty-five paces wide. They stared in wonder in the torchlight as they stood at the edge of the ledge. A waterfall flowed out of an opening near the top of the cavern's ceiling on the far wall to splash loudly into a dark pool below them. The constant influx of water falling into the pool flowed over a gap to the right of where they stood and down into the narrow limestone chasm.

The water was only a foot below the top of the ledge with steam vapor hovering and swirling above the surface. Taric knelt beside the ledge's edge and reached his hand into the water and felt the warmth of it on his skin. "The waters warm," he announced as he brought his hand up to his lips and tasted the water dripping from his hand. "And it's fresh too!"

"Oh my God! We have a warm pool to bathe in!" Jennifer gleefully exclaimed with growing excitement, knowing she'd never need to endure washing her body clean in the river's cold water ever again.

"Yes, we do!" Taric replied just as happily and added. "After you remove the stitches, let's take a swim."

"Sounds like a plan, my love," Jennifer responded and then kissed him lovingly in the torchlight.

He was so enamored by Jennifer's soft lips and glorious kisses, to him, their kisses always ended too soon. "You spoil me, and I love it," he said with a beaming smile on his face while wrapping an arm around her waist as they began walking back to the opening. Jaxx scampered ahead and quickly disappeared through the new passage into the middle cave.

By the time they reached the opening, Taric's mind was racing with possibilities for the area. Thinking of what he envisioned within his mind, he absentmindedly began saying what he thought. "We have to block any heat from entering this cave. We'll need to hang a hide over both entrances in order to keep our stores cold. I'll get another goroc hide stretched out on the frame and bore some holes over the openings to hang hides." Taric paused as his mind centered on an idea and impulsively suggested it. "Oh, or maybe, I can make the task easier and faster by stretching one out on the ledge." He then looked at her and asked, "What do you think?"

"I think you need to slow down," Jennifer replied, chuckling over his list of tasks. "How about if we just get our hide pegged over the front entrance tonight and not worry about what comes next?" Jennifer asked with a loving smile, clearly amazed by his mind's resourceful and creative imagination.

Jaxx was already curled up on their sleeping furs, wagging her tail as Taric sat down beside her. He knew that even though he was stroking and petting the back of Jaxx's neck, and on down her spine enjoying the physical contact, it was Jennifer who held her attention. "You know, I think you're right about Jaxx."

"Right about what?" Jennifer asked as she came over and placed a bowl of warm water with a cleaning hide on the ground and sat beside him. "Take your shirt off."

Taric did as he was told and continued to explain his thoughts. "I think Jaxx has bonded with me, but she has a stronger bond with you. I see how she reacts to your presence. She keeps her eyes and ears focused on you. In my mind, I can see Jaxx fully grown standing next to you, aware of every nuance of your body. She'll not leave your side.

Wherever you go, she goes. She won't worry if I'm not around. She's your friend and protector for her entire lifetime."

"You may have a good point, but don't sell yourself short on her affection and devotion to you," Jennifer answered as she easily pulled off the tattered, dirty bandage covering the stitches in Taric's hip.

"Hey, that didn't hurt!" he exclaimed, thinking it had become a part of him and would resist being removed.

Looking closely at his healed wounds with her tiny knots along their lengths, Jennifer hoped his reaction to removing the stitches would be the same. She began by slipping the tip of her knife beneath a knot and carefully guided the tip further under the line, letting the sharp edge do the cutting. She then pinched the knot between the knife and a fingernail and pulled. She looked up at Taric and grinned as two tiny droplets of blood formed over the spot of the stitch.

"Not bad, right? This should be over in no time," she said with a hopeful smile and went on to the next knot along the scar. Not all the knots were as easy as the first one, Taric learned very quickly as he flinched when a knot resisted at being pulled out. When that happened, he noticed the line always came loose with a tiny piece of his flesh clinging onto it.

"Are you okay?" Jennifer said when she finished getting the stitches out. As she washed his arm, she examined the horrible scars left on his beautiful flesh and started to cry.

"What's wrong? Why the tears?" Taric softly asked, confused by her unexpected tears.

"Oh, I'm sorry," she replied as she wiped her tears away with her hand and explained. "When I think back to the day you suffered these wounds, I feel as if I'm watching it happen to someone else. I can't remember me firing the gun. I just remember the kessra dead at my feet and you trapped in the rocks. I only remember what I felt within me, it was a dark and frightening fear of not knowing if you were alive or already lost to me. I never want to experience that kind of fear again."

Leaning into her, Taric smiled and said assuredly, "You won't! Now, stop thinking about it. Let's go hang the hide, then have ourselves a swim in our new pool."

CHAPTER 12

Winter's End

Taric was irritable and tired of the long winter as he watched big snowflakes falling onto the land. He felt trapped inside the cave, watching the snow swirl in erratic disarray in the air as cold gusts scattered it over the clearing outside of their cave. "The snow should begin melting soon," Taric said as he stood beside the partially opened hide, holding the loose end in his hand while looking outside at the waist-high snow. He shivered in his wrap, feeling the cold, bitter chill of winter air and ice against his skin. Even with the bathing pool and the additional space to move around inside the water cave, he was tired of winter's forced confinement, wanting the warm moons to return and an end to the cold.

"Oh, please close the flap," Jennifer pleaded with him as a slight shiver went down her body. Her arms wrapped about her tightly as the cold air blew into their home.

"I am. I just wanted a look outside," Taric replied as a strong gust forced the heavy goroc hide from his grasp, whipping it wildly about his head. The strong wind made it difficult to affix the hide back onto the pegs and close the cave entrance. When he finally managed to secure the hide back onto the pegs, Taric stepped back with a satisfied grin as the heavy hide billowed inward blocking the cold air from entering their cave.

"You didn't have to unpeg the hide. I would have told you. It's the same as yesterday and, every day since winter began, a whole lot of snow." Jennifer giggled her reply, knowing he was irritable and restless. He needed something to keep busy with, but Taric was such a neat freak, nothing needed to be done or made for days. Since the night she removed his stitches, Taric had spent his time improving their home, making new clothes from the hides of their summer kills, knapping new arrowheads and spear tips from flint. With heavy goroc hides covering the entrances, their stored food was well protected in the cold confines of the central cave. Taric's constant need to keep busy prompted him to sweep the entire ledge of the water cavern clean of the fine sand and small stones. When he had nothing to do, Jennifer noticed, Taric would walk the length of the water cavern to calm his restlessness, which always seemed to make him irritable.

On the northern side of the mountains, a boy was outside his tribe's campsite gathering firewood when he was snatched and dragged off by a fearsome beast. The men of the boy's tribe were out hunting in the area and heard the nearby roar of a kessra and a boy's shrill short scream. The hunters quickly returned to their camp to find their women, clutching their children, hysterically crying, and pointing in the direction the beast had taken.

Knowing the boy was lost to the tribe, the hunters had no choice but to follow the grim trail of blood. They had women and children to protect and could not allow a beast another opportunity to kill again. Tracking it up into the mountains, they discovered the beast perched on a tall boulder feeding on the boy's shredded corpse.

The kessra had chosen its spot to feed at the foot of a ravine running up the mountains. The hunters approached the kessra noisily, armed with lances, arrows, and torches. It was in its prime, busily tearing off strips of bloody flesh into its mouth. The hunters began to spread out, shouting, screaming, and shooting their arrows at the animal as they neared, trying to surround it.

The kessra didn't like hunters or their noisy shouts, watching them from its rocky perch while standing over its kill. A flying stick hit the ground in the grass below its feeding spot in the rocks. Loudly the kessra defiantly roared at the encroaching hunters, not wanting to give up its kill. It lifted and held the remains of the corpse's flesh within its fearsome forepaws and strong jaws. It then turned and fled from the hunters running on its four hind legs up the ravine, skirting around densely packed shrubs, trees, and rocks.

Unable to kill the beast, the angry hunters decided to use the steady wind that blew up the mountain ravine to their advantage. Using their torches, the hunters set fire to the dense growth of grass, shrubs, and trees. They watched with satisfaction as fire and smoke quickly blazed up the pass, preventing the deadly predator from escaping back down the ravine. Carrying its prize and smelling smoke, the kessra fled from the hunter's wall of fire, forcing it to undertake the arduous crossing of the mountain's jagged peaks.

Isolated as it was from the outside weather, the water cave turned into their own private resort. Taric spent days chipping away at the floor of the ledge near the edge to make a trail of small evenly spaced fat lamps dug into the limestone floor. Once the lamps were filled with melted fat and dry moss used as wicks, the combined light of the flames illuminated the ledge's boundary and reduced the need for a torch. In the center of the oval-shaped ledge next to the pool, Taric constructed a large firepit with stones he collected from inside the cavern. The water cave was their private place to exercise or simply relax and enjoy the muscle-soothing benefits of the pool's warm water instead of being constantly confined to the main cave.

Jennifer had been counting the days since her last cycle and smiled to herself as she cooked their breakfast. She was late, very, very late in fact, she thought happily, believing a new life was growing inside her.

"In the middle of spring," she heard Taric say, using her seasonal word for the weather. "We'll travel south down the plain to the wide grasslands beyond our sight. It should be exciting, we might even meet other people down there somewhere."

"Well, that's still a few months away. We can talk about it when the weather warms up," Jennifer replied, standing up with two bowls of chopped meat mixed with wild grains and an assortment of dried fruits in her hands after giving Jaxx her morning meal. Taric gratefully accepted the warm bowl, cupping the bottom with his hands, enjoying the warmth of it seeping into his cold fingers. They sat on their soft furs beside each other and ate their meal slowly, savoring it's delicious and delicate taste. Jaxx, who now has grown to the height of Jennifer's knees, quickly devoured her food, then turned and sat down to watch them, hoping to lick their bowls clean of leftovers.

Thinking Jennifer was still hesitant to meet people, Taric quietly asked, "Why must we wait to talk about this? Why not now?"

Jennifer stiffened as she evaded his question with another, knowing her argument was weak. "Why not stay here another cycle of seasons? I'll learn to hunt better and identify edible plants and when to harvest them as you do so easily. I have to pass as a native of this world. I don't know enough to survive here if something unforeseen should happen to you. I'm not ready to take that test," she argued, fully aware of what he thought of her fear. She played him and felt guilty doing so, but for the moment, she'd rather not tell him the truth of her condition because she was unsure how he'd take the news.

Taric stared at Jennifer in disbelief, seeing her body react to her lie as she spoke. Taric set his bowl down on the ground for Jaxx and asked her with a sad tone in the timber of his soft voice, expecting an honest answer. "Do humans always lie so easily? Is there something troubling you? Please, tell me, what is it? What are you afraid to say?"

Jennifer began to cry, ashamed and embarrassed for lying to him, knowing he saw through it and was demanding the truth from her. "Yes, and I'm sorry, I lied, but I'm not going to be able to travel in late spring."

"Tell me. What's stopping you, the people we might meet? How many times must I tell you, there's nothing to fear!" Taric exclaimed a little louder than he intended.

"I'm sorry, I didn't mean to be so loud," he added in a softer tone of voice.

Jennifer looked in his eyes and quietly whispered, "It has nothing to do with people."

"Then what is it?"

Whispering softly with a nervous hesitant smile, she announced, "I believe I'm with child."

A kind, loving smile instantly flashed onto Taric's handsome face as he leaned into her and softly kissed away her tears, wiping the moisture off her cheeks with his fingers lightly stroking her face.

"A child, really? Why that's wonderful news! Why didn't you want to tell me? What has you so upset?" he asked her, thinking it should be the happiest moment of her life, and yet he sensed there was something else bothering her.

"It may sound strange, but on Earth, a child born out of wedlock is considered by human society as a bastard child and an illegal birth. Two hundred years before the awful wars, our planet was past the brink of overpopulation. Strict marriage and birth controls were enacted by every nation on Earth. Marriages and births were approved and controlled by the government department of health. The penalty for violating birth control laws was the same worldwide, death for the parents and baby. Very few couples were permitted to have more than one child at that time in our history. The laws are no longer in effect, but the stigma of being a bastard still sticks with the child for its lifetime," Jennifer explained while trying not to cry.

"What does that have to do with us? The laws of your world do not apply here. You are free to have as many children as your heart desires," Taric answered her, hoping she'd understand and quit thinking as if she were on Earth and just be happy.

"I love you, and I enjoy living with you, but now I'm going to have a baby!" Jennifer exclaimed and then softly asked. "Will you marry me? I know this is just a stupid feeling and belief of my past, but it's traditional, a part of my culture."

Taric chuckled kindly and said to her. "Your world makes no sense to me. The word bastard is a human concept and has no meaning here. You need to put those concepts out of your mind. Our child's life can never be defined by a stupid human word. We are already bonded or married, if that's what you call it, didn't you know? I gave you my heart and soul on the night we made love for the first time. You and I are here. We are together, and we have been blessed with a new life growing within you. We've endured so much since you arrived. Isn't sharing our lives the same thing as marriage on Earth?" Taric asked her with a smile as he kissed her silly head.

Jennifer knew Taric was correct in suggesting she abandon her earthly prejudices, perceptions, and customs. "I guess it's a bit stupid of me to hold on to my past and human traditions," Jennifer replied while absently scratching Jaxx softly behind the ears as she slept beside her. Jennifer sighed, lifting her head up to look at Taric, only to see the joy of his love for her so deeply expressed in his handsome face and kind beautiful eyes.

"You're stuck with me," he teased her with a smile. "I'm yours for the remainder of my days. I will never abandon or abuse you. I'll raise our child with you at my side wherever you want to live. We'll teach him, or her, the knowledge of your world and mine," Taric said to her happily, seeing the worry drain from her face and body as she relaxed and leaned into his side.

"I'm sorry for being such a foolish girl," Jennifer said to him as she snuggled closer, liking his slight musky scent.

"You're a woman and allowed to be foolish once in a while," Taric answered with a chuckle as he wrapped his arms about her and guided her onto his lap.

"Well, my love, what shall we do now?" Jennifer asked him with a seductive and mischievous grin, while slowly loosening the laces of her blouse, exposing her breasts. Without words, Taric let his eager kisses and soft loving hands answer her question in the shadowy firelight of their cave.

Winter's chilly grip over the land finally began to diminish for Taric, as spring's rising temperatures slowly warmed the region day after day. Taking deep breaths of the chilly springtime air, Taric stood outside his home for the first time without a wrap. He was enjoying the sights of the landscape slowly change as scattered patches of bright green vegetation could be seen emerging from beneath a fading snowpack. He knew the massive herds of animals would soon migrate back into the lush high valley to have their young.

Jaxx nudged aside the heavy goroc hide hanging over the entrance and walked over to sit beside Taric. She nudged her nose into Taric's hand, expecting to be scratched. "Hey, girl, where's Jennifer?" he asked her, giving her chin a scratch with his fingers without leaning over to do so.

Jennifer came out dressed in leggings and a warm snug tunic that revealed a slight bulge in her belly as it draped just below her waist. "There you are. I should have known I'd find you here. Don't you feel the chill?" she asked, wrapping her arms around herself.

"I don't mind it. It makes me feel alive and excited for the animals returning to the high grasslands," Taric answered her, smiling broadly with the anticipation of the hunts to come, clearly expressed in his joyous rugged and handsome face.

"Well, standing in the chilly air is not going to make the animals get here any sooner. Until then, come back inside where it's warm, besides I need your help with Jaxx. She needs more training if she's to hunt with us," Jennifer replied, urging him back inside with an activity he liked to do, while she silently admired the view outside her home.

Catching her furtive glance at their beautiful valley, Taric asked her with a knowing grin as he turned to walk back inside. "It is pretty, isn't it?"

Following Jaxx and Taric back inside their warm and comfortable home, she jokingly replied with a grin, "It will be when the snow is gone, and the musky aroma of rutting animals permeates the air."

Inside the water cave, before their midday meal, the pair worked an eager Jaxx through Jennifer's series of silent commands. Jaxx responded to the hand signals as she was trained to do. With each successful response, Jaxx was given a small piece of their dried meat as a reward. The young half-grown lycur learned her lessons quickly and well over the long winter.

When Jennifer began training Jaxx at the beginning of winter, Taric found the hand signals confusing. But with time and familiarity, he and Jaxx soon had a firm understanding of her silent commands.

"She's ready," Taric commented as he and Jaxx walked over to sit on the furs Jennifer had laid out on the ledge between the firepit and the pool.

"I was watching. She'll be a big help on your hunts when I get too fat to move," Jennifer said with a chuckle, as she rubbed her belly and gasped in surprise as her baby moved inside her.

"Our baby is moving. Want to feel?" she said happily, reaching for his hand and placing it on her belly as their baby moved vigorously under his hand.

A wide smile appeared on his face as he felt their child move within her for the first time. "He's an active one! A sure sign of a strong hunter."

"It could be a girl," Jennifer said with a loving look in her eyes as she stared at her husband in the firelight and heard him say.

"Well, girl or boy, it doesn't matter to me. Our child will become a great hunter," Taric proudly boasted as any expectant father would do.

"Oh, yes! A mighty hunter to care for and protect us, when we're old and feebleminded," Jennifer laughingly responded as she placed Jaxx's bowl on the ground before handing Taric his bowl. She then retrieved her own bowl resting on warm stones beside the fire and joined him on the soft furs to eat her meal, snuggled up beside her mate.

"I was checking our stores, and we're getting low on supplies. We have a basket of tubers, a full leather pouch of grains, and two baskets of dried meat left. The dried fruit is nearly gone and will only last a few more days," Jennifer informed him with a tinge of worry in her voice as she ate her meal.

"You're worried about the baby. Aren't you? Well, you don't need to be. The grasslands will provide enough to keep our baby growing strong and healthy. Soon, there will be plenty of early spring greens and fruits ready to harvest. We'll have spring and summer to hunt for fresh meat. Grains, berries, and summer fruits will be plentiful during late spring to the end of summer," Taric calmly responded, soothing her worries a little bit but knew she would continue to worry.

"Well, you're the expert, and I'm just a student, so I'll place my faith in your knowledge and learn from you. I just wanted you to know what we have left. I didn't mean to sound alarmed or worried, but I guess I did," Jennifer admitted sheepishly, frustrated with herself for not paying enough attention to Taric's activities when she was recuperating from her broken leg.

"I know," Taric replied with a comforting smile.

"I'm going to help with the hunting until I can no longer hunt. In the summer, when I'm big, fat, and ugly, I'll help with gathering the grains, fruits, vegetables, and greens growing around here to fill the inner cave. Then sometime in the fall, we'll have our baby. I'm worried because there's so much to be done before our child's birth. Will we be ready?" Jennifer asked him, needing his reassurance that everything will work out.

"My love, the land is bountiful, and it provides everything we need to survive. Only the foolish and lazy suffer in the wintertime because they didn't take advantage of what the land offered them. I'm not lazy or foolish. We will have everything ready in time. Our child will be born in a comfortable home with all the food we need to keep her or him healthy. I've felt real hunger once in my life, and I don't want to feel that pain ever again," Taric assured Jennifer with a one-armed hug around her waist as they sat side by side.

"I've never felt that kind of hunger. What happened?" Jennifer asked curiously as she snuggled closer to Taric's side. "It must have turned out all right, you're still here. So what happened, why were you starving?"

"It's hard to remember much less tell without feeling its lingering sadness, but I will tell you. My father left the world when I was barely walking. I was told he was a fine man, a strong hunter, and a good provider. My mother chose her second mate poorly. She bonded to a lazy and foolish man who wasn't the best of providers. He went out hunting often and mostly returned with only small game. I was just a young boy of seven when he went out hunting late in the season and never came back. I don't know what happened to him, nor do I care.

"He left his mate, her son, and his newborn infant daughter in an empty cave with very little dried meat, grains, and fruit stored for the winter. Mother was still breastfeeding my sister and did what she could to add to our stores until the snows came, but it wasn't enough. That winter, our meals were few and days between them.

"When we did eat, my mother always gave me the most. She ate very little for herself, which over time caused her milk to dry up. I can still see the tortured tears streaming down my mother's face on the day she decided on the merciful choice. She told me to stay in the cave by the fire as she carried my sister out into the snow. I didn't obey. Instead, I followed her footprints in the snow, hearing my sister cry in the distance.

"When I caught up, I saw my mother crying out her sorrow for what she was about to do, as she knelt in the snow with my sister. She then leaned over and kissed her tiny head, while pushing a knife through her temple, forever silencing my sister's cries." Tears streamed down Taric's face as he slumped into Jennifer's lap after angrily pounding his fist on the ground. His recounting of the painful memory unleashed a torrent of grief blocked by his subconscious mind. He cried out angrily as the vivid memory within his mind played out to its grim ending.

Jennifer could only wrap her arms tightly about him, comforting and supporting him as he wept over the murder of his baby sister. She wept with him, feeling the heavy sadness of Taric's tale within her heart. Jennifer held Taric's head on her shoulder and rocked him in her arms as heavy mournful sobs shook his body in uncontrollable spasms. Her tears flowed freely from the corners of her eyes as she mourned over the lost life of an innocent child. Within the seclusion of the water cavern, she let Taric cry out his anger over the horrible memory until his body was spent.

When Jennifer was finally able to lay him down onto the furs, she whispered softly in his ear, "My love, listen to the water. Hear its rhythmic melody as it falls and splashes into the pool. Let your mind relax with the soothing melody of flowing water. Listen to the water dear heart and let your imagination free to dream," Jennifer crooned while inwardly wishing she hadn't asked to hear her question's heart-wrenching and tragic answer.

Jennifer laid down onto the furs and snuggled up behind him, wrapping an arm over his side to rest on his chest. She began to softly rub the palm of her hand in a small circle over the smooth skin of his chest. Holding him in a loose embrace, she began to feel his chest

105

expand and contract with each steady breath. Lulled by her warmth and closeness, Taric slowly drifted off into a deep, peaceful sleep, and as her lover slept, Jennifer prayed the horrible memory would fade over time and heal his wounded soul.

CHAPTER 13

The Signal

Jennifer rose quietly from the furs after Taric was soundly asleep. Motioning with her hand for Jaxx to follow, she left him to sleep by the fire and walked down the ledge and out of the cave. Once back in the main cave, Jennifer decided to clear her mind by taking a short walk outside to stretch her legs and test Jaxx's training by hunting for some small game.

She dressed for the chilly air of the afternoon by slipping on her fur-lined tunic over the soft leather halter she wore over her neck and breasts. Slipping on her heavy goroc boots and tying them securely around her ankles, she stood and unpegged the left side of the hide. Jaxx scampered through the loosened hide before Jennifer was able to grab her bow and quiver of arrows.

"Wait for me," she commanded as she moved the hide aside and stepped into the afternoon sunlight. Jaxx was running full speed in large oval circles with pure delight clearly shining in her eyes as she ran in and out of the trees in front of their home.

"You've been cooped up too long, haven't you, girl?" Jennifer said to Jaxx as her lycur ran up panting heavily from her exertions. Jaxx licked her hand as if to agree and then bounded off a short distance only to quickly spin around in her attempt to entice Jennifer into following.

"All right, I'll follow you," she said happily to the attentive lycur, extending out a cupped hand and then in a wave of her wrist opened her hand to a flat open palm, signaling Jaxx to begin her search of the area for small game. Immediately, the lycur trotted ahead sniffing the ground in search of an enticing scent.

Jennifer followed Jaxx up the valley within the trees. Jaxx's path led her near Peter's stone marker, and she unconsciously turned her head to look in the direction of the stone. When her eyes fixated on the spot, Jennifer wondered if Taric's mother had buried the tiny body or left it in the open for the scavengers to consume her flesh. Jennifer put the grisly thought out of her mind and continued following Jaxx in her search.

Jaxx's nose quickly turned her toward the open grass as she found a scent worth following. She was walking toward the crash site of her pod, when Jaxx suddenly stopped in her tracks and stretched out her neck and tail, signaling she was ready to flush out her prey. Jennifer notched an arrow to her bow and pulled the string back as far as she could. With a nod of her head, Jaxx quickly rushed the spot and stopped, instantly flushing a meaty burrower, which Taric called a skike, that leaped fearfully from the ground and ran abreast of where she was standing. Taking careful aim, Jennifer released her arrow. The arrow struck the animal in the hindquarters, causing it to tumble onto the grass near the open pod. Jaxx quickly ran over and finished the kill by clamping her jaws onto the wounded skike's neck and gave it a couple of hard biting shakes to break it, unconcerned by a faint blue light that briefly flashed inside the pod's shadowy interior.

"Good girl!" Jennifer happily exclaimed while walking to meet Jaxx as she carried the dead skike over to her and dropped it at her feet near the pod. When she stooped to retrieve the skike, Jennifer noticed the pod's tightly molded composite structure was beginning to break down with visible cracks and frayed fibers due to the sun's ultraviolet radiation. When she turned from the pod with her prize, Jennifer walked away with Jaxx scampering beside her, completely unaware the pods active emergency signal had been received by an imperial subspace communication relay satellite. The satellite, per its AI programming, sped the signal onward toward Earth, via the next relay in the empire's interstellar chain of subspace communication satellites spanning the vast distances between Earth and the newly colonized worlds of human habitation.

Pushing the loose hide aside with her nose, Jaxx entered the main cave with Jennifer stepping through the entrance right behind her. She stopped and pegged the hide back into place over the entrance, before walking over to the firepit with the skike. Using her knife from the pod, she quickly had the skike gutted, beheaded, skinned, and ready for roasting over the fire. She stuck a thick tree limb through the skike and secured it to the limb with lengths of string made from goroc fur. She buried the end of the limb in the ground beside the pit and supported it in place at an angle over the edge of the fire with heavy stones.

Jaxx walked through the hide covering the inner cave and disappeared. Jennifer assumed she went to check on Taric. She just smiled, knowing the close bond the animal shared with him as well as with her. After removing the entrails and head of the skike, Jennifer made a quick trip to their dump site outside the cave and tossed the remains for the scavengers to consume. She washed her blood-smeared hands clean as soon as she came back inside the warm confines of the cave before walking into the cool inner cave. From their stores, she brought out some tubers, the grain pouch, and some dried fruit for their evening meal.

The meal was nearly ready to serve, and Jennifer was just getting ready to go and get Taric when Jaxx bounded through the hide. She heard her mate laughing loudly before he entered the main cave behind the rambunctious animal. "She is something else!" he declared with a wide grin as he sat down on the furs beside the fire. "Want to know how she woke me?

"What happened?" Jennifer responded, seeing the mirth of the moment on his face.

"She started by pawing at my shoulder. I tried to ignore her and just waved her off, but it didn't work," he explained setting up his tale, trying to hold back his laughter.

"So what did she do?" Jennifer curiously asked, fully aware Taric expected her to ask the question.

"She laid down on my head and nearly suffocated me!"

Jennifer broke with laughter as she stared at Taric's comical expression while trying to fill his bowl with slices of roasted skike topped with grains and fruit.

"Oh, I was so mad when I stood up. I fully intended to toss her into the pool, but after seeing her scamper around trying to get me to play, I couldn't do it," Taric added as he lovingly scratched the lycur's neck as Jennifer gave him his bowl.

"You went hunting?" Taric asked, finally noticing the freshly roasted meat resting in a wide, shallow wooden bowl beside the fire.

"Yes, we did. Jaxx sniffed out and flushed a skike for my arrow. It wasn't a clean kill, so Jaxx finished it off. I think she did very well for her first hunt," Jennifer announced proudly for their lycur companion's success.

"Did you save the pelt?" Taric asked, thinking the skike's dense, fine fur and soft hide would be very useful after the baby is born.

"It's rolled up on top of the firewood. I was thinking it might be large enough to use as a baby blanket," Jennifer answered, seeing Taric's nod of approval as he hungrily devoured his meal. Night had fallen over the land by the time the couple finished eating their meal with a sated and alert lycur, lying on the furs beside them. Jennifer sighed tiredly as she leaned into Taric's side.

"Oh, how I long for a bar of lavender soap. I could use a long warm, soothing soak, but I'm stuffed and too tired to walk," Jennifer quietly remarked as she sat snuggled within Taric's warm embrace while watching the flames flicker and dance in the pit.

"What is a lavender soap?" Taric asked, liking the close contact of Jennifer's gorgeous slim body snuggled within his arms as well as the idea of a soak in the pool. But he was feeling an overwhelming sense of contentment at the moment and wanted to stay with her on the furs as they were and memorize the scene within his mind.

"Soap works with water when bathing and is often scented with lavender. It's a purple flower with a heavenly scent. When wet, soap slowly dissolves as you wash and turns into slick bubbles on your skin, and it makes you feel really clean when it rinses off," she answered, truly missing the simple pleasure a bar of soap provided.

"There is a water root that grows in muddy marshes and ripens in late summer. When mashed in water, it turns into a bubbly liquid. Maybe it could be used as soap. Now, about that soak," Taric suggested with a grin as he stood up from the furs.

"Maybe," Jennifer responded while wondering where a marshy area could be located as she looked up into his smiling face.

"Can we soak our cares away without soap?" Taric asked as he reached out his hand, expecting Jennifer to grab onto it.

"Why, thank you. What a marvelous suggestion," Jennifer graciously replied, accepting his assistance, and let his strength pull her up onto her feet.

Taric easily swept Jennifer into his arms and stared into her excited eyes. She happily wrapped her arms around his neck as he began to carry her out of the main cave, through the nearly empty storage cave and into the water cave. The fat lamps flickering along the ledge's edge guided Taric up the incline in their dim light. When he reached the firepit, he carefully lowered Jennifer onto the soft furs beside the low-burning fire. He added wood to the fire, and as the wood began to burn brightly, the giggling pair quickly removed their clothing and jumped naked into the warm pool.

Not to be left alone, Jaxx standing on the ledge launched herself into the pool. She splashed heavily and went under the water. When she surfaced, she swam easily across the pool to join her packmates sitting on a submerged outcropping of smooth limestone on the opposite side. The outcropping was a couple of feet below the water, making it a perfect lounging spot to enjoy the soothing warmth. Jaxx found her footing on the ledge and stood happily between them as her packmates sat on the smooth water-worn stone, letting their arms and legs sway freely in the flowing water.

Spring was in full cycle when the sun blessed the high grasslands with warmth and light. The herds returned slowly as the rains subsided and the season warmed. The big goroc bulls were the first to arrive, taking advantage of the fresh new blades of spring grass growing among scattered patches of snow. When all the snow had melted off, a steady advance of intermixed herds slowly filled the lush high mountain grassland with animals ready to give birth and raise their young. During the annual migration up to the grasslands, predators and scavengers followed behind their wandering source of food. The long trek provided predators with a bounty of stragglers, who were too old, weak, or injured to keep up with the pace of the herds.

Jennifer held a hand lightly on her bulging belly, feeling her child squirm beneath her palm as she stood with Jaxx in the warm sunshine at the edge of the grasslands. The herds were roughly a hundred yards downwind from where she stood with her lycur. Somewhere further down the grassy plain, Taric was hunting for runner's and wanted the goroc guardians distracted.

Jennifer stood upwind from the milling herd, letting the breeze carry her and Jaxx's scents downwind. She watched as the animals grazed on the grass and noticed when some of the animals detected their scents and called out an alarm.

Five goroc bulls moved out from within the mingled mass of animals to the outskirts of the herd, clearly agitated by their presence. The huge horned beasts stood abreast of each other, sniffing their scents in the air. They stared in her direction while stomping the ground menacingly with their massive front legs. Jennifer realized something must have happened earlier in the day to make the massive beasts act so aggressively.

Suddenly, the largest bull charged forward and stopped halfway between her and the line of bulls behind him. It bellowed out a challenge that was immediately repeated by the four bulls guarding the herd. Jaxx bristled with the challenge growling deeply in her throat as she stood her ground beside Jennifer. The big bull stepped forward a few paces, bellowing another warning while swinging its huge head from side to side, displaying long deadly horns. Jaxx's deep-throated growl increased to a full deep howl as the lycur answered the bull's challenge. In the distance, Jennifer heard a pack of lycurs howling in response to Jaxx's call.

Thinking the bull might decide to charge at Jaxx. Jennifer began to back away from the open grass and motioned for her lycur to follow her into the trees. Seeing the command, Jaxx relaxed her rigid stance and reluctantly turned to walk warily beside her. Jennifer kept her eyes fixated on the aggressive goroc bull as they made for the safety of the trees. The bull watched Jennifer and her lycur retreat from the grass as the distant lycur howls faded in the air. Once back in the forest within the shady foliage of the shrubs and trees, they quickly disappeared from the bull's sight.

The smell of fresh blood and death kept the herd at a safe distance while Taric quickly butchered his kill. He had the travois next to the carcass as he cut cleanly through the runner's flesh with ease using the extremely sharp knife Jennifer had found in the pod. A few bulls moved from inside the herd to keep watch as Taric worked quickly, tossing large portions of meat onto the travois. When the nearby animals suddenly ran away, Taric looked up from his task to see Jaxx exiting the forest and running swiftly onto the grass. He waved a hand at Jennifer when he saw her emerge from the trees as Jaxx ran over to take a defensive stance between Taric and the bulls. While Jennifer was walking over to Taric and the travois, Jaxx howled out a warning to any nearby predators to stay away and began pacing back and forth in front of Taric's kill while growling deeply at the nearby bulls.

The news of the *Fulcrum*'s demise with the sudden loss of the ship's AI subspace communications link preceded the pod's emergency signal to Earth by seven months. The signal was the foremost item on Empress Isabella Whitlock's morning agenda. High Counselor Thomas Grange waited nervously outside the private quarters of his sister, the empress. He wondered how Isabella would take the surprising news of survivors from the *Fulcrum* disaster. He had to read the message a few times to understand the full impact of the pod's emergency signal.

Within the message was the DNA identity of the pod's occupants, Peter and Jennifer Collins. The DNA profiles of the pair matched the names in the ship's manifest. However, per the profiles recorded in the imperial records of 2553, the DNA belongs to Peter Collins and his step-sister, Jennifer Hendricks. She was the Tyrant's heir who died before the last decade of the Great War. They were recorded as deceased, killed in a terrorist attack against the royal family estate a year before the *Fulcrum* left Earth's orbit in 2554. Where were they hiding during the year before the *Fulcrum*'s launch? It was obvious their deaths had been falsely recorded, but why? Thomas asked himself as he heard the click of the door unlock.

The door opened and was held by a servant who waited for his sister to pass. Isabella was extremely intelligent, barely five feet tall, and not very pretty. However, she possessed a personality that demanded and expected instant obedience to her commands by her subordinates. She was a cunning politician who was not afraid to make hard decisions when it came to preserving the empire. She was an uncommonly stern woman who would not tolerate excuses for failing. But sometimes, Isabella could be a compassionate and understanding confidant to someone who had failed in their assignment. She rarely granted second chances, but Isabella had a way of seeing into the heart and soul of people for her young age of twenty-six, and it made her a good ruler.

"What's the opening item on the agenda? Anything interesting?" she asked as he fell in step with her.

"Well, it just so happens there is, Izzy," Thomas said, using her childhood nickname and continued on with the informal briefing. "Apparently, our cousins from a few generations back, Peter Collins and Jennifer Hendricks, did not die in the year 2553 with their guardians as is widely believed."

Isabella stopped walking, remembering a secret her mother revealed about that particular year as she lay on her deathbed. So she faced her brother, pretending ignorance, and asked, "What do you mean they didn't die?"

"We received an emergency signal from a life pod located in star system WLF1954. Yes, it's the Planoian system, the *Fulcrum*'s last known position." Thomas said, answering Isabella's anticipated question when he saw her reaction to the star systems identification.

"How do our supposedly dead cousins end up marooned on a planet thirty-two lightyears away?" Isabella curiously asked, fully aware Thomas's sharp mind would have a plausible theory to explain everything.

"Well, when Jennifer was born, she became the Tyrant's heir to the throne. It's rumored Jennifer is the product of an incestuous affair or rape of Kera by the Tyrant. But, there's no proof either way. The Tyrant erased his DNA profile along with his grandparents, parents, and sisters from the imperial records. Anyway, Jennifer's assumed death along with her brothers in 2553 must have been part of Kera's elaborate plan to escape the planet. Michael and Kera disappeared in 2541 right after Peter's birth. They were outspoken critics of the war and of the Tyrant's imperial policy of mass prisoner executions, which made them traitors of the empire. They were rumored to have been secretly killed by our uncle's assassins, but there's no evidence of him denying or confirming the validity of the rumor.

"Our great-uncle may have been a cruel man, but he didn't regard the sins of the parents as sins of the children. Peter and Jennifer were his sister's children after all. By his order, they were sent to an imperial estate in Wyoming in 2543. They were raised and educated on a cattle ranch by highly trained imperial guardians, who portrayed themselves as their biological grandparents.

"The estate compound was destroyed in a presumed terrorist attack in 2553. The attack was a tragic blow to the royal family. Before the attack on the royal estate, Michael and Kera disappeared and were rumored to be dead. Somehow they changed their last name to Collins and were able to alter the imperial DNA profiles to match their new names. It takes nearly a year to get all of the colonists into hypersleep. Kera was the senior engineering officer aboard the *Fulcrum*. It was her job to oversee the compliance to the hypersleep procedures. Kera's children were listed as dependent passengers, so there were no fees for their boarding. I assume when they boarded the *Fulcrum*, they were immediately placed in hypersleep. When Jennifer's death was reported it left the Tyrant with his youngest sibling Ella, as his heir and we know how that worked out," Thomas said, ending his informal briefing.

"What are the odds of them being alive right now?" Isabella asked as she continued walking down the corridor toward the imperial palace's main conference room.

"It's hard to say. Who knows? The planet is referred to in the Imperial Scientific Charter as Planos. It's a protected planet," Thomas answered, letting the significance of it register within her mind.

"There's a dominant humanoid species? How many? What level of technology do the inhabitants of Planos possess?" Isabella asked her little brother, knowing he held an astrobiology degree and chaired the imperial scientific communities' yearly conferences.

"The Planos planetary survey is nearly three hundred years old, but at the time it was taken, the survey recorded a worldwide population of two million souls. They live on only one of the three major continents on the planet. Planos is a raw and wild world. The odds of them surviving in the wilds are not in their favor. However, they were raised in the country, trained in the use of basic weapons, and were known to hunt frequently. Jennifer was a creative young girl, able to work with her hands, and known to be an excellent shot with a bow and arrow. Maybe, she has the skills to survive. I honestly don't know," Thomas admitted with a shrug of his shoulders as they reached the door to the briefing room.

Isabella smiled with a thought that entered her mind as Thomas opened and held the door open. "My empress," she heard him say softly with a smile as she entered the packed briefing room, hearing the scuffle of chairs being quickly pushed back as the men and women in the room stood to attention.

"Good morning, everyone. Please sit as we have a busy day ahead of us, so let's get going," she said happily as she sat down in her chair. "I'm sure you've read the meeting agenda. I'm just as surprised as the rest of you of the signal received from a life pod off the *Fulcrum* that landed on a planet called Planos. However, the morning's brief didn't give any further details, except a message was recorded by our subspace communication satellites. The DNA analysis taken at the time of the pod's launch matches the DNA profiles of Peter Collins and Jennifer Hendricks, distant cousins to Thomas and me. Judging by the astonished looks on your faces, you recognize Jennifer was once the Tyrant's heir to the throne until she and her brother were reported as killed in a terrorist attack in 2553.

"Jennifer has no valid claim to the throne and is not a concern of mine, but her life is. Peter and Jennifer are members of my royal family and I'll not turn my back on them. They're stranded on a wild, primitive planet and we're going to search for them. We have two new warp drive starships in orbit nearing completion with faster than light speed capabilities. I want one of the ships ready to depart in two months. If construction crews need to be doubled to finish the ship, then do so. Ladies and gentlemen, this is a top-secret priority one mission. The Hendricks name still evokes a deep hatred in the hearts of the Tyrant's enemies to this day. Contrary to popular belief, Jennifer is not his daughter. The Tyrant's line is dead, just as he is. Jennifer and Peter are innocent victims of chaotic times. If it's at all possible, we're going to rescue them. Make it happen.

"Thomas, you'll oversee the final preparations for flight as the starship's captain. I think you're the ideal person to lead a rescue mission to Planos. If they're alive, they have the option to continue on to Opalla or return to Earth. You're to render any and all assistance they require to begin a new life on Opalla if they choose. We'll talk more about it tonight at dinner.

"Now, to the next item on the agenda, the introduction of genetically engineered sperm whales to the oceans. What's the progress?" Isabella asked her current scientific administrator overseeing the restoration of the Earth's oceans while watching Thomas's shocked, confused mind comprehend her orders and finally seeing an elated expression flash within the depths of his blue eyes with the sudden and unexpected promotion.

On Planos, as Taric and Jennifer were eating their morning meal and planning their next hunt, Thomas was sitting at the dinner table with his sister on Earth and asked, "You really expect our cousins to be alive on Planos?"

Isabella sighed heavily, set her fork on her plate, and then looked at him. "I truly hope they are alive, but no, not really. At most, we'll abide by the charter's bylaws and salvage the wreckage of the life pod. No evidence of human existence on Planos can be left behind. The planet and its inhabitants must be allowed to evolve naturally."

"You know, Izzy, I've been thinking. The pods are designed to follow a strict glide path during reentry to a planet's surface. Now imagine, the pod's descent carried our cousins to the inhabited continent. Their chances of survival do increase considerably if they landed in close proximity to the natives. What if one or both of them survived and were able to integrate themselves into a Planoian tribe? What am I to do? Am I ordered to force their extradition in order to comply with the Imperial Charter?" Thomas asked her, wanting to know how far her orders went.

"I'm bound by the charter. No human contact can be permitted to contaminate the natural evolution and development of the Planoian species. It's highly unlikely your imagined scenario can happen. I expect they died in the wildlands of Planos shortly after landing. But I'll leave any unforeseen predicaments and consequences to your capable judgment," Isabella answered and added as an afterthought, "Stop thinking of impossible scenarios of what might happen. If they're alive or not alive, whatever you discover, you'll deal with it as humanely as possible."

"You're right. I'll concentrate on the ship right now, and our cousins after we launch," Thomas replied after swallowing a bite and added, "Do you realize, over the last four hundred years, hypersleep starships have been our only means of traveling to and exploring M1-class planets? The scientific exploration missions launched in the early twenty-second century became footnotes in our history books. The scientists and the crews who manned those pioneering starships were forgotten over the years and were considered lost. Until the starships began returning to Earth with their amazing discoveries in the twenty-fourth century. With the new warp drive engines, we will be able to cross the galaxy to our colonized worlds in days instead of hundreds of years. We estimate it will take us thirty-one days to get to Planos. That is if the new drives are as effective as our engineers claim them to be."

"Thirty-one days to Planos. Remarkable!" Isabella exclaimed, aware the starship drives would change human history and possibly answer the single most poignant question recorded in the charter concerning the protected worlds: Why do the alien life-forms on those worlds look so similar to life on Earth? Do the planets follow a natural cosmic process to generate life or have all M1-class planets been seeded with the genetic materials to evolve life by an older more advanced race of beings?

"What about afterward?" Thomas asked as he finished his dinner and looked directly at his sister.

"What do you mean?"

"Will I remain as captain of the ship or is this a onetime deal?" Thomas elaborated, needing to know, wanting to know his future.

Isabella saw the hopeful expression on her brother's face. She was aware of his obsession with science and his desire to explore the galaxy. But she didn't know if she could spare his services as her high counselor as he was the one person on Earth she trusted completely.

"I'm aware of the answer you want to hear. But I don't know if I can rule the empire without you by my side. Will you allow me some time to decide? Can we put this on the table until after you return?" She saw his disappointment and knew she had hurt him deeply.

"I didn't ask to be your guy Friday, you made me high counselor! I hate it! I'm an astrobiologist, a scientist of alien life-forms. I'm a seeker of life beyond Earth. Why can't I be what I'm educated and trained to do? I've dreamed of space exploration since I was a kid and now it's within my reach. Everyone else on this godforsaken rock gets to choose their life's profession! Why can't I?" Thomas furiously argued back at her.

"Do you believe I had a choice to become empress of the empire? Do you? We're royals! We don't have the luxury to do what we want! We're servants of the people of Earth and of the colonies. We're bound by family obligations. Do you understand?" she countered hotly, then softened her tone and said, "Give me some time, please."

Thomas stood from his chair, intending to leave the room. He paused to lean on his chair and faced his sister. "Did you ever wonder why Kera and Jennifer left? Maybe they just wanted the freedom to live their own lives. Think about it." He said angrily, before leaving her alone in the room.

On the far side of the planet in an unassuming house isolated on the African coast, a charterist cell leader had been ordered into activation from his superiors. He was a thin old man with a plain, craggy, weather-beaten face and long white hair that hung down below his shoulders. He stood proudly in front of his three disciples, looking at their familiar faces. From babies to adults, he had raised them as if they were his own children.

Like his birth so long ago, their births were never recorded in the imperial birth records. They were living ghosts, raised, educated, and trained to faithfully serve the charter. Two men and a woman waited silently and respectfully for the nameless old man to give them their orders.

"From this day forward, you will act like strangers and give no outward sign of recognition until you board the imperial starship that is set to launch next month and accomplish your mission. Here are credentials denoting your occupations and rank. These documents will get you past the security checkpoints at the spaceport. You'll receive your individual assignments after you're aboard the starship. Perform your assignment for the glory of the charter," the old man said to the three, handing each of them their authentic yet untraceable imperial credentials in dismissal.

The old man stood sadly at a window, watching as the three young people he'd grown to love drove away in separate vehicles. With his lifelong assignment complete, the nameless old man sat down in a chair and removed a small remote from his pocket. He settled himself comfortably into the chair's soft cushions and pressed down with his thumb on the remote's only button. A micro bomb implanted at the time of his birth exploded with a barely discernible pop, rupturing the jugular vein in his neck.

CHAPTER 14

Observations

Leaning into a dense thicket of thorny vines, Jennifer carefully picked a yellow docal off a vine and bit her teeth through the fruit's thin outer skin. Sugary-sweet juice burst in her mouth with a delightfully flavorful tangy taste. *Taric knows his stuff,* Jennifer thought to herself while chewing on the oval fruit's sweet, tangy pulp. Docals grew on the vine's stalk in three equally spaced rows and were protected down the length of the vines by rows of finger length thorns in between the fruit. Looking at the tangled mass of fruit and thorns, she cautiously reached into the thicket of thorny interwoven vines.

Jennifer's arms paid a small painful price for each piece of the sweet fruit she picked off the vines. No matter how careful she was, she couldn't avoid the thorns pricking and scratching her arms as the fruit broke free of the vine. For each sweet reward, a few more tiny red droplets of her blood appeared on her skin. She set her hard-won, tasty morsels into a basket as she continued to pick the docals from the thorny vines. During their conversation the night before, Jennifer had asked about the local fruits and vegetation ripening and ready to collect. Taric had casually mentioned the docals and told her where to find them. She remembered him smiling as he told her docals were one of his favorite fruits, but he didn't get to enjoy them often, and she wondered why.

"No wonder it's his favorite!" Jennifer remarked sarcastically with a little frustration expressed in her voice as she talked to herself and picked another docal, feeling the thorns sharp prick into her skin as the fruit broke free. "He's not the one who had to pick them! No! Docals are his favorite! Why? Because anyone in their right mind would look at the thorns and say, screw that! Pick 'em yourself!"

Their storeroom was quickly being restocked from the bounty of fresh greens, fruits, and tubers of late spring. Jennifer was now too far along in her pregnancy to actively hunt, so she spent her time dehydrating the gathered fruits and vegetables she collected along with the ample amount of meat Taric and Jaxx brought back to the cave from their hunts. She had planned on spending her day weaving loose reed baskets and grass mats. Her needs for the growing supply of preserved meat hanging on the drying racks and new grass mats for the cave floor outweighed the need for the docals. "I must be crazy," she said to herself, as she picked another docal while suffering the painful thorn pricks on her arms for a piece of fruit she'd rather leave alone.

With her basket finally full of sweet fruit, Jennifer gratefully carried her prize back toward the cave. As she neared her home, she looked down at the tiny blood spotted thorn pricks wounding her arms and swore with an amused malicious smile. "Oh, how he owes me big time for these," she said to herself while thinking the next time Taric mentioned docals, she was going to hand him a basket and let him do the picking. The mental image of him being pricked repeatedly by the nasty thorns made her laugh out loud as she entered the cramped confines of the main cave with her basket of hard-won fruit, debating within her mind whether to share them with him or not.

Jaxx took her position between Taric's kill and the scavengers drawn by the smell of warm blood. Taric worked quickly as Jaxx's fur bristled with her hackles raised and growled so deeply at the milling scavengers that the sound of her sent shivers down Taric's spine. Jaxx's hunting instincts and prowess surpassed his expertise when it came to tracking down their prey. The ease of their partnership as they hunted was like nothing he'd experienced in the past.

Taric subconsciously compared Jaxx to the wild lycurs he'd seen from time to time roaming on the outskirts of the herds. Jaxx was large for her breed, but the difference between them was shockingly apparent when she stood on the grasslands. Wild adult lycurs were shorter, thinner, and leaner compared to his nearly fully grown companion.

Jaxx was much larger than her wild cousins, probably due to her never having missed a meal in her young life, unlike the lycurs living in the wild. Living with Jennifer and himself, Jaxx grew to be broader in the chest with well-developed muscular shoulders and strong powerful hindquarters that could swiftly carry her across the grass. When Jaxx stood beside him, her shoulders were equal to his waist, allowing her to easily touch his elbow with her nose.

He didn't believe it at first when Jennifer adopted the helpless puppy by the riverbank, but time, care, and love for the animal did indeed lead to the fulfillment of everything she predicted. He remembered how upset he'd been with her at the time, only to be sternly rebuked for his callous attitude toward a helpless animal. Now, he couldn't imagine life without Jaxx hunting with him or sleeping within the confines of their cave at night.

Taric was nearly finished butchering the last of their three kills, a bovuck, a burly knee-high short-legged scavenger covered in a saggy fatty coat of short brown fur. Their fleshy face with black bulbous eyes and flabby nose set atop a wide flat protrusion of a skull was covered in wrinkled loose pink skin sagging below a wide toothy mouth. The bovuck's loose, wrinkled skin with a thick fat layer underneath made it difficult for predators to securely hold them and inflict deadly harm.

Along with a steady diet of grass, bovucks ate nearly everything they could find abandoned on the plain. Their hard flat teeth could easily grind through the thickest of bones from an abandoned carcass into a fine pulp for the blood-rich marrow. Their powerful jaws deterred all but the biggest of predators from attacking.

Tossing the last leg of the butchered animal onto the travois, Taric began to roll up the hide with its thick fatty layer that, once it was rendered to oil and cooled, would fuel the lamps along the ledge in the water cave. A lycur howled close by and Taric quickly turned his head toward the river, looking for the source of the howl. Jaxx made no move to advance toward the intruder, but her attention was clearly fixated on a lycur standing alone on the river's embankment. It stood motionless on the crest staring curiously at Jaxx, uncertain of the strange yet familiar scent of her breed. Jaxx stood stiffly, growling low in the throat as she watched the wild lycur intently. The lycur howled once again at Jaxx before it moved off into the woods above the embankment and quickly disappeared from their sight.

"Yes, you're one of them," Taric said to Jaxx as she looked back at him as if asking a question. Jaxx ran back to Taric's side when he lifted the travois poles and began to drag the load back to the cave. As Taric pulled the travois, he soon became unconcerned with whatever may be following the dripping blood trail behind him. Jaxx's presence, strong scent, and keen awareness kept the scavengers at a safe distance as Taric dragged the travois behind him over the grass. When he and Jaxx entered the woods, the scavengers quickly advanced toward the blood-soaked site, viciously fighting over the choicest scraps of meat left clinging to discarded bones scattered on the grass.

After the day's work was done and their evening meal consumed, Taric sat lounging in the water with Jennifer looking at the fire's flickering flames dancing wildly in the air above the pit on the opposite side of the pool. The blazing timbers were surrounded on three sides with staggered racks of meat drying in the heated air of the naturally warm cavern. Taric watched Jaxx lying next to the wall behind the racks, gnawing and ripping off small strips of meat from a bone. Seeing their lycur busily gnawing on her prize reminded Taric of the lycur they saw on the far side of the river. He thought Jennifer would like to hear about Jaxx's first sight of her own kind in the wild.

"Take your bow and Jaxx with you when you leave the cave from now on. There was a lycur standing on the far bank of the river today, and it was very curious about Jaxx and gave her a good look. Last spring the lycurs mostly stayed out of the high grasslands, because the kessra pride claimed the territory as their own. Now, since the kessras are no longer around some lycurs have moved into the area. I don't believe an individual lycur would dare attack with Jaxx standing beside you, but hunting as a group, who knows? I want you to keep a sharp eye out for them," Taric said as a warning of their new neighbors living and hunting in the area.

"What was Jaxx's reaction to seeing a wild lycur?" Jennifer asked, concerned for her lovable and furry companion.

"Jaxx was curious but growled really low in a deep continuous rumble as if she were saying, 'Stay away from me.' I thought she might be thinking of running after it, but she didn't. Jaxx just stood there looking across the river at it, watching very closely to see where it went into the woods. After the lycur disappeared, she no longer appeared curious or concerned by its proximity. To be honest, if she had decided to run, I wasn't sure if I could have called her back," Taric admitted, thinking of his observation of the differences between the two lycurs.

"Our Jaxx may look like her wild cousins, but that's where their similarities end. Because of you, Jaxx has never gone hungry. She eats regularly living with us, unlike her wild cousins. Jaxx is not quite fully grown, but she's already grown into the largest, strongest, and fastest lycur I've seen roaming the grasslands," Taric added proudly, smiling at Jennifer for teaching him the wonderful benefits of having Jaxx living with them as a member of their family.

"Having lycurs in the area could be a problem for Jaxx," Jennifer commented with a worried expression on her face as she thought about the habits of wild wolves on Earth.

"Jaxx is a monster compared to the other lycurs. What kind of problems can they cause?" Taric asked, curious about what she was thinking. "Tell me."

"I don't know enough about the habits of wild lycurs. Would they challenge Jaxx in an attempt to drive her out of the area? Wolves on Earth roam and hunt within their territory in family packs. Wolves are known to be very protective of their hunting grounds. They do not accept outsiders within their territory. A lone wolf trespassing into a pack's territory is often driven away or hunted down by the alpha male and killed by the pack. The similar physical characteristics between wolves and lycurs are incredibly remarkable," Jennifer said, pausing her narration as she thought about the guidelines of alien life within the Imperial Scientific Charter's bylaws and then quietly asked herself. "Or is it?"

"Is it? What?" Taric asked, slightly confused by her pause and unexpected question.

"Think about the physical similarities between us," Jennifer said, prompting Taric to stretch his imagination and really compare their species. "Our bodies represent a version of our species sex. I'm a woman of Earth, and you're a man of this world. Our worlds are twenty or more lightyears apart. Our appearance is slightly different because of our DNA, yet we're very much the same creature and I've noticed that many of the animals here seem to be similar variations or counterparts of animals on Earth.

"The Imperial Charter's planetary surveys are highly classified secret documents. Their contents are not known by the average citizen, except the discovery of four solar systems with planets supporting a dominant humanoid species in varying stages of technological development. Those systems and planets are protected by the Imperial Scientific Charter's bylaws.

"I think our scientists discovered human DNA is not as unique as they once believed. Instead, maybe our DNA follows a common cosmic formula for the evolution of life to exist on an M1-class planet. I'm not sure if that's the reason why, but from a cosmic perspective, we might very well be variations of the same genetic DNA code. Somewhere in the galaxy, there could be an older human variation more advanced than humans on Earth. The evidence is there to support what we already know and if it's true, the charter is concealing the truth.

"No human contact or interference of the natural evolution of a protected planet is permitted. Any human concept or exposure to human technology by a native is regarded as a contamination of the species. If human contamination is discovered on a protected planet, it's eliminated to the fullest extent of the contamination, even if it involves killing natives of the worlds the charter is supposed to be protecting," Jennifer added, explaining the reasoning behind the consequences of human contamination.

"The land is vast, and we are the only two people around. How can they discover you here?" Taric asked her, suddenly alarmed and concerned for her safety as he sat with her in the soothing water.

"Oh, they can easily find us, believe me. They have the technology to distinguish the differences between us in space without having to land. The empire believes everyone aboard the *Fulcrum* is dead. Any debris from the *Fulcrum* will be pulled down toward the surface by the planet's gravity and burn up entering the atmosphere, long before your people develop into a technological society. So I don't think anyone will come looking for survivors. How would they know? Besides, we'll be long dead before humans from the Earth can get here," Jennifer reassured him, confident her perspective of the *Fulcrum* tragedy was the prevailing belief on Earth.

"You may be right," Taric said before pushing himself away from the outcropping to swim freely in the water. Gliding effortlessly with the flow of water back toward Jennifer, he touched the wall and spun around to sit once more on the outcropping beside her and asked. "What other similarities between our worlds have you noticed?"

"Well, now that we're thinking about it and because you asked. I'd say everything. The birds are just as varied here as they are on Earth. There are thousands of species living in every region on Earth and from what I've noticed, it's probably the same for this world. We are so familiar with their sights and sounds, we hardly notice them as we go about our daily routines. This planet's birds may look and sound different than Earth birds, but their instincts and habits are nearly identical.

"Also, skikes are very similar to rabbits. They're both harmless animals that eat grass and flowers for their food, which makes them an ideal meal for many meat-eating predators. Skites run, hop, eat grass, and dig just like rabbits. They raise their young in burrows just as rabbits. Although, the two animals share similar life characteristics, their appearance is completely opposite. Skikes don't have a soft cuddly body, innocent face, adorable long ears, and a white fluffy ball for a tail on their bottoms, which make humans think rabbits are appealing and cute. Frankly, I think the skikes got shortchanged when it comes to looks. They're ugly little creatures compared to rabbits.

"I think I might be correct in my assumption. Before we were able to actually travel to new worlds, our imagined descriptions of alien life in the galaxy were that they would look nothing like us and varied from benign to hostile toward us. But the worlds discovered so far with their varied plant and animal life are nothing like what we expected. Every M1-class planet discovered so far are very much like Earth. How can this be on so many worlds spread across the galaxy? It can only happen if our worlds share a common cosmic genetic formula, our DNA codes. It's a mystery and I don't have the education to back up my theory, so who knows?" Jennifer declared with a chuckle and pushed off the outcropping and swam the few strokes it took to get to the other side of the pool.

Taric watched her swim away, thinking about what she had said, then put it out of his mind. He was waiting with anticipation for her to climb out of the water and stand in front of the fire. With her back to the smooth ledge, Jennifer lifted herself up and sat comfortably on the ledge with her swollen belly resting on her thighs. She slowly got to her feet and walked toward the heat of their fire. Standing in front of the fire, Jennifer raised her arms above her head, stretching and arching her naked body toward the ceiling, silhouetting her extended tummy with his child in the firelight. He loved seeing the water droplets fly off in the firelight, as Jennifer whipped her long red hair from side to side. Every droplet reflecting the fire's color and appeared from a distance as if she were spraying tiny balls of flame all around her. Jennifer was so beautiful to behold that the sight of her standing naked in front of the fire astonished his senses and fueled his desire every time he looked at her.

As Jennifer dried off and began to dress, Taric let out a sigh, pushed himself off the outcropping, and swam over to the opposite ledge. He easily climbed out of the pool and immediately felt the onslaught of the fire's heat on his dripping skin. He was nearly dry in the few steps it took to retrieve his clothes.

Jennifer handed Taric a soft drying hide. "Thanks, don't know if I need this or not," he replied with a chuckle but used the hide to dry off the damp areas under his arms and crotch. He dressed quickly to get away from the heat and join Jennifer who was waiting for him kneeling beside Jaxx, busily scratching the lycur vigorously up and down her spine.

Jaxx's tail pounded the limestone floor, soaking up the attention Jennifer was giving her. When Taric finished dressing and came up to her. Jennifer stopped her scratching and happily cooed to her adoring Jaxx, "You're a good girl. Yes, a very good girl!"

Jennifer then stood up and greeted Taric with a kiss, when Jaxx suddenly ran down the ledge at full speed. "What the hell?" Jennifer stammered as Jaxx disappeared through the opening.

Immediately alarmed, the pair took off running after Jaxx. "She's outside!" Taric exclaimed, hearing the unmistakable roar of a kessra somewhere nearby when he entered the main cave. Grabbing his bow and quiver of arrows before handing a frightful Jennifer hers, he quickly unpegged the hide with one hand to hang limply against the stone. "Stay in the light by the entrance. Don't step into the darkness!" Taric warned her and left the cave after Jaxx. Jennifer could do nothing in her condition but nodded in compliance with his order.

Taric followed the howls and growls Jaxx barked out as she ran to eventually find her in the moonlight within a clearing challenging a kessra, defending some purloined meat from their cave. Jaxx was as tall as the kessra, but she was no match for the six-legged predator. Taric's arrow was ready to launch as he called out, "Jaxx, come!"

Hearing his voice, the kessra turned to face him, and when he did, Jaxx charged in, biting deeply into the kessra's hind leg before quickly jumping back out of the way.

"Jaxx!" Taric shouted in warning as the kessra spun on four of its six legs toward Jaxx with its forearms reaching out slashing at empty air. But Jaxx stayed easily out of the kessra's range of motion as it stood over the meat, trying to defend its prize. Jaxx kept darting around and behind the kessra, biting its hind legs whenever a flank was exposed.

Taric maneuvered for a clear shot without risk to Jaxx. "*Ahhhh!*" he shouted loudly above the growls and roars of the dueling animals. The kessra reacted as Taric had hoped, turning its head to look at him. Instantly, Taric let his arrow fly and almost had another notched in his bow when the arrow struck the kessra below the chin. His arrow lodged in the neck between the bones of the spinal column, severing the animal's spinal cord. The kessra fell to the grass, clawing weakly at the arrow as it lay on the ground, slowly choking on its blood. Taric loosed his second arrow into the kessra's chest to end its suffering and silence the creature forever.

"Jaxx, come!" Taric ordered angrily, retrieving his arrows from the kessra's corpse and wondering if there were others about. He left the kessra and the stolen strips of meat where they lay for the scavengers to fight over, keenly aware the corpse would be shredded to pieces before first light. Jaxx sensing Taric's anger submissively followed behind him with her tail between her hind legs all the way back to their cave.

"Get in there," an exasperated Taric ordered Jaxx, watching her slink down low to the ground as she passed by him to get inside before saying to Jennifer, "Dumb thing went after a kessra! She could have gotten herself injured or even killed! What was going through her crazy head?"

"Don't you be mad at her! Jaxx did what she's been taught to do. She chased it out of our home," Jennifer countered authoritatively, pointing a finger down at the floor, where clear deep impressions of a kessra's paws could be seen.

Taric's eyes followed the deep paw prints leading into the inner cave, realizing the animal had followed the blood trail from his hunt and into their home. Jaxx must have taken off after the kessra at the same time it entered the inner cave and found their stockpiles of the season's fruits, vegetables, and dried meat. Aware his anger was misplaced, Taric softly called to their lycur lying on her bedding. "Jaxx, come here, girl. I was wrong, sorry," he said softly, seeing her rise from the bedding as he knelt to scratch and rub his fingers up and down her spine.

"I killed the pride of kessras. Where did this one come from?" Jennifer asked, concerned for the safety of her baby as she looked at Taric.

"The kessra we killed tonight might have been a scout for a neighboring pride. The scent of the old pride has been washed away by the winter snows. It's unusual for lycurs to roam this high on the grasslands, and kessras can sense when a territory is abandoned. It was only a matter of time before a new pride moves in to claim the high grasslands. We'll know when a kessra pride is in the area before we see one because the wild lycurs will suddenly vanish from the area. A lycur isn't just a hunting competitor, it's food to a kessra," Taric answered Jennifer's questions with the hard truth as he pegged the heavy hide in place and noticed the bottom two peg holes in the hide were torn. He held it up to show Jennifer how the kessra got in. "It tore the hide to get in."

"I don't want another of those ghastly beasts entering our cave. We're going to start building a barricade in front of the opening and secure our home," Jennifer demanded, cradling her tummy with her hands as she looked to Taric for assurance their baby would always be safe.

"I was thinking the same thing, my love," he said softly. "But in the morning, let's get some sleep first, it's been an eventful day." Jennifer nodded while leaning into his strong embrace for a reassuring hug and soft kiss.

CHAPTER 15

A Conflict of Interest

Captain Thomas Grange stood at the threshold of the bridge of his starship with the calm assured demeanor of a leader, but now that his ship was fully operational, he suddenly felt apprehensive. Shrugging off the annoying sensation, he entered the bridge with the confidence of a leader ready to embrace his destiny.

"Report," he ordered his first officer as he walked to the front of the bridge and turned to face his crew before taking his place in the captain's chair.

First Officer Commander Kelly Sterling, a tall, slim woman with oval blue eyes, narrow nose, crescent moon eyebrows, and long blond hair tied back in a ponytail, announced in a clear voice to her captain. "The imperial starship is prepared for launch. Dignitaries from all four kingdoms are observing from the viewing rooms inside the space dock. They are awaiting your command to proceed with the ship's christening."

"Very well, let's not keep our guests waiting any longer. On-screen," he ordered and turned around to face the imperial delegation appearing on the view screen.

"Welcome, ladies and gentlemen. We're pleased you could attend the festivities and witness this historic first mission launch of this amazing starship. Now, without further ado, let's discover the name of this beauty, Commander Sterling," Thomas announced to his first officer with a smile. "The honor is yours."

Commander Sterling paused momentarily as the screen changed to an outside view of the starship resting at her moorings, with a large green-and-white tarp covering the starship's identification.

Sterling pushed a button on her console, releasing the locks securing the tarp in place. The tarp swiftly rolled away to reveal in bold green italics, "*IFS Maleficent*."

"Honored guests, please welcome to the fleet, the imperial starship *Maleficent*," she said somberly as the dignitaries clapped their hands within the viewing room and added. "Captain, the imperial starship *Maleficent* is yours to command."

"Helmsman, release all moorings. Ten percent impulse power out of spacedock," Captain Grange ordered as he sat down in his command chair for the first time.

"Moorings are retracting, the ship is free of the dock. Initiating 10 percent impulse power," the helmsman answered as the ship slowly began to glide out of the orbiting spacedock.

"Captain, we're now clear of the spacedock," Thomas heard his helmsman call out from his console.

"Well done, Helmsman Carter. Ladies and gentlemen, thank you for coming to the christening. Please stand by to witness our departure," Captain Grange announced to the dignitaries before ending the broadcast from the bridge.

"Commander Sterling, please set course for Planos in star system WLF1954," Thomas calmly ordered from his chair.

"Sir, that system is under the charter's protection," Sterling pointed out and added, "It's forbidden."

"Commander, I'm fully aware of its status," Thomas answered her without further discussion.

"Sir, I—" Sterling questioningly stammered only to be cut short by her captain before she could say another word.

"Commander, is there a problem with my order? Set our course or transport yourself back to the docks. Please decide! We'd like to get underway," Thomas quietly but sternly emphasized so there was no misunderstanding of his intentions. "Well, Commander?"

"There's no problem, Captain. I apologize. Setting course for the Planoian system. The course is set," Commander Sterling quietly complied, knowing the captain's order was violating the Imperial Charter's bylaws.

"Cooper, maximum warp. Let's go!" Thomas exclaimed as the AI obeyed and initiated the warp drive.

From the perspective of the royal dignitaries, who attended the christening and launch. The *Maleficent*'s warp engines glowed a bright red as enormous power surged within them. The starship floating in the vacuum above the Earth then disappeared in a blinding flash of multicolored light followed by instant darkness, leaving the dignitaries blinking their eyes repeatedly as they collectively gasped in awe and wonder.

"Status, Commander?" Thomas asked, looking at Sterling from his chair.

"The ship is functioning within design parameters," Commander Sterling answered curtly.

"Open a shipwide channel," Thomas asked his young communications officer, Lieutenant Tim Brooks. Tim had what is known as a baby face, making him appear much younger than his actual age of twenty-five years.

"Channel's open, Captain," Tim calmly responded to the order.

"This is your captain. I'd like to welcome you all to our new starship, the *Maleficent*. We are beginning a shared destiny of discovery aboard this magnificent vessel. Some of you may think *Maleficent* is an odd name for a starship, but I beg to differ. Maleficent is a deity capable of causing great harm by supernatural means. Although this starship is primarily a scientific exploratory vessel of the imperial fleet, she contains an arsenal of weapons for our defense, which can cause great harm. I believe *Maleficent* is a great name for our starship and I hope you agree. Ladies and gentlemen, today is June 20, 2640. A day our history books will someday say planet Earth became the home world of a true interstellar species.

"I'm proud to say, our maiden flight is a rescue mission. We're traveling to the planet Planos, a world located in star system WLF1954. It's the last known location of the ill-fated colonial starship the *Fulcrum*. Two months ago, we received an emergency signal from a life pod that escaped the tragedy and landed on Planos.

There are possibly two survivors still alive and we're going to rescue them. I can't imagine a better first mission for this ship and crew. I expect your fullest assistance in this charitable endeavor. Thank you," Thomas said, ending his briefing by waving a hand under his chin to kill the broadcast. He then stood up from his chair and motioned for Commander Sterling to follow him off the bridge.

"Lieutenant Dan Carter," Thomas announced in a clear voice, matching the young man's face with his name within his mind. "You're next senior officer, take the chair," Thomas ordered as the captain's door on the bridge opened to reveal his ready room. A private office, which served to buffer his living quarters from the continuous activity on the bridge.

Sterling followed behind her captain in silence until they were alone in his private office. Hating she had to swallow her pride, she said, "Sir, I apologize for questioning your commands. It was wrong of me to do so."

"Yes, it was, Commander Sterling. I'll attribute your hesitation as a simple case of first launch jitters," Thomas replied kindly from behind his desk, studying his first officer closely.

"Thank you, Captain."

"Oh, I see Admiral Harrington has a very high impression of your leadership and piloting skills. Very impressive, Harrington is not known for openly praising young officers. Your name, Sterling. Are you a member of the Sterling royal family in the European kingdom or is your last name simply a coincidence?" Thomas asked while indicating with a pointed arm for her to take a seat opposite him.

"Thank you, sir," she said, taking the offered seat as she continued to answer her captain's question. "Yes, sir, I'm a third cousin from a minor branch of the Sterling family tree to King Alexander."

"I see. Why did Alexander order you aboard this ship?" Thomas asked, catching her off guard with the question, watching her reaction very closely.

Kelly involuntarily flinched in her seat when she heard the unexpected question. "Sir?" she stammered, knowing she'd been caught.

Thomas stood from his chair and leaned over the desk while motioning for her to lean forward. As Thomas looked directly in her eyes, he spoke softly yet very sternly, "You are second-in-command and I don't know much about you, but I know your king very well and I've never trusted him. So, Commander Sterling, tell me your king's orders or be ejected out of an airlock."

"That's murder! You wouldn't dare!" Sterling accusingly countered, angrily staring back at him.

"Oh, I wouldn't, but accidents happen all the time. I'm sure your cousin, the king, would give up a minute or two of his busy day to mourn your family's loss. Now, what are your orders?" Thomas demanded from his entitled first officer.

"Alexander requested an interview after my appointment to the *Maleficent*. He wanted to emphasize that I'm to uphold the charter's bylaws to the letter," Sterling answered, hoping it was enough to satisfy the captain, but she immediately saw in his face that it wasn't.

"Really, Commander? You expect me to believe Alexander gave you a lecture on the charter's bylaws? How gullible do you think I am? Now, Commander, tell me what the vile leper ordered you to do!" Thomas angrily stated, furious with her stupid evasion.

"I've been ordered to eliminate the Tyrant's daughter, Jennifer Hendricks. Must I remind the captain, it's a condition of the 2561 treaty? No direct blood offspring of the Tyrant is permitted to live. His bloodline is held accountable for the execution of twenty-seven million prisoners during the Great War. One life is a small cost to uphold the lasting peace currently existing on Earth. Don't you think?" Sterling countered, not liking her captain or the mission they've been ordered to conduct.

"You're a goddamn charterist!" Thomas declared, accusing his first officer of being an active member. The charterists, a feared worldwide militant group, which grew out of the general populace during the later years of the war. Charterist enforced the empire's compliance with the stipulations of the 2561 treaty and the charter's strict by-laws to the letter.

"No Sir! I'm not a charterist! But, I suspect my king is." Sterling exclaimed angrily denying the Captain's accusation.

Thomas quietly looked at her, trying to decide if he could trust her to obey his mission orders. "Commander, Empress Isabella regards Jennifer Hendricks as an innocent pawn of a terrible era in human history. There's no proof she was the Tyrant's daughter. Her birthright is based on rumors of incest or rape against the girl's mother. Whichever one you tend to believe makes no difference. Kera Hendricks gave her child her maiden name as she refused to identify the child's father. Jennifer if she had survived the war, is blameless and could not be held accountable for the Tyrant's war crimes. However, we're not talking about Jennifer Hendricks, because she's been dead for over ninety years," Thomas stated, letting his statement, indicate to her the perspective the empire has decided to embrace.

"King Alexander told me there's proof in the imperial records to back him up," Sterling proudly defended her king, countering her captain's claim.

"Did Alexander show you the imperial records?" Thomas asked, knowing the DNA profiles in the imperial records had been changed to match the ship's manifest long before either of them were born.

"I asked," Sterling quietly answered.

"And?"

"I was rebuked for questioning and sternly given my orders, then dismissed," Commander Sterling finally admitted. "No proof was provided."

"Our mission, Commander Sterling, is a simple one. We're to rescue two young passengers marooned on Planos, Peter and Jennifer Collins, as identified by the DNA profiles listed in the *Fulcrum*'s passenger manifest, which matches the imperial records. The *Fulcrum* was sailing toward Opalla. If they are alive, we're ordered by the empress to take them there. We will provide them with the pioneering equipment and livestock to successfully homestead anywhere on the planet. In this endeavor, I believe you have an alarming conflict of interest that may jeopardize the success of our mission," Thomas explained, letting her decide within her mind, which orders were best to maintain the peace within the empire.

"Permission to speak freely, Captain?" Sterling asked from across the desk.

"Please, by all means," Thomas hopefully replied and waited to hear what she had to say.

"Captain Grange, as an officer of the Imperial Fleet, I'm bound by my oath of loyalty to the empire. However, you're asking me to ignore the orders of my king. What if Alexander is right and she actually is the Tyrant's daughter? Are we to ignore the stipulations of the 2561 treaty? The crimes charged against her bloodline are still active. There's no statute of limitations for mass murder," Sterling asked him, torn by her conflicting loyalties.

"Commander, I sympathize with what you're going through. It's hard to balance family loyalties with the demands of the empire. But ask yourself, what's really best for the empire as a whole? Jennifer Hendricks is dead and must remain dead and buried in the minds of the people alive today. The past is gone forever and cannot be changed. I beg you for the welfare of the empire. Leave Jennifer Hendricks in the past where she belongs. Help me in rescuing the survivors of a tragic accident, Peter and Jennifer Collins," Captain Thomas Grange asked his proud officer and waited for her response.

"Captain, I'm not a charterist, nor am I an assassin. I'm an officer of the Imperial Fleet. I can see the wisdom, compassion, and even logic behind Empress Isabella's insightful perspective. Our duty is to maintain the unity of the empire for the benefit of all people. So Jennifer Hendricks died in 2553 and her name must remain as a footnote of our history.

"Captain, I believe King Alexander has been swayed by his father's and grandfather's old lingering hatreds and was wrong for ordering me to kill a child simply because she lived during that horrible era and shares a common first name. I cannot follow my king's orders as they obviously conflict with the interest of our mission and the empire. I will be proud to assist you with the rescue of the Collins children.

"However, we must consider the possibility that there might be a charterist aboard this starship. If so, we may have an assassin, who's most likely been ordered to kill the survivors, regardless of who they are, simply because they're on Planos. Also, I recommend having the ship's life pod's planet-side destination be preprogramed to the same location as the emergency beacon, just in case," Sterling truthfully answered while changing her initial opinion of her new captain from dislike to one of respect.

"Thank you, Commander, for your renewed oath of loyalty to the empire and for being so open-minded to see the possible future ramifications of our actions. To be honest, Isabella and I believe the Collins children are already dead, unable to survive in the wilds of Planos. Isabella made it quite clear, I'm to abide by the charter in assessing the situation. However, compliance of the charter's bylaws on Planos is mine alone to determine, for any and all unforeseen contingencies that may exist on the planet.

"Now, about that last statement of yours. You must understand something, the charter's bylaws concerning protected planets were written after the first hypersleep exploratory starships returned to Earth. We've never been able to go back to those worlds until now. This ship, along with her sister ships under construction, will one day form our Imperial Fleet. We'll become explorers of our galaxy and guardians of the empire's colonized worlds.

"The Imperial Fleet cannot allow charterists to extend their hate-fueled influence beyond Earth. I personally don't like charter-ists. They're violent militants who continue to dwell on the wrongs perpetrated in our past. The hatred of the Tyrant still lingers after all these years. It's an incurable cancer that thrives within the poor frag-ile souls of their misguided followers. If there are charterists aboard this ship, we have thirty days to discover who they are. Any sug-gestions?" Captain Thomas Grange asked his first officer, with the respect she had earned during the interview clearly emphasized in his casual tone of voice.

"Not at this time, sir."

"Nor do I, Commander, nor do I," Thomas quietly replied to her as he pondered the problems they may face.

"Is there anything else you wish to discuss?" Commander Sterling asked, convinced the captain's personality profile King Alexander had presented to her was nothing more than an attempt to discredit him within her mind before they even met.

"No. I believe we've reached an acceptable accord on the pur-pose of our mission. I'm looking forward to serving the empire with you as my number one," Thomas said ending the interview with a slight smile on his face as he stood from his desk to offer her his hand and escort her over to the door.

Kelly Sterling honestly liked the man she saw standing in front of her and proudly clasped her hand in his and said. "I'll not disappoint you, Captain. As far as the other thing, I think I just might have an idea after all."

"Oh, please tell," Thomas replied with a genuine and open smile.

"I know a couple of trustworthy low-ranking officers aboard ship. They're well-liked and approachable to the crew, unlike you or me. You're aware the mess halls are a gossip's home on every ship in any fleet. Ours is no exception to the rule. The officers I'm thinking of are former students of mine from the academy. They were the funniest two guys in the mess hall, always joking around and clued into everything happening on campus. The pair were widely suspected of being competing masterminds behind many of the successful pranks perpetrated on the underclassmen. They're always invited to share a meal at their crew's table. By observing and listening to the conversations around them as they eat, they may hear a casual slip of the tongue, which might reveal a person's ulterior motives. It's a long shot I grant you, but we might get lucky."

"Commander, I love long shots because every once in a while, they pay off. Proceed with your idea, but be very discreet and make sure each officer believes they alone are your eyes and ears aboard ship. Now, if you'll forgive me, It's been a very long day and I need some rest. The ship is yours to command," Thomas suggested as he guided Commander Sterling toward his ready room door, which automatically opened to admit her back onto the bridge.

"Mr. Carter, if you don't mind. Please, resume your post at the helm," Commander Sterling announced with a smile, stepping onto the bridge as she purposely strode toward the captain's chair and took possession of it for the remainder of her watch.

With her watch over, a medical assistant entered her quarters, kicked off her shoes, and sat down in a recliner within her living space. Turning on the vid's, she leaned back in her chair to watch a show and relax before going to sleep. On the screens upper-right corner, an envelope icon was slowly pulsing. Taking the remote, she clicked on the icon. Only a photo of a young redheaded girl appeared on the vid screen. She guessed the girl in the photo was about sixteen years of age and it appeared to be a happy moment in the young girl's life. She sat cross-legged in tall green grass with a couple of tiny shepherd puppies playfully jumping onto her lap. "Pretty girl," she said, memorizing every detail of the girl's young face before deleting the photo from the screen, aware that in another apartment an engineering technician didn't give a damn about the ship's mission but secretly worked to accomplish his part of their mission for the glory of the charter, no matter the cost.

CHAPTER 16

Waning Days of Summer

From late spring through to the last days of summer, Taric hunted large to small animals and a variety of birds nearly every day, while Jennifer and Jaxx gathered the edible fruits, vegetables, and grains when they came in their season. Their storage cave was nearly at its capacity and could not hold much more food. Only a narrow pathway leading through the inner cave to the water cave remained open between Taric's neatly stacked baskets and pouches of their winter supplies.

Taric had assured Jennifer in the early days of spring, everything they required to survive another winter would be done by the time she neared the end of her pregnancy in the fall. Jennifer was in the main cave kneeling beside the firepit cooking their evening meal, reflecting on his promise and loving him for all the hard work he did to keep it.

She looked around the cave and was truly impressed with how much everything has changed since her first day. The entrance was the most noticeable change as the stout barricade of narrow tree trunks lashed together with strips of leather in front of the entrance kept the predators out but also blocked any natural light from streaming inside. To compensate for the loss of natural light, they made a series of holes for lamps along the walls by chipping away at the limestone with a flint hammer and bone scrapers. At the bottom of each one were scraped-out depressions roughly two-inches in depth. Once filled with moss and rendered fat, the scattered lamps illuminated the entire interior of the main cave.

Taric's endless energy, coupled with the ease in which he was able to hunt with Jaxx, was astonishing to behold. As more large animals were brought down and their hides processed, they soon had more than enough cured hides to cover the main cave's hard lime-stone floor with a thick layer of soft furs, instead of woven grass mats. Taric also cut a tough goroc hide scrapped clean of fur to fit snugly around the outside stones of their firepit. The hide provided Jennifer a wide cleanable area to prepare their meals and store her utensils and bowls.

Not to be outdone, Jennifer gathered some of the cured small furs and sewed them together to make comfortable pillows stuffed with the colorful soft feathers plucked from the many game birds Taric had brought home over the spring and summer.

Jennifer had never met a man so joyful, loving, or hardworking than Taric. She knew the stress of her arrival last spring had made it a difficult challenge for him to gather the supplies they needed to survive the winter. It was his constant activity, which made it possible for them to outlast the snow but not by much.

However, with the preparations they've accomplished during spring and summer, she actually looked forward to the forced seclusion of winter. Since the end of her first winter, she and Taric had truly transformed their three caves into a cozy, comfortable home. "Not bad for Neanderthal chic," Jennifer proudly admitted, happily joking with Jaxx, who was listening, wagging her tail and watching her every move from her bedding.

A large wooden bowl rested in the center of the flat cooking stone surrounded by hot coals within the smoldering firepit. Using a hand-carved wooden spoon, Jennifer stirred her vegetables and wild rice. "Almost ready," she announced with anticipation to Jaxx, who patiently watched and waited from her bedding. Jennifer replaced her cook stones with hot new stones to keep their food simmering in the large cooking bowl. To round out their dinner, Jennifer had three crudely cut goroc steaks resting on a wooden platter beside her as she waited for Taric to return from his bath.

Jennifer used a pair of leather-wrapped tongs to lift the bowl from the cooking stone and set it outside the firepit. She then covered the hot bowl with a small but heavy piece of leather to keep their vegetables and rice warm. She lifted the steaks one by one and placed them onto the cooking stone. The meat instantly sizzled and snapped as they began to cook on the heated stone.

Jaxx's head popped up and looked toward the inner cave as Taric entered, clean and refreshed from his bath. He was bare-chested and holding on to a shirt in one hand while running open fingers through his long damp hair with the other. Jennifer's smile quickly faded as she saw his scars on his skin exposed by his innocent pose, reminding her of that terrible day. Hiding the memory within her mind, she smiled and hoped he didn't notice her reaction.

"Hi. I'm all finished back there. The meat from today's hunt is now drying on the racks, and the hide is stretched tight on a frame. I was so covered in blood, I thought I'd never get clean," he said with a smile, sniffing the enticing aroma of their food drifting in the air while sitting down in his usual spot by the fire. He watched as Jennifer flipped their steaks using a long two-pronged fork he had carved from a leg bone of a runner. He ran his fingers through his long hair a few more times before tying it back in a ponytail and out of his way.

"Why don't you sit down and relax while I serve you dinner?" Taric suggested, wanting to help and started to rise from his spot but was waved off by Jennifer.

"I got it," she replied, stabbing the fork into a steak and lifted if off the stone. When she had all three steaks on the platter, she began to cut the meat into bite-sized pieces using the knife from the life pod.

"I wish the pod had held more than one knife. It sure would be nice to have another one," Jennifer commented as she easily cut the thick steaks with the steel blade. She filled their bowls with vegetables and rice halfway to the brim and topped the bowls with pieces of cut meat. Per her habit, Jennifer gave Jaxx her bowl first before handing Taric his and then joined him on the furs.

"Oh, this is really good," Taric complimented Jennifer as he enjoyed the savory, rich taste of her meal in his mouth.

After their dinner, they talked about the baby and what their child's name should be, without success. Jennifer preferred to wait until her child was born before deciding on a name. Outside in the darkness of night, the herds slowly quieted down, settling in for the night as they began to sleep secure and safe within the tall grass as goroc bulls roamed around the outskirts watching over the herds. The silence in the valley, combined with the incessant musical chirping of insects, slowly lured the couple to their bedding for a long night's sleep.

A persistent slow pawing from Jaxx on his shoulder awoke Taric from a deep, dreamless sleep. Sleepily leaning forward, while propping his torso upright with his arms as Jaxx ran over to the hide covering the entrance to the inner cave. He watched through groggy eyes as his lycur turned around and looked back at him. Jaxx then loudly barked at him twice, before pushing the loose goroc hide aside with her nose and disappeared into the inner cave.

Taric looked over at Jennifer's empty bedding, before realizing he was alone in the cave. "Jennifer!" Taric shouted out in alarm and sprang naked from his bedding and onto his feet. He ran in and out of the inner cave to sprint up the ledge as fast as his legs would carry him to find Jennifer, quietly sitting at the pool's edge with her legs swaying in the warm water. Jaxx was panting loudly and sat on the ledge beside her, watching him.

"What's wrong? Are you okay?" he frantically asked her as he neared, straining his eyes in the dim firelight looking for harm or injury. He came up behind the pair to see Jennifer happily scratching Jaxx behind the ear with one hand while rubbing a warm damp fur over her swollen belly's tight, itchy skin with the other.

"Did Jaxx frighten you? Oh, I'm so sorry, it wasn't intentional. I just sent her to wake you up for breakfast," Jennifer calmly answered without looking at him as she continued rubbing her itchy skin. "Were you really worried about me?"

"What? Yes! I was!" he exclaimed, staring at the back of her head with a confounded look on his face.

"So, so you're really okay?" Taric asked her, trying to slow his breathing and calm his tightly wound nerves.

"You know love, you really need to relax a little bit. Kids are born every day, it's a natural process of life. Our child has been restless and has kept me awake for most of the night, but everything is fine. I'm good and the baby is doing great, growing bigger by the day. Trust me, my love, I'll let you know when our baby is ready to be born.

"I've made our breakfast. I need to eat a little before I sleep and wanted some company. The bowls are sitting beside the fire keeping warm," Jennifer replied, turning her head to face him in the dim light with a slight pouting apologetic smile on her face. But one look at Taric was all it took for her to suddenly burst into uncontrollable laughter.

Jennifer laughingly asked him in between painful intakes of air, while supporting her heaving belly with her hands. "Where are your clothes?"

"I was concerned for your safety!" Taric stiffly exclaimed, realizing he had run through the caves naked because Jaxx had awakened him with a terrible fright. Looking down at himself and then at Jaxx, sitting calmly beside Jennifer, who looked back at him with her dark expressive eyes as if to say, "What?"

"Next time," he said warningly to the lycur. "Lick me in the face!" An embarrassed and angry Taric then turned and walked down the ledge and out of the cave with all the dignity he could muster. All the while, hearing amid her laughter, Jennifer praising the dog. "Good girl, good girl, Jaxx. Oh, you're such a good girl."

It didn't take Taric long to get dressed and return to the water cave. Jennifer was still sitting at the ledge with her feet dangling in the water as Jaxx rose to greet him as he walked up the incline to rejoin her.

"Oh, thank goodness, you're back. Can you help me up? I'm kind of stuck," Jennifer sheepishly asked, cradling her heavy belly with her hands as Taric came up behind her.

"How'd you manage to sit down, if you can't get back up?" Taric asked as he knelt behind her, placing his arms under hers and slowly began to lift her up to her feet.

"Well, gravity and having a fat ass helped." Jennifer chuckled her reply, feeling her torso stretching upward as Taric lifted. Taric immediately realized Jennifer was heavier than he remembered and had to brace himself to support her weight as she rose off the ledge. Jennifer braced her body against Taric's as he lifted her up and over the edge of the ledge. When Jennifer had both feet back underneath her, she assisted Taric's efforts by using her leg strength to stand upright.

"Oh Lord, I'm so fat," Jennifer remarked, looking down at her belly to discover for the first time, she was unable to see the toes of her feet.

"You're not fat, you're very pregnant," Taric replied as he kissed the back of her neck.

"I can't see my toes!" Jennifer exclaimed happily as she tried to look down at her feet, realizing her baby had dropped within her and would soon be born.

"I'm so hungry," she said enthusiastically, wiggling and squirming her way out of Taric's comforting embrace to waddle laboriously over to the fire and her waiting breakfast bowl.

"Obviously," Taric quietly whispered to himself as he walked a few steps behind her toward the fire and his morning meal.

"What was that?" she asked him, hearing Taric mumble something behind her back, unable to decipher within her mind what he had said.

"Oh, nothing," Taric quietly replied as Jennifer settled on a high mound of furs piled up so she could recline comfortably.

Then she asked Taric, "So what have you planned to do today?"

"Collecting some more firewood and later I'll work on finishing the hides I'm in the process of curing," he answered her after swallowing a bite of his breakfast bowl of warm grains and fruit.

Jennifer looked at the caves back wall to see three rows of neatly stacked firewood as high as Taric's shoulders. "Don't we have enough?" she asked him, thinking it would take more than a winter to burn that much wood.

"Winters are unpredictable. You can't tell how long the land will be covered in snow. So it's best to have more than enough firewood to last the season," Taric answered.

"Well, I really think you've gathered enough firewood. It's definitely more than we had last winter," she commented, knowing he'd go out and get some more anyway. She knew he was worried about the baby and was trying to keep busy and have everything perfect by the time their child was born. Taric was adamant she enjoy their child's first months without care or worry during the cold of winter, secure within the warmth and comfort of their home.

"Well, okay, but don't go too far. You need to be able to hear me if I shout out. Or I'll have to send Jaxx after you again," she said with a giggle, setting her empty bowl down beside the fire, unaware an imperial starship had just dropped out of warp and came to a stop, a million miles outside their planetary system.

"Captain on the bridge," Commander Sterling announced, rising from the command chair as Thomas exited his ready room and stepped onto the bridge. He glanced at the view screen as he walked over to his chair. Starlight radiated outward from the system's sun, illuminating the darkness of space for millions of miles around, revealing the orbital paths of the planets held by the star's gravitational pull.

"Cooper," Thomas said, addressing the ship's AI as he took possession of the command chair. Instantly, the standard imperial AI Cooper persona appeared to stand beside him.

"Captain," Cooper's holographic image replied and waited for instructions.

"Verbal communication only, Cooper," Thomas ordered, disliking the projected image.

Instantly the hologram disappeared in compliance with the order. "Very well, Captain."

"Track the emergency signal to its source and plot our course into the system. I'd like a geosynchronous orbit three hundred thirty miles above the planet," Thomas ordered, letting the AI calculate the best flight path for the ship.

"Coordinates are set, and the flight path has been sent to navigation," the bodiless voice of Cooper announced in compliance with the order.

"Lieutenant Carter," Thomas said to his helmsman with a smile. "Take us in at full impulse power."

"Yes, sir. Taking over flight control from the AI," Carter answered excitedly from his station and began to manually fly the *Maleficent* into an alien system following the AI's recommended flight path toward Planos.

"Commander Sterling, please report to the hangar bay. Have a shuttle loaded with camping gear and a three-day supply of rations for one. You're to accompany me to the surface to help locate the life pod. Have the shuttle ready for launch as soon the ship is in orbit around Planos. Once on the ground, we'll attach the life pod to the shuttle. You'll fly back to the ship and take command. I'll use the time on the surface to search for any sign of survivors," Thomas calmly announced his intention of exploring a wild, untamed world alone.

"Helmsman Carter, how soon before we're in a stable orbit around Planos?" Thomas asked his officer.

"About thirty minutes, Captain," Carter answered from his station.

Thomas rose from his command chair and looked at his crew stationed around the bridge. On their faces, he could see their puzzled questioning looks. He could especially tell by the hard look on Commander Sterling's face, she clearly disapproved of his planned activity but said nothing except. "I'll see to the preparations, a shuttle will be waiting for our departure at your convenience."

She then stiffly walked off the bridge with the intention of accompanying him to the surface and to remain on the planet with him, regardless of his orders. It would be a violation of her duty to allow him to recklessly endanger his life on the surface of a wild world without a partner. But she had to wait to get him alone on the shuttle and privately remind him that as his first officer, she goes wherever he goes. Sterling had no wish of ending her career facing an angry empress if harm should befall her captain.

Thomas was very good at reading people's body language, and seeing Sterling march stiffly off the bridge, he knew another insightful discussion with her was forthcoming and the thought of it made him smile.

"Cooper, center the view on Planos and magnify the image," Thomas ordered the AI.

At their current distance, the view of Planos was much like Earth. It appeared as a blue-and-green world partly obscured by clouds of patchy white to the threatening dark-gray shades of scattered storms swirling around the planet. As they flew further into the planetary system more detail of the planet was revealed on the screen. The beautiful green and brown landmasses were separated by wide swaths of dark blue oceans as Planos spun on its axis. The planet was home to three very distinct and isolated continents, two of which, stretched from the north's mountainous glacial wall down to within a few hundred miles of an expansive southern polar ice cap. The central landmass extended down from the northern glacial mountains to the hemisphere's lower latitudes. The landmass stretched horizontally across the planet with ocean waves rolling onto its eastern, western, and southern shores. The startling beautiful view of the planet reminded Thomas of a dragon claw gripping tightly around a treasured crystal orb.

"Open a shipwide channel," Thomas requested in a quietly subdued tone of voice.

"Channel is open, Captain," he heard from across the bridge.

"This is your captain speaking. Today, we make history together as the *Maleficent* takes her position to orbit around an alien planet. We'll be orbiting for three days to comply with the charter's bylaws. If we're fortunate enough to locate the *Fulcrum*'s survivors. We'll journey on to Opalla and enjoy a few days of R&R on the empire's first colonized world. When you get a chance, please take some time to admire the magnificent view of Planos. Our beloved home, Earth, was once very similar in appearance, thirty thousand years ago. It's a rare sight few will ever see in their lifetime.

"I'd also like to commend you all for your outstanding efforts and wish for you to enjoy the next three days of light-duty aboard ship. Thank you," Thomas stated and then began to walk off the bridge. As the door to his ready room opened, Thomas smiled and ordered as he passed the threshold. "Lieutenant Carter, until Commander Sterling returns, the *Maleficent* is yours."

CHAPTER 17

Landfall

Once inside the hangar bay, Thomas walked across the open floor to the rear access ramp of the shuttle and boarded the small craft, noticing an extra backpack among the gear stowed aboard. Commander Sterling pushed a button on her console to close the access ramp behind him. As the ramp retracted, a slight hiss could be heard as the air pressure stabilized within the shuttle. Thomas's ears popped within his head adjusting to the sudden change of pressure as he sat in the copilot's seat next to Sterling and buckled the seats restraining harness about him. "Whenever you're ready, Commander."

"*Maleficent* shuttle, ready for launch," Sterling said into the comm unit notifying the hangar's flight control technician monitoring their launch.

Their small craft rested on a motorized track leading to a launch tube door, which opened in front of the shuttle. The shuttle secured to the track slowly began to move across the floor through the door and into the crafts launch position inside the tube. Once in position, the inner door closed behind the shuttle, sealing the hangar bay from the vacuum of space as the outer door opened in front of the shuttle.

"Prepare for launch." They both heard and felt the restraining locks disengage, releasing the shuttle from the track for flight. "Shuttle, you're free to launch." They heard the launch control technician announce over the speaker.

"Roger, hangar control," Sterling answered and then announced, "*Maleficent*, shuttle away."

Thomas braced himself against his seat anticipating the rapid acceleration of the impending launch. He watched with a little envy as Sterling pushed the accelerator handle on her console quickly forward to maximum thrust. In a blur, the tube walls flashed past and disappeared as the shuttle flew like a bullet down and out the barrel of a gun. Sterling calmly controlled her craft as it shot out of the ship into the open vacuum of space.

"Whew, what a rush! Just like a rollercoaster back home!" Thomas excitedly exclaimed with a huge smile on his narrow face as Sterling smiled back at him as she expertly flew the shuttle toward the planet.

"Planos looks a lot like Earth, except the continents are all wrong, but it's a beautiful world just the same," Sterling commented as she angled her craft's flight to enter into a stable orbit around the planet before descending into the atmosphere.

"Yes, it is," Thomas agreed, stunned by the incredible natural beauty of Planos shimmering within the blackness of space like a sparkling gem.

"Permission to speak freely, Captain?" Sterling questioned, turning her head to stare at him with a serious "don't mess with me" attitude expressed on her face.

"Granted," Thomas calmly replied, anticipating the topic of their conversation, and waited for her to speak her mind.

"Captain, before I say anything that may lead me to a court-martial, I want you to know I truly like and respect you. However, you're not qualified to be a captain of an imperial starship. It's harsh to hear, I know. But allow me to explain? Please?" Sterling asked him, apologizing to him, respecting the man sitting beside her but not the rank he held.

"Proceed, Commander, I value honest communication with whomever I interact with. It's a rare commodity to discover in people," Thomas replied, caught off guard by her statement, and added, "If we're going to be open and honest, let's forget about the formality of rank. Okay? Let's start by defining what you meant when you said the word 'qualified.'"

"Really? You want to go there?" Sterling asked him, staring at him with incredulous disbelief.

"You brought it up," Thomas calmly answered, allowing her to continue.

"I'm aware of your occupation and educational degrees support the appointment of your rank. You're a highly regarded world-re-nowned academic and politician, but you lack the basic command skills taught at our fleet academies on Earth.

"I've been observing you since we left. The first thing the acad-emy teaches prospective officers is maintaining an effective distance from the crew. You're too easygoing and jovial. Your approachability and friendliness with the crew is a detriment to your command. A captain's chair is positioned to be an island on the bridge for a reason. It separates you from the crew. Your orders are to be instantly obeyed without question.

"In a crisis, the men and women aboard the *Maleficent* expect their captain to make the difficult life-and-death decisions, not a nerdy science academic appointed by the empress. They have to trust and believe in their captain to get the ship safely back home, even at the risk of their life or the life of someone else. That's why a captain cannot be a friend to his crew!"

Thomas, having heard similar criticisms in the past, forced himself not to chuckle or smirk at her, knowing it would be an insult if he did. He thought about his words carefully and then replied as honest with his answer as she was with criticizing his command style.

"Well, Kelly, that's quite a lesson, but I don't agree. Any officer can stiffly bark out orders, but it doesn't make them a better officer. That's military conditioning in discipline, always follow the chain of command. A true leader is someone who's able to draw out the untapped potential of his peers, regardless of their rank or status in life.

"An effective captain should encourage, empower, and reward his people with praise from time to time and listen to the ideas of his subordinates. Observation and interaction with the people under your command, provides a positive means of assessing their capabil-ities. A good leader inspires others to excel and sometimes take the initiative, even if it violates a direct order."

Thomas paused, letting his last statement linger in the silence. "I'm sorry, if you don't approve of my command style. You're correct, I'm an imperial appointee with no formal military education or training. Just the same, I hold the rank of captain and expect military discipline in following my commands."

"I didn't mean to insult you. I understand your perspective, but I don't see how it qualifies you to be captain of the *Maleficent*," Kelly responded while casting a quick glance at the gear stowed behind them.

"Do you know what I do for Isabella?"

"No."

"People think I'm her errand boy, her guy Friday. I'm not. I'm her scientific advisor for the colonization of planets. I'm her enforcer of the charter on Earth and now, for the first time, in space. Isabella and I are working to ensure the survival of our people on Opalla, Rema, and Garoff, and I'm coordinating all of it. Are you aware all the colonists from your kingdom is sent to Opalla? Each kingdom is solely populating one of the three habitable planets that have been declared suitable for colonization. We're still searching for a planet for the Americas to colonize.

"When the survey ships returned to Earth, we did nothing with the information until my great-grandmother commissioned the construction of the colonial starships. She envisioned Earth as one day becoming the governmental home of a Union of Planets. Each planet sovereign unto themselves but united as one intergalactic human society. The peace of the empire on Earth is held together by the kingdom's adherence to the charter's bylaws because of her inspirational dream.

"Isabella and I are working to complete our great-grandmother's vision for us as a species. It takes patience, understanding, and imagination to accomplish a goal that grand. It's my easygoing and jovial personality and education that has made it possible for us to succeed. My leadership skills are more subtle but just as effective in getting the best out of people, even kings, queens, and a hardheaded empress. There are many ways to lead and inspire others. Discipline is only a tool of leadership, not the foundation of leadership," Thomas explained, ending his narration. He then quietly looked out the window at the magnificent planet below them, letting his words fill the silence between them.

Sterling still didn't get him, but she was beginning to understand him as she went about preparing the shuttle for entry into the atmosphere of Planos. "Prepare for entry, activate the window heat shield," she ordered as she aligned her craft for the descent.

"Activating window heat shields," Thomas nervously stated, while pressing a button on his console. A hazy transparent ceramic based heat shield slid over the windows surface from opposite sides and sealed seamlessly in the center.

Sterling flew the shuttle on a preset optimum glide path to safely fly through the planet's many atmospheric layers and informed her captain. "We'll be out of contact with the ship for approximately seven minutes during our descent through the mesosphere."

"This is the one aspect of space travel I don't care for very much. Passing through the mesosphere always frightens me," he tensely admitted, controlling the nervous tension within him while holding tightly onto the armrests of his chair with white knuckles. It was a frightening sensation to him, seeing flames engulf the nose of the craft and flow violently over the window. It made Thomas imagine he was inside a crematorium being consumed by an intense unrelenting fire.

Witnessing her captain's anxiety, Sterling offered him some advice. "Captain, I've logged over a hundred flights to and from the construction docks in orbit above the Earth. There's nothing to be worried about."

"I'm well aware of that, Commander!" Thomas tensely replied, fighting to control his lifelong fear of fire.

"I used to be like you. All white-knuckled and stiff. Believe it or not, before the academy, I grew up in the two orbiting space docks during their construction. Every month, three weeks in space, one week at home. I loved living in the docks, the shuttle trips up from Earth was exciting and thrilling to ride but the return trip down to the planet, not so much. I had a deathly fear of reentry into the Earth's atmosphere every single month. Why don't you try what I used to do before I became a pilot," Kelly suggested with a slight smile on her lips.

"What was that?" Thomas hopefully asked her.

"Well, close your eyes and imagine you're camping and sitting around the nightly campfire watching the flames dance high in the air. Now, take slow deep breaths, and when you're comfortable and relaxed, open your eyes."

"That really helped you get used to reentry?" Thomas asked her with a serious tenseness expressed within his questioning eyes.

"Oh, hell no! But everyone thought it was funny to watch," Kelly laughingly replied with a sympathetic look of understanding.

"Thanks," Thomas replied with a hearty chuckle and then relaxed his tight grip on the armrests of his seat, deciding to trust in the skills of his pilot.

The view through the hazy transparent shield changed quickly from red flames to steaming white water vapor flowing over the surface of the window as they entered the stratosphere of Planos. Thomas gratefully retracted the hazy heat shield covering the window. As the shield slowly retracted, they were greeted by a clear view of deep blue oceans with a faint silhouette of a landmass far below on the eastern horizon.

Sterling flew her craft toward the surface in a wide spiraling gradual dive, constantly banking the body of the craft against the air in slowing the shuttle's speed.

"Leveling off at ten thousand feet. Our airspeed is eight hundred fifty miles an hour," Sterling announced with an easy smile on her face.

"I've got a fix on the beacon's signal, alter our course thirty degrees northeast. Activating shuttles cloaking device," Thomas said, pressing a button on his console while reading the signal's strength increase as they flew invisibly toward the pod's location.

Sterling flew the shuttle following the beacon to its source as Thomas monitored the signal strength and direction. "Signal strength is rising fast. We better slow down to cruising speed. Alter course five degrees north, toward that far mountain range," Thomas stated, listening to the beacon in his headset while pointing toward the far peaks to the north, feeling the shuttles airspeed decrease.

"Aye, Captain," Sterling responded, turning her craft five degrees north in a wide bank to help reduce her ship's speed without using the air brakes or thrusters.

"Estimated range to objective is fourteen hundred sixty-three miles. The signal has to be on the southern side of the mountains to be reading this strongly," Thomas remarked as the shuttle swept over the land bringing the mountain range rapidly into view.

"Dropping down to three hundred feet," Sterling said as she brought her craft to the desired elevation and slowed, giving clarity to the land and animals living on a wide expansive plain that stretched upward into the mountains.

"Range to the pod is fifty miles up the open plain. We should see signs of where it landed very soon," Thomas said, taking off his headset, no longer needing to hear the beacon.

"Look at that!" Sterling exclaimed in awe, looking out the window as she flew over massive herds of unfamiliar animal species roaming over the plain of grass. "I've never seen anything this amazing or beautiful."

"Agreed," Thomas replied, totally wonderstruck by the view. "This is what our home must have looked like before the first cities of men were built, open and extremely wild. With the size of the herds, there must be some predators roaming around the outskirts of the animals. We'll have to be on our guard once we're on the ground."

It was near sunset on a hot day without the slightest hint of a breeze in the air to cool the valley. Taric busily worked in the sweltering heat, chopping off sections of a branch from a fallen tree with his stone bladed ax. Severing the final section in half, he picked up the chunks of wood and threw them onto his pile.

As he wiped his sweaty brow with the back of his arm, he felt a sudden gust of hot air whip over him, but before he could lower his arm back to his side, the air was once again as still as it was a moment before. It made him feel uneasy and apprehensive for no apparent reason as he scoured the area around him with his eyes searching for signs of danger. He saw nothing and heard nothing but the normal sounds of the land, which made him shiver under his skin. Lifting the loaded travois, he began to pull his load of wood quickly back to the cave with an unnerving sense of urgency, he couldn't explain.

Jennifer and Jaxx were resting outside the barricade on a fur spread over the grass in the waning sunlight. They were waiting for Taric's return when Jaxx suddenly stood and ran to the right of her as Taric came into sight, dragging a heavy load behind him. Relieved to see him return from his labors, she walked over and greeted him home with a kiss.

"Whew, you stink," Jennifer said with a kind smile as she pushed herself away from his sweaty embrace, wafting the air in front of her wrinkled nose with a hand. "Leave the wood! Go and cool down with a bath."

"Yes, let's get inside," Taric agreed, quickly ushering a confused Jennifer toward the door of their barricade with a worried expression on his face.

Seeing the alarm in his eyes, Jennifer asked, "You look as if you've seen a ghost, what's the matter?"

"You know, that's exactly how I feel. I was chopping wood when I felt a sudden gust of hot wind blow over me and then nothing. I didn't see or hear anything. It made me feel as if a spirit had passed through me. I don't know why, but it did," he superstitiously replied while quickly closing the door behind them and tying it securely for the night.

"Don't be silly, it was probably a dirt devil that flowed over you," Jennifer commented, leading him by the hand through the caves toward the pool and their evening meal cooking beside the fire in the water cave.

"That's the strange thing, dirt devils blow around you. I felt a gust of wind blowing directly over me in a straight direction and then nothing. There's no wind outside, no breeze whatsoever, and it gave me the creeps. That's the word you use, right?" Taric asked her as they walked up the ledge toward the fire and the pool.

Jennifer smiled, never having seen him spooked by unexplained sensations, and she found it amusing to witness. "Yes," she answered and then tried to comfort him by saying, "Well, with a warm bath to soothe your nerves, your unusual and unnerving sensations will pass quickly. I think you're stressed is all, it's a very natural feeling of expectant fathers. By morning, the feeling will pass, and you'll feel just fine."

"I hope you're right," Taric remarked while removing his leggings and loincloth before jumping into the warm pool. He swam over to the opposite side and sat on the outcropping, relaxing in the flowing water with his arms stretched out and resting on the smooth limestone ledge.

Sterling saw the depression left by the pod's impact before Thomas. She slowed the craft, switching her controls over to hover mode. She then glided down to thirty feet above the trees and brought her craft to a stop, hovering above the wreckage of the pod. With expert ease, she lowered the ship to the grass-covered ground and opened the access door to the fresh, stuffy heat of late afternoon summer air. "Welcome to Planos, Captain."

"And you, Commander," Thomas replied as he uncoupled the harness and rose to his feet. He walked over to the gear and lifted two backpacks. He handed one to Sterling and said, "I understand why you disregarded my order and had the shuttle prepped for two. I shouldn't have put you in a position, which forced you to disobey an order. I'll try not to repeat mistakes like that in the future. It's fortunate for me when I say something stupid, you have the strength of character to act appropriately. I'm glad you're here."

"Thank you, Captain," Sterling replied and then asked as she slung her backpack onto her back and strapped it in place. "Do you think there's a chance the Collins kids are alive?"

"I honestly don't know, but we have an obligation to search for survivors," Thomas said with a hopeful smile while inwardly believing they had already perished.

"Well, let's get our gear outside and get the pod secured to the bottom of the shuttle for recovery," Sterling announced, grabbing a large duffel containing their camping supplies and walked down the ramp.

Thomas followed her down the ramp into the tall dry brown grass, dropped his load onto the ground, and turned around to enter the shuttle once more. From the foot of the access ramp, only the interior could be seen as the cloaking device was still activated around the shuttle's exterior hull, mimicking the natural colors of the landscape.

He went up the ramp and walked over to the weapons locker and entered the authorization code to gain access to the weapons inside. Opening the locker, Thomas removed two rifles, two steel-bladed knives, a pair of handguns in holsters, and ammunition for both. The rifles were remakes from ancient America's historic old West, the Winchester repeating rifle. Whereas the pistols were military remakes of the famous Colt .45-caliber handgun. As Thomas carried the weapons down the ramp, he hoped they'd not have a need for them.

Sterling had already climbed under the shuttle and was positioning four restraining cables to the pod's grappling rings. She wiggled herself free from beneath the shuttle after connecting the cables securely in the rings. Standing next to the ramp, she pressed a button to activate the combination winch and pull the pod free of the ground. Upon contact with the hull, the winch automatically switched off, securing the pod to the underside of the craft.

"That was quick. Well done, Kelly," Thomas said as he walked around to the visible pod, which appeared to be floating in the air due to the cloaked ship. Thomas looked into the opening and saw a thin stream of light penetrating the shadows inside. He walked around to the other side and knelt down on his knees to see the reason behind the tiny beam of light. "Hey, check this out," he called over to Sterling and pointed to the small hole in the side of the pod. "Does that look like a meteor strike to you?"

"Yes, that's definitely a meteor impact," Sterling said, seeing the position of the hole in relation to the interior. "Whoever sat on this side was struck by the meteor after the pod entered the atmosphere and might have died during the remainder of the flight down to the surface."

"You might be right. The angle of the meteor's path would have struck the upper torso of the person like a bullet. The emergency medical kit is gone, and there are no human remains inside. I can only assume one or both of the Collins kids survived the landing," Thomas answered with more hope in his voice and heart than he originally had for the marooned children.

"So we're staying?

"Yes, Commander. We're staying for a while," Thomas answered with an adventurous grin on his face, eager to explore the area and observe the varied animal life Planos supported.

Sterling smiled and spoke into her comm unit on her wrist. "*Maleficent* shuttle one reporting."

"Roger, shuttle one. We hear you," a bodiless voice responded to the call.

"Have Cooper return the shuttle back to the ship. The captain and I will be staying on the surface. We've found plausible evidence indicating one or both of the Collins kids may have survived landfall. We'll report our progress daily in twelve-hour intervals. Sterling out," she said into the unit as the access ramp slowly began to rise off the ground.

They stood side by side, watching the shuttle slowly lift off the ground with its contaminating cargo secured to the underside of the craft. Within seconds the life pod disappeared from view as the shuttle streaked into the darkening sky.

"Well, we best get our campsite set up before it gets dark," Thomas said, looking at the darkening sky on the horizon.

Without much more said between them, the pair went to work setting up their base of operations on the planet beside the depression. Nighttime had descended over the valley by the time they finished getting the gear and campsite organized. Only the amber light from their lanterns penetrated the total darkness around their camp.

In the depths of the darkness, Thomas and Kelly listened intently to the nightly commotion of countless animals restlessly roaming near their camp. The alien animal noises, unfamiliar to human ears, became less unnerving as the night grew late, noticing a gradual decline of the animal's ambient noise as they started settling down for the night. Every so often, they'd hear a long low bellow from a goroc bull disrupting the rhythmic nocturnal melodies of the grasslands varied insect life.

"How could I forget to gather wood? I knew we were staying!" Thomas exclaimed, venting his frustration and kicking himself in the ass for his blunder.

"Thomas, the lights will do just fine. We'll get wood in the morning. Don't worry so much, enjoy the moment and try to relax," Kelly replied with a slight chuckle and an encouraging smile, completely at ease with the darkness of the night, a natural camper since childhood.

Beyond the reach of their amber lights, absolute blackness, a total absence of light that blanketed the land. Only by looking up into the night sky could his eyes detect the comforting sight of faraway starlight. But the stars were not aligned in the familiar constellations that filled the night sky above the Earth. The stars above Planos were a comforting sight to be sure, Thomas thought, but they were roughly eighty lightyears removed from their home, giving him nothing to indicate the direction of true north.

Thomas could not see into the darkness and hated having to rely on the bright amber lights to keep animals at a distance. He preferred a large fire to deter animals, especially predators, casting a reassuring glance at his rifle leaning against the tent. Unaware, a predator had roamed over the high rocky peaks and made its way down to the mountain base and stood looking over the river at the rich abundance of the expansive grasslands.

CHAPTER 18

Introductions

Lured by fire like amber lights, the kessra moved cautiously from the rocks and into the trees without a sound. It walked down the river's embankment in search of a favored prey on the opposite shore. It stood at the water's edge, sniffing the air while peering through the darkness with its keen eyes. Entering into the water's swift current, the lean, muscular kessra began to swim across.

The swiftly flowing water carried the kessra quickly downriver as six legs fought the current with each powerful stroke, propelling it through the water and into the shallows on the opposite shore. It stood still and silent, dripping streams of water from its thick fur onto the sand, listening intently in the darkness to the various animals roaming the grasslands.

Ignoring the noise and strong musky scents of the animals, the big male in his prime violently shook the remaining water from its fur and crept slowly up the embankment to the rivers grassy crest. It stood in the sand below the tall blades of brown late summer grass and peered over to see a strange object within the distant glow of amber light. Silently, the kessra crept into the cover of shrubs and trees to circle the area and search for a place that would provide him with an advantage in attacking its favored prey.

During the night as the kessra walked through the dark forest, it encountered a fortified den of its favored prey but could not get past the barrier with the desirable smells inside. The kessra's mind stored the information for a later time. Instead, it continued on with its roaming toward the exposed easy prey on the open grass. It stayed out of sight of the goroc bulls as it stealthily maneuvered around the open plain. The predator moved with ease through the thickets of shrubs and trees undetected by the alert bulls. By the time the oppressive darkness of night gave way to the bright rays of the morning sun. The big male predator found a hiding spot near its prey in which to rest, watch, and wait for an opportunity to strike.

Jennifer awoke with Jaxx pawing at her shoulder and licking her in the face. "Jaxx," she drawled out sleepily, pushing her dog's head aside with her hand to stop her from licking. Jaxx backed off, sat patiently on the furs beside her, and waited.

"Taric, wake up. Jaxx has to go outside," Jennifer said, nudging him gently with her arm to wake him up, but she heard no reply from him.

"Come on, wake up. Jaxx has to go out!" she whined sleepily, nudging him once more a little harder with a bony elbow, wanting nothing more than to linger in the warmth of the furs and drift back to sleep while listening to the waterfall.

"I'm awake," Taric quietly grumbled in the dim firelight of the cave, while rising slowly to his feet and stretching his arms out and upward to loosen up. He dressed quickly, added more wood to the fire, and then came back and knelt beside their bedding to lay the top fur neatly back in place on the bed. He leaned down over Jennifer and softly kissed her on the forehead. "I'll be right back," he whispered in her ear as she dozed off to sleep, returning to the fantasy of her dreams.

Taric rose from his knees and back to his feet, smiling down at the totality of his world, feeling a sense of contentment within himself that he hadn't felt for a very long time. He then looked over at Jaxx and smiled, seeing her sitting patiently beside Jennifer, waiting for his hand signal to follow.

Taric flicked his wrist, giving the dog permission to follow. Instantly, the fully grown lycur leaped over Jennifer's sleeping form in a graceful arch and landed softly beside him without a misstep.

"Come on," he said with a smile and began the short walk through the caves to their barricaded door. Jaxx walked beside him down the ledge, but first Taric needed to relieve himself, so he walked to the low end of the water cave near the end of the ledge and passed his stream into the gaping black hole.

Walking back to the opening, he pulled the heavy goroc hide aside for Jaxx to pass through to the storeroom. He watched as Jaxx pushed aside the next hide on her own with her nose and disappeared into the main cave. Following the dog, Taric lazily stepped into the main cave and became immediately alarmed.

Jaxx was standing stiffly halfway through the entryway hide, growling low and deep in her chest. Taric walked up behind her and quickly pulled the light summer hide off the pegs while wondering what had suddenly gotten the dog so aggressively agitated.

Staring intently through the tightly lashed branches of the door, Jaxx continued her low menacing growl. As often as they hunted together, Taric knew something dangerous had prowled around their cave. Hanging on a wooden peg stuck into the wall next to the entryway, Taric snatched his bow and quiver of arrows, before warily untying the door from the frame to swing outward with an easy push.

Taric had pushed the door halfway open and immediately noticed the reason behind Jaxx's aggressive behavior and almost slammed the door back into the dog's face. In the soft dirt in front of the barricade, Taric could see clear impressions of six unmistakable paw prints of a kessra that had paused by the barricade sometime in the night.

Looking into the depths of the trees beyond the clearing of their firepits, Taric could not detect any danger nearby and slowly pushed the door fully open, allowing Jaxx to pass through the door ahead of him. The experienced pair of hunters stood side by side in the bright morning sun, scouring the brush and trees with their eyes for danger. With Jaxx watching the clearing in front of the cave, Taric turned his back to the trees and tied the door tightly onto the frame.

Where the kessra stood in the middle of the night, Jaxx was busy sniffing at the ground, breathing in the strong scent of the nighttime prowler into her sensitive nose. Jaxx pawed at the ground and growled deep and low, giving Taric the signal she was locked onto the kessra's scent. Jaxx lifted her head, growled aggressively eager to be off. Taric flicked his wrist with his fingers pointing forward. Seeing the signal, Jaxx stopped her low growling and began to silently follow the hated scent at an easy pace, always staying within Taric's line of sight as she advanced through the shrubs and trees.

Jaxx tracked the kessra's scent to the edge of the grasslands with Taric following a few steps behind her. When Taric walked out of the trees, he quickly knelt beside Jaxx in the tall grass. He saw a square tent erected near the depression but trained his eyes to follow Jaxx's line of sight to see a kessra's barely perceptible movements in the tall grass. Jaxx's eyes fixated on the slowly advancing predator that was continuing to creep steadily through the grass, unaware it had been tracked and was being watched.

Jennifer's pod no longer rested half-buried in the overgrown depression. It was gone, and in its place, a flimsy blue tent gently billowed with the breeze flowing over the open grass. With the pod's sudden disappearance, Taric knew humans had returned and were obviously searching for Jennifer. A woman was speaking to someone inside the tent as he slowly notched an arrow to his bow with the slightest of movement.

Taric ignored the voice and tried not to think about the ramifications of their presence as he pulled the arrow tightly back across his bow. Watching the parting tips of the tall grass as the kessra advanced toward the human's tent. Taric then thought, asking himself, was it chance or fate that had Jaxx track the kessra to this spot on the morning of their return? Taric admitted he didn't have an answer and put it out of his mind so he could concentrate on the moment. Taric slowed his breathing and aimed his weapon, targeting the beast's movements through the grass, aware it would not attack its prey until assured of a quick kill.

"Oh God, I have to pee!" Kelly said to Thomas in the stuffy confines of their tent, wiggling out of her sleeping bag fully dressed. She sat on her bag, pulling her legs up so her arms could reach her feet, then she slipped her shoes on and tied them. She stood and strapped a gun holster around her waist, grabbed a rifle, unzipped the tent, and stepped outside to the fresh cool air of the early morning. Kelly felt the sunlight warming her skin as she stood on the trampled grass in front of their tent.

"Thomas, you've got to see this!" she exclaimed happily as she watched the different herd animals peacefully grazing on the grass, no more than fifty yards from their campsite. Picking up a camera, she pointed it at the animals and began taking pictures, never realizing peace in the wilds was only a temporary interlude between extreme acts of deadly violence.

Taric kept his bow aimed at the unseen animal as it crept within striking distance of the woman. Seeing its chance to strike, it sprang roaring out of the tall grass running toward its prey with quick, easy strides. Jaxx instantly ran forward as Taric held his breath and prepared to shoot.

Frozen by the terrifying roar, Kelly had no chance to react to the advancing deadly predator, except to turn around with her hand frozen on the camera's shutter, clicking pictures of death coming to claim her. She managed to step back a pace and scream as the animal was reaching out for her with its deadly claws. Her death was upon her, when suddenly, out of nowhere, a streak of black angry fur rushed in from the tall grass and struck the attacking beast as it slashed a single claw across the flesh of her forearm.

She watched, transfixed with terror as the big black doglike animal turned away from the snarling six-legged beast and bravely stood in front of her with its hackles raised and growling frighteningly low. The two strange animals faced each other and began to circle, growling aggressively no more than ten yards apart. As the furious animals circled, Kelly kept herself behind her apparent defender. The kessra roared loudly as the lycur stood defiantly in front of the woman howling back at the deadly predator.

From out of nowhere, Kelly saw an arrow strike the beast deeply in the side and was followed by another a split second later, hitting the snarling beast beneath the head in the neck, killing it. Kelly backed away from the frightening doglike creature, afraid the fierce animal would then turn on her. Instead, she watched it cautiously approach the dead beast, sniff it, and paw the carcass sharply with a foreleg, before running off in the direction it had come from.

Thomas ran out of the tent to see Kelly frightened to death, pointing at a big black dog running swiftly toward the trees. Thomas looked in the direction Kelly was pointing and for a brief instant, he saw a man with copper-colored skin and the black doglike animal disappear into the shadows of the trees. Thomas turned back to see Kelly's pale ashen-white face slowly fading back to her light coco-brown skin as she cried unable to recover from the harrowing experience.

"What the fuck is that thing?" she shrilly asked him, with her arm bleeding, terrified of the dead animal that wanted to kill her.

"I don't know," Thomas replied, holding Kelly in his arms as she cried helplessly, unable to cope with the terror raging within her mind.

Thomas held her tightly against his chest and tried to calm her by whispering. "It's over. It's over. Try to relax, take slow, deep breaths." Kelly's sobbing began to quiet down, but she held on to him, afraid to let go.

Thomas spoke into his comm unit strapped to his wrist. "Cooper, pilot the shuttle with a doctor and a med tech to the surface. There's been an animal attack."

Five minutes passed before Cooper's voice emitted from the unit. "Shuttle one is descending and should be arriving in fifteen minutes."

"Copy," Thomas replied as he looked down at the dead animal at their feet with two arrows sticking out of the body, marveling over the strength and accuracy of the mysterious shooter to kill at such a distance.

"I'd sure like to meet the man who killed this thing," he said, searching the trees for a glimpse of Kelly's saviors, but they were nowhere to be seen.

Kelly backed out of their embrace, feeling uncomfortable by their closeness as she fought to regain control of her senses. Without a word, she dropped the camera to the ground and grabbed her pistol out of the holster to examine it. Shaking her head from side to side, she removed the magazine from the grip checking the bullets, before loading the full clip back into the handle. She then pulled the slide back to insert a bullet into the chamber before slipping the gun back into the holster.

"You were worried about wood last night. I didn't even think to load a bullet in the chamber. Talk about stupid!" she exclaimed, knowing even if she had, the animal had been too quick in its attack for her to get off a shot.

"If I had Aladdin's lamp, I'd wish that doglike thing a mountain of steaks," Kelly said in a croaking voice as she looked in the direction of the nearby trees, where the native man no longer stood with his big black dog. Feeling as if she had a debt to repay, Kelly requested, "Captain, don't send me back to the ship."

"I'm not. I sent for a doctor to treat your wound. I need you here. But I need you to be fit. Right now, you're a mess. It's completely understandable, but you can't stop shaking and could use something to calm your nerves, besides you're bleeding," Thomas answered giving her a look that refused to be argued with.

"Yes, sir," Kelly replied, aware he was watching her hands involuntarily shake at her sides.

Wrapping her arms about herself, Kelly sat on one of the stools and waited for the doctor to arrive. Kelly saw the camera lying on the trampled grass of their campsite and walked over and picked it up. She faced the grassy plain, seeing where the animals had scattered during the attack. They had not gone far, and once again, they grazed on the tall grass as if nothing had happened. Kelly searched the grass with her eyes, wondering if there were other beasties lurking nearby? The silent question chilled her heart and sent a shiver down her spine as goose bumps rose on her skin.

"I wonder why he saved you and then disappeared without so much as a howdy-do?" Thomas asked himself, pulling the pair of arrows out of the creature, examining their craftsmanship before sticking them carefully into the ground, not wishing to damage them.

"We best drag this thing away from our camp, or we'll be overrun by scavengers." Kelly heard Thomas say as if it was an afterthought.

"I'm not touching that thing!" Kelly adamantly exclaimed, taking a few backward steps increasing the distance between herself and the corpse.

"Okay, I'll drag it away," Thomas conceded, bending down to grab the animals back legs. "Damn thing is heavy!" Thomas complained as he slowly dragged the corpse to a safe distance from their camp.

Taric sprinted through the trees heading back toward the cave with Jaxx leading the way. He opened the door of the barricade and flew through the caves in a run. "Jennifer!" he shouted when he entered the water cave and ran up the ledge toward her.

"What?" Jennifer groggily replied, propping herself up onto an elbow.

"People! Your people! Out on the grass!" Taric breathlessly exclaimed to her.

"People? Here? What people? Really?" Taric heard a sleepy and confused Jennifer respond slowly from underneath her warm furs.

"Yes, yes, and yes," he answered excitedly, shaking her gently to rouse her from sleep. "A kessra attacked them!"

Hearing *kessra*, Jennifer's senses instantly awakened to full comprehension beneath her warm furs. She pushed the top fur down and looked into the eyes of her husband.

"Are they hurt?" she asked worriedly, fearing the worst.

"No, I think they're fine. Jaxx prevented a kessra from harming a woman, giving me a chance to kill it with a couple of arrows," Taric answered, giving her a brief account of the incident.

"Then what?" Jennifer asked him, motioning for Taric to help her onto her feet. "I swear, our baby better come soon, I can hardly move," she tiredly complained as Taric helped her onto her feet and steadied her with his arms.

"I came back," Taric answered, clearly concerned they may try to take her away.

"Where are they?" Jennifer asked him, seeing his worried expression, knowing he was already suspicious of their motives.

"They are where I found you."

"Ah, thank you, my love," Jennifer said with a smile as Taric held her in his hands. He had a loose-fitting, ugly leather dress draped over his shoulder, knowing it was the only garment she could comfortably wear. He held the garment as Jennifer slipped into it, letting the soft, thin leather slide over her swollen breasts and belly to fall loosely down to her knees.

She then turned to walk beside Taric when their baby suddenly squirmed violently within her, making her feel as if she'd been kicked in the bladder. Silently cursing her unborn child, she winced in pain, while saying with a sense of urgency. "Oh Lord, I have to go pee!" Jennifer left Taric standing alone on the ledge, trying not to laugh at the comical sight of her waddling her way down to the end of the ledge to use what she referred to as the naturally built-in facilities.

"Well, Commander, other than the slash on your arm, you're no worse for the ordeal you've experienced. The cut skin is regenerating nicely and should be completely healed within an hour. However, I'm giving you a hypo to calm your nerves," Dr. Mencia kindly stated inside the shuttle after the examination and treatment of his patient while applying the hypo to Kelly's neck.

"Thanks, doc. I appreciate it." Kelly said, feeling the slight pin-prick as the medicine entered her system.

"You'll be right as rain in a few minutes," Dr. Mencia assured her, closing his portable medical bag and handing it to his tech Tina Marlowe before walking out of the shuttle looking for the captain. He found him looking toward the trees and stood beside the man and said to reassure the captain. "It was a minor wound and will heal within an hour."

"Thank you, Doctor. I have an idea. I'd like you and your tech to stay planet-side. I believe there was a survivor of the *Fulcrum* tragedy, and I have a hunch—Kelly's savior may know where they are. I may need your services. Do you mind?" Thomas asked the portly middle-aged doctor.

"Not a problem, Captain. In the meantime, my tech Tina and I will help out by gathering some firewood for tonight. Commander Sterling told us inside the shuttle, she never felt such oppressive darkness before in her life," Mencia said, volunteering his services beyond medicine as Kelly stepped out of the shuttle and walked over.

"Where do you think he went?" Kelly asked Thomas as she stood beside him.

"Kelly, stay in the camp with the doctor and have the shuttle return to the ship. I'll be back soon," Thomas ordered, walked over to the tent for his rifle, picked it up, and walked away.

"You're not going out there alone, are you?" Kelly asked, disapproving of the idea while staring at the back of Thomas's head as he marched toward the trees.

"Don't get lost!" she shouted out after him, following him with her eyes until he disappeared into the shadows of the trees.

Thomas sarcastically replied to himself as he advanced deeper into the trees, searching the area for footprints in the dirt or signs of habitation. "How am I supposed to know? He went this way, and so, I'm following. Hell, I may get lucky and bump into the guy."

Thomas stumbled upon what he hoped was a footpath through the trees. Placing his faith in blind luck, he followed it for over a quarter mile before pausing to look behind him through the gaps in the trees. "Maybe, he doubled back and is watching me right now," Thomas said to himself as he scanned the area behind him with his eyes.

"Why am I looking back there?" Thomas quietly asked, talking to himself as he stepped through a thorny thicket into a sizable clearing with scattered firepits and a barricade of thick straight poles lashed together with wide strips of leather. The poles appeared to be set into the ground and were leaning securely against the stone of the mountain's base.

"Wow, I know why that was built," Thomas said with confidence, remembering Kelly's horrified face after her near-death experience from the morning and wished they had met the occupants inside, the night before.

Thomas walked up to the barricade and was suddenly uncertain of what to do, when the doorway quickly opened outward, revealing an entrance to a cave. Standing just inside the open doorway was the man from the morning. He held a bow with an arrow poised for instant release.

Thomas slowly removed the holster from around his waist and dropped it to the ground. He then set his rifle to lay beside the holster. Raising his hands to show the two blood-tipped arrows. Thomas smiled in greeting, hoping he wouldn't shoot his arrow and said quietly to himself. "Oh Lord, now what do I say?"

Hearing the man, Taric's eyes flashed suspiciously and gruffly said to the Earthman standing outside his home. "Why are you here?"

Thomas smiled even wider, knowing his hunch was right and was about to answer him when he heard a woman's soft, pleasant voice coming from inside the cave. "Taric, don't be so rude to our guest. Hang up your bow and invite him inside."

Taric lowered the bow but held it firmly in his hands before slowly easing the tension from the bow. "My mate welcomes your visit inside our home," he announced, sliding the arrow back into the quiver of arrows that hung on a peg before hanging up the bow.

Thomas heard the woman speaking from inside the cave. "Please come inside. Taric, my love, back away so he can come inside."

"Tie the door shut," Taric commanded him as he backed away from the barricade door and walked over to stand protectively behind Jennifer.

Thomas stepped through the doorway and tied the door behind him as requested. He then stepped inside and stood staring at the unexpected clean, plush interior of the cave and the shockingly obvious condition of his hostess, who was reclining uncomfortably on a huge pile of furs with the black doglike animal lying beside her, silently watching his every move. Behind her, he saw from floor to ceiling a storehouse of firewood. The neatly stacked piles of wood extended six feet out from the back wall. Thomas couldn't help but think how long it must have taken to gather such a supply of wood.

Gathering his wits about him, Thomas introduced himself. "Good morning. I'm Captain Thomas Grange of the imperial starship *Maleficent*. I'm here in response to the *Fulcrum* tragedy. A little over three months ago, we received an emergency signal from a life pod. I'm pleased to find you alive as I was sent by Empress

Isabella Whitlock to rescue you, but it seems you have more pressing concerns at the moment than to worry about what the empress wants."

"This is Taric, my husband, who rescued me from certain death upon my arrival. Therefore, I don't need to be rescued," Jennifer replied and indicated with a hand for him to sit beside the fire.

"I'm assuming you're Jennifer Collins, the daughter of Michael and Kera Collins, the *Fulcrum*'s lead engineering team. Is your brother Peter around?" Thomas stated, looking at the flickering lights around the ceiling that ringed the cave.

Jennifer's face involuntarily frowned at hearing Peter's name and replied, "No, Peter didn't survive the landing. Is your starship a colonial ship bound for Opalla?"

"No. My ship is the first warp drive starship of the imperial fleet. We flew from Earth to Planos in thirty-two days. I called my ship for a doctor to come down to the surface after this morning's incident. I don't mean to be intrusive, but may I ask, how soon do you expect your baby? The doctor and his med tech are still at our campsite. I'm sure, he'd be happy to assist with the birth of your child," Thomas offered, knowing by the look of her that her water was going to break very soon.

"You're very kind to offer his services. It would make me feel better having a doctor present. Yes, please have him come here. Taric can show them the way," Jennifer said, squeezing Taric's hand, letting him know it was all right for him to leave her alone.

Thomas spoke into his comm unit. "Commander, the gentleman from this morning will meet you at the trees. Inform the good doctor to come along, he may have to deliver a baby."

"A baby?" Kelly's questioning voice could be heard from the comm unit.

"Your camp is too exposed on the open grass. You'll stay here during your visit. I'll go and lead them back," Taric said, signaling with a flash of blurry fingers for the dog to stay at Jennifer's side before retrieving his bow and quiver of arrows from the wall peg.

Jennifer knew Taric was out of earshot when Jaxx slowly lowered her head back down to the furs. She then looked at the man sitting in front of her and asked him directly. "What are you really here for? Did you really expect me to believe the empress wants to rescue the Tyrant's daughter?"

"So the rumors about you are true. You may be surprised to know, your birthright has been a long-debated topic on Earth for nearly ninety years. We and I mean, Isabella and I always believed you were the Tyrant's daughter," Thomas admitted, aware the young woman in front of him was a very discerning and perceptive woman.

"My father, whom I try not to think about, was a demon of death. He may have worn the skin of a man, but he was born a demon of Satan's army. He is solely responsible for the murder of millions during his decades-long reign of war and terror. This world is my home now. I'll not be dragged back to Earth to stand trial for his crimes," Jennifer warned, knowing active warrants had to have been issued after the Tyrant's death.

"Truly, that is not our intention. Isabella has no wish to harm you," Thomas honestly replied, knowing she could tell if he were lying.

"Why should I believe you?" Jennifer quietly asked as she softly patted the doglike creature lying quietly beside her with a slow stroking hand.

"Because Isabella is my older sister. You and I are related, we're cousins. Ella, your mother's little sister is my great-grandmother. Do you remember her?" Thomas asked, seeing the flash of memory in her eyes.

"Yes, I remember her. How could I forget my sweet auntie Ella? To me, it's only been a year since I last saw her," Jennifer answered, with a slight pang of regret for not being able to thank her for getting Peter and her away from the estate and onto the *Fulcrum*.

"Isabella revealed a family secret to me. I wasn't aware of it until the night before our departure. I'm going to tell you what she told me. Ella provided Kera and Michael the false identification documents and changed their imperial DNA profiles to gain the senior engineering officer's positions during the *Fulcrum*'s construction four years before launch. Three years later, Ella was the mastermind of the terrorist attack on the estate. She asked seven of her most trusted and loyal officers to free you from the Tyrant's control by staging the attack against the estate. Ella committed treason, so her sister and her family could escape the Tyrant's death order and disappear among the stars, forever beyond his reach," Thomas stated, watching her closely, as he was unsure if she knew the truth of the situation at the time, which lead to her exile from Earth.

Jennifer tensely stared into the man's eyes as she remembered the most frightening night of her life. She knew he was speaking honestly and could see no deception in his face or mannerisms. She then relaxed and asked, showing a pleasant smile on her face. "So is it Thomas, Captain, or cousin? How do I address you?"

"For now, call me Captain. My crew is comprised of people from all four kingdoms on Earth, and they've been told your name is Collins, and it must remain that way. It's been over sixty years since the Tyrant's death and the hatred of his name still lingers to this day," Thomas replied with a smile of his own, feeling the kinship to his cousin from a time beyond his imagination and then asked curiously, "What is that creature's name?"

Jennifer smiled while softly laughing and said, "Why, this is Jaxx. She's called a lycur by Taric's people. I found her when she was just a puppy, no bigger than my hand."

CHAPTER 19

Sabotage

Aboard the *Maleficent*, a technician reported for his shift in engineering. There were only a handful of people on duty while the ship's drives were functioning at minimal power output. It wasn't hard for him to disappear and be alone among the maze of machinery, pipes, and computer consoles comprising the entire engineering section of the ship. During the course of his shift, the technician opened and inserted the last five of twenty-five microchip processing boards into an empty auxiliary slot of five widely spaced computer consoles, which were in close proximity to the *Maleficent's* warp drive.

When his shift ended, the technician was walking to his quarters down a busy corridor, when he saw an old familiar face among the many faces he passed by in the corridor each day. He raised an eyebrow in recognition, signaling the completion of his assignment and palmed the master processing board into the officer's hand as he walked past without a word spoken between them. Moments later in the solitude of his quarters, he fired a phaser through his brain, leaving no evidence of his clandestine activity.

Jennifer was in the middle of telling Thomas a comical story of Taric's initial resistance of accepting the animal when a voice was heard coming over his comm unit interrupting their conversation. "Captain, this is Lieutenant Carter."

"Yes, Mr. Carter, what is it?" Thomas asked as his hostess waited patiently across the floor from him.

"Sir, a crewman committed suicide." They both heard the bodiless voice of the young officer say.

"Who was it?" Thomas asked into the unit, shocked by the unexpected report.

"Ensign Cole Mason of engineering and there wasn't a note in his quarters to be found to explain why he did it. In fact, security remarked that his quarters were impeccably clean and organized, which is unusual behavior for a suicidal person."

"Have they checked his private communications? There might be something to indicate why he took his life," Thomas suggested, thinking it might help.

Carter immediately replied, "They did. He's had no communication with anyone since boarding the ship. Security found it odd, so they asked Fleet Academy to check his records, and this was their reply. There are no records of a Cole Mason ever attending Fleet Academy or any school on Earth. According to fleet headquarters, his DNA profile does not exist in the imperial birth records. In fact, the man's DNA profile does not exist anywhere, but in the ship's crew manifest."

Hearing the response set Thomas's mind reeling as he wondered how the man had obtained the credentials to pass security scrutiny and board the ship as a member of his crew. He then asked himself what the consequences of his mysterious life and suicide could lead to.

"Place engineering on full alert until they can verify all systems are functioning within the parameters of the ship's design. Have security, interview his coworkers, and do a detailed sweep of the man's quarters. There has to be something left behind to explain why and how he came to be on the ship. Find it! Call me back with their report," Thomas said, ending the communication with a furrowed brow and worried expression on his face.

Jennifer had been listening intently to the open exchange between Thomas and the officer aboard the ship. She was saddened to hear of the death but noticed the mysterious presence of the man and his actions aboard the starship, concerned the captain deeply, and so she commented, "I'm sorry, Captain, but why did he come this far out from Earth to commit suicide?"

"Why? Well, there could be many reasons, but I doubt we'll find out. Hell, right now, I'm not sure if Ensign Cole Mason is the man's actual name," Thomas admitted while wondering what was going to happen next.

"Captain, would you mind helping me up?" she asked him, feeling her water suddenly break and gush out of her soaking the fur she was sitting on as the first painful contraction of labor hit.

"Are you sure?" Thomas asked, seeing her convulse with the contraction.

"Yes, Captain, I'm sure. Help me please," Jennifer responded between breaths as Jaxx suddenly jumped to her feet and growled low.

Thomas rose from the furs to help her up, when he turned to see what had the dog's dander up. Hearing the low growl, Dr. Mencia stepped into the cave, blocking the doorway, and asked as he stared warily at the large black animal. "Ah, does that thing bite?"

"Jaxx, hush," a very pregnant woman said as he watched the animal instantly obey and lay down quietly in its bedding.

"Doctor, please tend to your patient," Thomas stated as he saw Jennifer convulse with another contraction.

Doctor Mencia ignored the animal and stepped up to his patient's side. Taric came into the cave next, followed by a young girl. "Hello, I'm Dr. Mencia, and this is Tina Marlowe, my med tech. How long between contractions?" he asked while kneeling beside her.

"Thank you, Doctor. I'm Jennifer Collins. They've just started," she replied and then looked at her husband as she doubled over in pain. "Ahhhh!" she yelled as Taric's strong arms lifted her easily off the furs.

"Follow us," Taric ordered as he turned with Jennifer in his arms and walked through a loose heavy hide into the next cave.

"Ah, where are you going?" the doctor asked, confused as to where he was taking his patient.

"Just follow," he heard the native say from inside the back cave.

"Come on, Doc. They must have a place already prepared for their child's birth," Thomas said, moving the hide aside, letting the doctor go first into the chilly inner cave. He followed the doctor and assumed the med tech was following him. Tina just stood and stared at the cave as light from flickering flames cast multiple shadows on the stone ceiling from lamps dug into the cave wall. She then noticed the captain's weapons lying in a pile by the door. Alone for just a moment, she bent down and removed the pistol from its holster before pushing aside the hide to enter the inner cave.

There was barely room for them to walk as they passed between baskets full of dried meats and fruits stacked neatly to the ceiling. They also noticed pouches full of grains hanging from pegs high up on the walls and cured furs and hides stacked neatly in piles below them.

The trail through the inner cave lead to another heavy hide, and as the visitors pulled it aside, they gasped in wonder at the water cave. They noticed lamps flickering along the edge of a ledge leading up to a large smooth area where a fire illuminated the area.

"My Lord!" Thomas exclaimed as he took in the sight of the amazing cave with a waterfall pool and a river flowing out of the cavern into a dark hole in the stone, a sight that had become commonplace to the couple.

Taric stood in the pool, reaching out with his hands to help Jennifer into the water. Once she was in his arms again, he guided her over to the outcropping and let her recline back against the smooth limestone edge.

"Oh, a water birth. How marvelous!" Dr. Mencia exclaimed with a delightful smile on his face as he entered the pool, surprised by the warmth of the water soaking his clothes.

"Ahhhh!" Jennifer yelled out again, breathing hard between contractions. "I don't want to have a baby today!" She screamed loudly, fighting the contractions, wishing they'd disperse and go away as her voice echoed off the cavern walls.

"It's all right, most new mothers say that. I think your child is impatient to be born! This will be over quicker than you think," Dr. Mencia reassuringly replied, calming his patient while noticing the father's shocked expression as he looked on helplessly supporting her in the water.

"Mrs. Taric, in my line of duty within fleet medical services, I don't often get the opportunity to deliver a baby, but rest assured I'm very capable. Unfortunately, I don't have an epidural to ease your discomfort, so we're going to have to deliver your baby, the old-fashioned way," Mencia said with confidence, appreciating the forethought of the young couple to think of having a water birth.

"Take slow deep breaths between the contractions," he instructed Jennifer as a contraction subsided, allowing her to breathe. He breathed along with her setting the pace of her breaths between contractions. Seeing that she was doing well, he said to her mate. "Mr. Taric, could you help me? If you'd be so kind and lift her up, I can get her dress out of the way."

Taric thought that "out of the way" meant he wanted it off. So he let go, and as Jennifer rose off the outcropping by the flow of the water, he lifted the garment completely off her, exposing Jennifer's nakedness to everyone's eyes.

"Oh, my word. Ah, I meant up to her waist," Mencia said, slightly embarrassed, and caught off guard by the native's actions.

Jennifer smiled at his reaction while softly chuckling between breaths at the doctor's comical expression on his round middle-aged face and said, "It's all right, Doctor."

"Oh, yes. Of course. I'm going to dip down under the water to see how far you're dilated," he announced, recovering from his embarrassment of the moment, and disappeared below the water.

Jennifer noticed her cousin watching her from the opposite side of the pool. When Taric removed her garment and exposed her ample breasts, he quickly turned his eyes away from the birthing scene. She felt the doctor's hands pushing her thighs wider apart, and she tried her best to hold them there as another contraction started. "Oh God! I feel it coming!" Jennifer screamed and pushed.

"That's it. Push, this kid wants to be born!" Mencia exclaimed as he popped his head above the water. "Push down hard on the next contraction. You're almost there," he ordered as she relaxed from the subsiding contraction.

When the next wave of pain hit, Jennifer bore down, pushing with all her might, when suddenly, she felt her baby slip out of her and into the water. She sighed with relief as the doctor rose from beneath the water, holding her baby in his hands. With a gentle tap on the rump, she heard her baby cry as the doctor announced with a beaming smile. "Congratulations, it's a beautiful baby girl!"

Dr. Mencia happily placed the little girl in her mother's arms and said, "You'll feel another contraction to expel the placenta, but it won't be as bad."

He turned around in the water to talk to his tech, whom he saw was standing behind the captain on the opposite edge. He noticed she held a weapon in her hand, and it was pointed in his direction and at the captain's back.

"What the hell!" he yelled out angrily at his tech. "Tina, lower the gun!"

"The charter must be upheld," she said as Thomas turned and faced the young girl, bravely staying within her line of fire as Jennifer fearfully turned around on the outcropping, shielding her baby with her body.

"Move, Captain! You know what must be done!" she screamed shrilly, alerting their pet, which had quietly slipped off to lay down against a cool wall and sleep.

"Marlowe! Put the weapon down!" Thomas loudly ordered as he saw Jaxx running out of the shadows toward the girl. "Noooo!" he shouted as the animal rushed in, clamping its sharp teeth into the arm holding the weapon.

He saw the animal sinking its sharp teeth deeper into the girl's flesh. Tina struggled against the animal's strong grip. She pulled the trigger, firing the gun at the creature, but missed as Jaxx threw her onto the ground. Jaxx did not lessen her hold with the report of the gunshot as she vigorously shook and tore into the pink flesh of Tina's arm. The gunshot reverberated repeatedly off the cavern's stone walls and slowly faded, leaving only the sound of rushing water, Jaxx's angry growls, and Tina's terrified screams to be heard.

Unable to hold on to the gun with her shredded arm and hand, Tina managed to switch the gun to her other hand between Jaxx's relentless painful tugs on her arm as she pulled, shook, and dragged her along the stone floor away from her packmates.

Aware she had failed to carry out her assignment and could not risk capture but must still do her duty to ensure the success of their mission, Tina Marlowe, a charterist assassin, placed the gun against her temple and fired. Jaxx let go of her, backing away from the body and growled as the gunshot echoed off the stone walls until it finally faded away.

Taric couldn't believe the scene he'd just witnessed. The open hostility and deadly violence humans contained within themselves confused him as he stared at the body of the young girl. He then noticed the man they called Captain, lying on the ground pressing his hand against his side and he knew, because of his bravery, Jennifer and his daughter were safe and alive.

"Doctor," he called out and pointed at the captain. "I think he's hurt."

Mencia looked at the frightened mother and gave her a comforting pat on her thigh. "It's all over now. Just push with the next contraction, and you'll be fine. I'll be back in a few minutes. Why don't you put something on while I see to the captain," he said to her with a warm, gentle smile as he pushed away from the outcropping.

He then swam quickly to the other side and easily lifted himself out of the water. In a few paces, he was at Thomas's side. He pried the hand away from the wound on his side and saw two small holes, no more than two inches apart slowly seeping blood from the wounds.

"You're a very brave and lucky man," he said, reaching into his bag pulling out a spray canister that he had used to treat Kelly's arm and snapped the cover off. "Do you feel any internal pain?" he asked as Thomas shook his head.

"No, not really. Is it unusual?" Thomas asked Mencia, liking the doctor's easy calm demeanor in a crisis.

"It means, none of your organs were harmed," he said with obvious relief as he sprayed the contents of the canister over the wounds. Within seconds of application, the wounds began to heal by rapidly regenerating the missing tissue on a cellular level. Placing a new skin bandage over the open wounds to keep them clean, Mencia knew within a few hours his skin would be fully healed, without the slightest trace of a scar.

"Now, if you'll excuse me, I have an umbilical cord to tie off," he said, giving Thomas a hearty pat on his shoulder before rising to his feet while snapping the cover back onto the canister and dropping it back into his bag.

"Thank you," Thomas replied with a nod of understanding as the doctor turned and then jumped back into the pool. Thomas then looked at the prone body of the young girl as comprehension hit him with a fright.

"Where's Sterling, didn't she come with you?" Thomas asked the doctor as he performed his final duty to the newborn child.

"She stayed at the camp with the shuttle," Thomas heard the doctor reply.

"I'll be back," he said with a hopeful expression on his face as he dashed away down the ledge and out of the cave. Once Thomas was outside, he activated his comm unit. "Kelly, please respond," he said into the unit, waiting impatiently for her to respond to his call.

"Captain?" he heard his commander calmly ask.

"Are you with the shuttle?" Thomas asked her and went on talking without allowing her a chance to answer him. "I think the ship is in danger. Prepare the shuttle for launch. We've got to get back."

"Captain, I felt ill after the doctor left and thought, I might be feeling the effects of a toxin from my wound. So I returned to the ship with the shuttle. I just arrived at the bridge from the sick bay. Is there something amiss?"

He heard Kelly's plausible explanation for returning to the ship and confided in her. "The tech Tina Marlowe is dead. She tried to kill the Collins girl. I think the Mason suicide and her assassination attempt may be connected. Check her background. In fact, send all personnel profiles to the fleet for comparison. We have to know if another impostor is aboard. They're both charterist ghosts, I'll bet my command on it," Thomas stated with a sureness of conviction in his voice.

"I'll send the shuttle back down for you," Kelly replied, knowing he'd want to be aboard.

"Thank you, do it. But have Cooper fly it down. I need you on the bridge. What's the status of the ship?" Thomas asked her and waited to hear her reply.

"The ship is functioning within design parameters, everything is operating normally," Thomas heard Kelly's calm, confident voice say over the comm unit.

"Have Cooper land at the campsite. I'll meet it there," Thomas replied, severing the link and hoping she'll be able to discover the identity of the impostor by the time he returned. He then turned around to see Taric carrying Tina's body in his arms.

"I will bury your dead per your custom?" Taric sadly said to him, abhorring the notion of murder. "Can't humans control their urge to kill? Individually or as a group, I think your people are unbalanced. You should leave us and never come back," he stated flatly, showing no emotion on his face other than sadness. He then turned and quietly walked off into the woods with the girl's body hanging limply in his arms.

"That's exactly what I plan on doing," he said to himself in response to Taric's comments as he gathered his weapons and headed into the woods in the opposite direction toward the campsite on the grass.

Thomas began running through the trees, wanting to meet up with the shuttle as soon as it landed. But before he cleared the trees, his comm unit emitted Sterling's frantic voice.

"Captain, Cooper has gone offline throughout the ship! The shuttle is burning up in the atmosphere. We've lost it, sir! There's no way to get you back aboard. I was able to alert the fleet of our circumstances prior to losing Earthlink subspace communications," Kelly stated to him, knowing that without the AI's extensive mathematical computations, the ship was stuck in orbit above Planos.

"Sterling, you're *Maleficent's* captain. Find the impostor and get Cooper restored!" Thomas adamantly responded to the unit.

"Will do. I'll keep you informed of our status," Sterling replied from the captain's chair on the *Maleficent's* bridge.

"*Fuck! Fuck! Fuck!*" Thomas raged, shouting out his anger as loud as he could, because he sure as hell believed there was another impostor aboard the *Maleficent*. Pissed off as he was unable to stop the impostor's from sabotaging his starship. Thomas stood within the shadowy solitude of the trees, angrily ranting, yelling out his rage for being marooned on the planet's surface. With his temper once more under control and feeling as if he'd been played, Thomas started walking back toward the cave. As he slowly walked through the trees tired and hungry, he questioned his fitness to command for the first time since he left Earth.

After his captain ran from the cavern, Dr. Mencia watched as Taric reverently lifted the dead girl into his arms. He heard him sadly ask while looking at the face of the young girl. "Why is there so much violence and hatred in your people? Why did this girl seek to kill Jennifer?"

"I wish I knew. I'm sorry, but I don't have an answer. Only God knows why. Maybe we're a little off-balance," Dr. Mencia replied, knowing his response was of little comfort to the man.

With nothing left to be said between them, Taric walked away down the ledge, intending to bury the girl's body near Peter's under the tree overlooking the plain. He hoped the place would give the girls spirit some peace in the afterlife.

Taric reached the tree where Peter's bones were laid to rest and set his grim burden onto the soft grass in the shade of the tree. Using a stick to loosen and break the ground, Taric began the arduous task of digging a grave. He cleared a space to fit the girl's body before walking up the slope toward the mountain's rocky base. Taric was looking for a thin flat stone, one large enough to dig with and hold comfortably in his hands. With a little luck and a sharp eye, he soon spotted a stone that could be used as a shovel.

It was midday by the time Taric laid the body in the grave. He was angry, tired, and hot from his exertions, but he couldn't stop. He had to bury the girl. By doing so, Taric buried his feelings of hatred toward humans with the body of the girl. He stared once more at the girl's face and wondered why before using his hands to scoop the loose soil over her face and body. He finished by covering the grave with a layer of heavy stones to prevent scavengers from digging the body up. With his task complete, Taric vowed as he stood over the grave to never think of her again and walked away.

CHAPTER 20

Betrayal

Thomas was sitting on a log outside the barricade in the cool afternoon sun waiting for Taric's return to the cave. After the events of the day, he owed the man an apology for putting Jennifer and his newborn baby in danger. How could everything go so wrong so quickly? Thomas was asking himself, thinking he'd only been there for a few hours, and everything had instantly gone to shit.

He realized his mission had been compromised at its inception. The charterists knew exactly where to place their ghost agents aboard his ship. He was accountable for the conduct of his crew. It was his responsibility and he failed the one person he was sent to protect by bringing an assassin into their home.

He saw Tina's eyes when she pointed the gun at him, she had every intention of killing him. If Jaxx had not intervened and saved his life, they'd all be dead. He knew it, and so did Taric. How could he blame Taric for wanting him to leave and never come back?

Jaxx stepped out of the barricade, stood in the sun, shook her fur, and glanced at the forest bordering the clearing. She then trotted over to where Thomas was sitting and sat down beside him within easy reach.

"Hey, Jaxx, what brings you out here?" he remarked to the lycur, completely surprised by her easy approach.

"How do I tell someone who dislikes me that I'm marooned, huh? Can you tell me, because I haven't a clue?" he asked the animal, reaching down giving her a well-deserved back scratching with his hand. The lycur wagged her tail in appreciation for the vigorous rub down.

He continued to scratch Jaxx's back, admiring the domesticated wild animal sitting calmly beside him, marveled by the smooth softness of her midnight black fur. As he scratched beneath her thick fur, he could feel Jaxx's strong lean muscular body under his fingers. Thomas spoke to the lycur as he continued scratching her back. "You're an amazing creature, Jaxx, and I owe you a life. How can I repay a life debt to an animal?"

"You can leave us," Thomas heard Taric say once again from behind him as he stepped into the clearing.

Thomas stood and turned around to face his host, deserving of the man's ire. "I can't fault you for feeling that way. If I were you, I'd want us gone as well. Taric, I'm truly sorry for what happened. I came here to rescue Jennifer and Peter. I had no intention of harming them, much less place their lives in danger.

"Before I left Earth, I hoped Jennifer had survived, but it was a long shot. We've lost the skills you possess to live in this world. The average person from Earth would not survive their first winter in the wilds. So much of this planet is uninhabited, it's a miracle you were here to rescue Jennifer, it's only because of you, she beat the odds and survived."

"So if you believed Jennifer and Peter were dead, then why did you come here?" Taric asked him, confused by their conflicting human ideologies, motives, and the trouble they cause.

"The charter prohibits humans or our artifacts to contaminate developing worlds. We came here to investigate the *Fulcrum* tragedy and remove any evidence of our presence orbiting above or down on the planet," Thomas answered, watching Taric's body language closely seeing the tenseness of his stance.

"Your words sound like orders to me. It may be a truthful answer, but it's not the truth. The *Fulcrum* is not the real reason you're here. It's an excuse! You're seeking something else," Taric declared and then turned away from Thomas to walk into his home, wanting nothing more than to see his mate and newborn child.

Thomas reached out with his hand grabbing Taric by the arm and held it, restraining him while saying, "You're right. We know how the *Fulcrum* met its fate. Jennifer's colonial starship was destroyed by rocky debris from a rogue planet collision with a planet on the outskirts of this system. But it was the excuse I needed to come here."

"Why?" Taric asked, shaking his arm free of the man's grip.

Thomas released his grip on Taric's arm and answered, "Because on Earth, I'm Isabella's full-time political advisor. I'm really a scientist, an astrobiologist. It's the study of where and how life is created and evolves within the universe. Earth has known life existed here on this planet for a little over three hundred years. We've been here once before. But we couldn't come back until we developed a faster way to travel through interstellar space. The *Maleficent* is our first starship with a warp drive. It has made it possible for scientists like myself to actually travel to your world without the requirements of hypersleep.

"I wanted to see the similarities of animal life on Planos compared to animal life on Earth. Isabella couldn't trust anyone to protect Jennifer if she was found alive, except me. She knew I'd accept the mission as the *Maleficent*'s captain to see Planos for myself."

Impatient and uncaring, Taric replied as he walked away toward the barricade's doorway while talking over his shoulder and signaling Jaxx to his side. "Then go see it and leave us alone."

"I can't, I've lost my ship! I'm marooned here! I need your help!" Thomas shouted at Taric's back, watching him slam the door in place. Thomas heard Taric's cold, angry reply as he stood behind the door, tying it shut.

"I should have left you to the kessra, it's always safer to hunt when their bellies are full."

Thomas recognized a curse when he heard one. The tone of Taric's voice made it perfectly clear he was not welcome within his home. Regardless of his kinship with Jennifer, entering Taric's home uninvited would only make matters worse between them.

"Well, I'm fucked," Thomas said to himself, trying to decide what to do when the barricade's doorway was opened once more. A flustered and confused doctor stumbled through the door into the clearing, while hearing Taric say, "Leave, go back to your camp."

"What in the hell is going on?" Dr. Mencia asked as he approached Thomas, expecting some answers.

"I'll explain our situation on the way back to camp," Thomas replied, picking up the rifle he had leaning against a log. "There's a footpath through the trees, it should lead us to the open grass," Thomas told him and then walked off, not caring if the doctor followed or not.

Isabella slept very lightly, and the slightest sound would easily awaken her, making restful sleep difficult. Her bedchamber was completely soundproof from outside noise. Every night as she went to bed, she'd hand off her phone to Freddie, her manservant and confidant. She trusted him to gauge the importance of nighttime communications; rarely was she awakened in the middle of the night. It was nearly two in the morning when Freddie softly knocked on Isabella's bedroom door and quietly said, "Empress, a call has come in from fleet headquarters."

Deep in slumber, Isabella heard the knocking from beneath her blankets and slowly came awake. Hearing Freddie's familiar voice, Isabella sat up in her bed, pulled the blankets up to her lap, and then covered her thin lace nightgown with a robe. "Come in, Freddie," she sleepily answered her trusted aide.

Freddie opened the door and came into the room wearing green plaid pajamas and an old blue bathrobe hanging loosely about him. He held her phone in his hand and walked up to Isabella's bedside. "It's Admiral Harrington," he said, handing her the phone.

Accepting the phone with a smile and nod, Isabella looked at the screen to see a tall slim black man with short black hair with distinguishing strands of gray at the temples, nervously staring back at her. "Admiral, I'm sure there's a good reason for calling at this hour."

"Empress, I apologize for waking you, but we've lost contact with the *Maleficent*," Harrington stated, then saw Isabella's face come wide awake on his side of the screen.

"What happened?" Isabella asked, fearing the worst and hoping her brother was all right.

"We don't know, but before we lost contact, we learned the *Maleficent* may have a charterist cell operating aboard ship," Admiral Harrington stoutly replied, seeing Isabella's worried face instantly change to an icy-cold serious expression on her pale pink skin.

"A charterist cell on my brother's starship? What makes you suspect a cell is operating on the *Maleficent*?" Isabella asked the admiral's proud image and could see by his prideful stance, he had a theory.

"There's been a suicide. An engineering technician by the name of Cole Mason. He fired a phaser through his brain inside his quarters. The problem is, Cole Mason's entire life is a very detailed and artful work of fiction. He doesn't exist. Upon notification of Cole Mason's death, fleet's imperial records could find no listing of his DNA. There's no record of him anywhere on Earth. No DNA, no fingerprints, no retina scan of his eyes, nothing at all. And yet this person held authentic Imperial Fleet credentials to pass security and board our starship. He's a ghost and we have no idea what he was doing on the ship." Admiral Harrington paused in his briefing, letting the information sort itself out within her sharp mind.

"I'll accept the idea of a charterist cell. If that's the case, then someone has spent a long time planning this clandestine operation. The other starship under construction, it's operational, correct?" Isabella asked the admiral and waited.

"Ah, yes, it's fully operational, but the interior is still under construction. It's mainly the finishing touches to humanize the environment in the corridors, living quarters, and common areas that remain to be done," Admiral Harrington answered, wondering where this conversation was leading.

"What if their intent is to steal the starship. How many people does it take to fly a starship? Smallest number please?" Isabella asked the admiral, trying to formulate a plan of action within her mind as he turned to his subordinates for the answers.

Harrington turned back to face his screen and calmly replied, "To fly the *Maleficent* with AI assist would require a minimum crew size of fifty. Eighty if you expect to fight the ship. Without an AI assist to perform the thousands upon thousands of calculations, it requires to travel from one point in space to another point is impossible. My advisors have assured me, stealing a starship is impossible!"

"So you say. Now, imagine a charterist cell of three or five agents. What can they do to a starship, if they can't fly it?" Isabella asked him, curious as to what his answer would be.

"Ah, Empress, I'm sorry, but there's no way I can specifically say. There are many ways a ship can be damaged or destroyed. However, without the *Maleficent's* AI, the ship is stuck in orbit, they can't leave. So all we have to do is go there and take the *Maleficent* back," he said, stressing his last point to make the mission appear easy.

"Harrington, listen closely. It's obvious, this agent Cole Mason was given forged imperial credentials to board the ship as an engineering tech. It makes sense, his mission was to disable the AI's link. He did his job and then killed himself. His death is part of their plan. We know, they have succeeded in disabling the AI's link, but what about the AI itself? What if the AI is still functioning?" Isabella asked him, ignoring everything he said after the word, however.

"AI's cannot function without Earthlink subspace communications, it's part of their loyalty programming!" Harrington adamantly answered, sure of the fact.

"Admiral, I need facts. Are you certain the ship is disabled? Or are you speculating based on what the experts claim? When you lost contact, what was the ship's status?" Isabella asked, thinking the constant stream of information sent to Earth by the AI's subroutine programming should be helpful.

"Yes, my empress, there was one more thing," Harrington admitted, biting his tongue, and added, "I'm sorry to say, Captain Thomas Grange is most likely marooned on Planos. The *Maleficent's* shuttle was flying down to the planet to retrieve him when the AI's Earthlink went offline. We're assuming the shuttle was destroyed during reentry."

"How amazing everything is working out so well for the charterist. It's like they've found a magic lamp with a genie trapped inside. For his freedom, the genie grants them not one, not two, but three magic wishes. Boom! Ghost agents mysteriously inserted into the *Maleficent's* crew. Boom! The AI's Earthlink goes offline. And boom!

The captain, my brother is marooned on the planet! This is a convenient list of circumstances for them to simply destroy a starship. The charterist have something else in mind for our ship. Don't you think?" Isabella irritably stated, angry over Harrington's lack of imagination and then wondered if he should be retired.

"Admiral, let's move on. We have some questions to answer. Number one, how could someone obtain and forge authentic Imperial Fleet credentials? Perfectly forged credentials are not cheap. Whoever is funding this has very deep pockets.

"Number two, can an AI's loyalty program be circumvented to sever Earthlink subspace communications and remain operable? Talk to the experts once more and find out. I'm always worried when experts say something is impossible to do. I don't believe them. Our species has done the impossible throughout our history. If we hadn't, we'd still be hunter-gatherers and living in a cave.

"Now, my number three is hypothetical. Let's say they intend to steal the ship with the AI disabled. What if the charterist discovered a way to fly to a known position in space without an AI assist? Is it even possible? Find out what it would require to perform the complex computations for a single point to point warp drive flight using an alternate means of computing?

"My number four issue is simply a question, but it's the most important question of all. Can an AI's loyalty programming be compromised and remain fully functional and allow the charterist to fight the starship against us?

"Admiral, get your people searching for the answers. In the meantime, have the new starship fully armed and prepared for launch. Make damn sure the officers you select are loyal to the empire. Recruit your crew from cadets currently attending Fleet Academy. You've got three days admiral, make it happen," Isabella ordered while seeing Harrington's eyebrows arch upward as she ended their conversation.

Taric was relieved to find Jennifer and the baby asleep when he returned from burying the girl's body. It made it easier for him to remove the human doctor from the cave. The harrowing turn of events had pushed his mental state over the limits of his tolerance.

Why did the girl want Jennifer dead? Kept invading his mind. He almost lost his mate and daughter because of them. He was so confused and angry, he didn't want to look at them anymore or think about their problems. The humans were not his responsibility. They traveled here on their own accord. They knew the risk. Jennifer would agree with him. Why should he worry?

Taric looked at his new family sleeping peacefully on warm, soft furs. Jennifer slept with their child snuggled up inside the crook of her arm. Focusing his eyes on his beautiful baby girl. Taric noticed her skin was a pinkish copper color, a perfect blending of her parents' vastly opposing skin tones. Thick reddish-brown hair crowned her tiny head with finely sculpted facial features. Taric knew with a father's pride, his daughter was destined to grow into a stunningly beautiful woman just like her mother. Expecting Jennifer to be hungry when she woke up, Taric got quietly to his feet and went into the storage cave to gather ingredients for their dinner.

"Charterist! Marooned!" an angry Dr. Mencia bellowed out, startling the animals grazing on the long dry grass near their camp.

"Yes, marooned. The shuttle is gone. It burnt up in reentry because the AI is offline. Sterling has no way to get us off the planet. We're stuck here until Isabella sends the *Maleficent's* sister starship. It will only be a month or so. In the meantime, we have weapons to hunt and defend ourselves with. So I see no real problem. Water is nearby, and as long as we keep some fires burning around the camp, the animals should stay away and not bother us." Thomas explained, outlining their situation to a very angry doctor, who was used to the comforts of modern living.

Aboard the *Maleficent*, Sterling sat behind the desk in the captain's ready room, trying to send an update to the fleet, but was unable to send the message due to the AI's severed Earthlink. "Cooper? Come on dammit! Answer me!" She called out to the empty air in the room, but nothing happened. With no response coming from the AI, Kelly felt like the walls of the room were closing in around her with no way out.

Knowing she couldn't hide in the captain's ready room much longer, Kelly stood up from the desk and walked purposefully toward the door to the bridge. As the door opened, Kelly confidently walked onto the bridge.

The *Maleficent* had been operating on autopilot since entering orbit above Planos, holding the ship to a preset course and speed without the need for human assistance. "Lieutenant Carter, I'll take the chair. Why don't you take some time off and get some rest," Kelly said with a smile, knowing the young man had extended his watch.

"Thank you, Commander," Carter said as he rose slowly from the chair, relinquishing command of the starship to her and left the bridge.

Kelly stood beside the captain's chair, looking around at the tired faces of her three officers working at their station consoles. "I'm aware you've all been on duty far too long and suspect something is going on with the loss of the shuttle. You're right, the captain and I suspect a charterist cell is operating aboard the *Maleficent*. We're not sure of their numbers or intentions. The Earthlink is offline. We can't send a message to the fleet, nor can we attempt warp flight. The AI's Cooper persona is not responding to spoken inquires. And yet our chief engineer insists the ship's diagnostics program confirms the AI's system is functioning properly. So we have a dilemma, and I need sharp minds and alert officers to help me solve this problem. I'll monitor the bridge, while you go and get some sleep. Report back in six hours. In the meantime, I'll try to think of a way to get our AI responding to vocal commands."

Kelly watched her officers leave the bridge with grateful expressions of thanks on their faces. She followed her officers to the door, reassuring them as they passed the threshold that everything was under control. Kelly locked the door behind them, restricting access to the bridge.

Kelly walked off the bridge to the ready room, letting the door close behind her before locking it as well. She had been thinking about Cole Mason's mission. With his extraordinary engineering skills, Kelly knew Mason was responsible for cutting the AI's Earthlink.

The AI's complex programming was considered infallible and hacker-proof, making the AI Cooper persona the most widely used AI program on Earth. After sixty-odd years of operation, the AI system had never failed until now. Her ship has been hacked and she didn't have a clue how Mason had done it.

"Cooper? Can you hear me?" she asked the empty room as she sat at the desk and activated the computer. She then mumbled to herself as she typed, "Well, let's see if you can answer a query?"

"Cooper? Can you respond?" she typed on her screen, addressing the system directly, hoping for a response. The silence in the room felt heavy and barren to her as she waited, holding her breath when an error text appeared on the screen: "System offline."

"Shit!" Kelly said out loud to the empty room, then decided on another tactic by using a low priority subroutine and typed, "Show security footage of corridor outside of Cole Mason's quarters ten minutes before his death." The screen changed to show pedestrian traffic moving up and down the corridor. After three minutes of playback, she saw Mason get out of a lift and turn toward the security sensors mounted into the corridor ceilings. He walked toward his quarters shifting himself around people as they passed without a casual greeting or comment but then saw him reach for something in his pocket. He held a small device of some sort in his hand when he suddenly arched an eyebrow and palmed it to a passing officer without anyone the wiser walking in the corridor.

Kelly replayed the handoff in slow motion to verify her eyesight and suspicion. "Who the fuck are you?" she asked the back of the officer's head. She then typed, "Show reverse angle."

The view changed to show the back of Mason's head as he set up the exchange with the officer walking toward him. The sight of the officer accepting the device saddened and infuriated Kelly as she recognized his face and loudly shouted, "Carter, you bastard!"

In the corridor outside his quarters, Carter yawned loudly while sucking in gulps of air as he stepped up to the sensor operating the door to his quarters. He was stretching his limbs outward as his body shook, making his tired appearance a comical sight to others in the corridor. He walked into his apartment hearing their amused chuckles behind him as he waited for the door to close. His feigned tiredness instantly disappeared as he walked with a calm assurance into his bedroom. With Commander Sterling's return to the *Maleficent*, the prerequisites for his mission were now in place.

Stepping up to his built-in wardrobe drawers on the left side of his closet, Carter withdrew from the top drawer, the device Mason had expertly palmed him and a hand-held screwdriver that was powered and adaptable for multiple uses. He split his uniforms and civilian clothes hanging on a rod on the right side of the closet with his hands and pushed his clothes out of the way. He saw just above the floor, a gray two-foot square steel access panel held at the corners to the closet wall by four stout screws. He set the device on the floor beside him as he knelt down to open the panel. Using the screwdriver, he quickly removed the screws and set the panel aside leaning against the wall. Hidden inside the wall was an environmental suit with magnetic boots and a helmet. He assumed the suit had been secretly smuggled aboard by another charterist cell during the ship's construction.

Carter wasted no time in changing into the tight-fitting environmental suit and secured the helmet into place. His ears popped with the artificial air pressure inside the helmet. He quickly reattached the panel to the wall, making sure the screws were tight and secure.

With the calmness of foreknowledge, he laid himself onto the floor, placing his feet up to the panel and activated the magnetic boots. Instantly, his feet were pulled to the panel as the boots strong magnets secured his feet in place. Carter pulled with his feet testing the magnets hold to the steel plate. Lying on his back, he picked up the device from the floor and activated the device in his hand by pressing a button and speaking a code phrase: "Glory to the charter."

Cooper's AI persona appeared standing above him in the closet and asked, "What are your orders?"

Replying to the hologram, the charterist soberly stated, "Purge the ship."

Instantly alarm klaxons sounded as every door opened simultaneously, exposing the interior throughout the starship to the freezing cold vacuum of space. Carter felt the strong pull of the ship's air escaping into the vacuum as he lay on the floor of his closet. Releasing his boots from the access panel, he rose to stand on his feet. Believing he was the only one left alive aboard the ship, he walked out of his quarters into the corridor, where the instantly frozen bodies of the crew floated in the airless vacuum. He then began the task of clearing the ship of its dead, one deck at a time.

Kelly was about to inform security of Carter's involvement with the sabotage of their ship when the alarm klaxons for a hull breach sounded off, and both doors of the ready room opened to the adjacent rooms. Suddenly aware Carter was purging the ship, Kelly knew she only had a few seconds before the pull of the vacuum would take her. She scrambled as fast as her legs could move toward the emergency escape pod in the captain's sleeping quarters. Kelly felt the air quickly thinning within her lungs with the force of the vacuum trying to pull her backward. With one last breath of the rapidly thinning air in her lungs and the last of her strength, she frantically struggled to step into the escape pod and seal herself inside. Kelly fought to hold her breath as the pain within her lungs became almost unbearable to endure while continuing to hear the loud whoosh of air escaping the ship as the pod's hatch slowly sealed her inside.

Her lungs were near the verge of collapse when Kelly blacked out into the depths of oblivion. She didn't feel the expulsion of gasses from her chest as her lungs exhaled, relieved of the straining pressure. She lay as still as death and appeared through the pod's viewport to be dead, showing no signs of life. When suddenly, Kelly came back from the brink by sucking in the pod's limited oxygen supply, in painful chest-pounding gulps. Once she was able to breathe in a slow easy rhythm, her oxygen-starved body quickly recovered from her near-death experience.

With each successive breath, awareness of her situation returned to the forefront of Kelly's mind as her eyes slowly focused on the pod's interior. Weakened from the frightening experience, she slowly snapped the pod's restraints into place, securing her to the seat.

Without an environmental suit's additional oxygen supply, Kelly knew she didn't have much time. Thankfully, Captain Grange had approved her idea of synchronizing the pods with the coordinates of the *Fulcrum's* landing site. With a prayer in her heart, Kelly hit the launch button and swiftly fell away from her lost starship.

CHAPTER 21

Reconciliation

The pod's thrusters pushed it safely away from the ship for a few seconds before shutting off, then activated the preset coordinates for entry into the planet's atmosphere. Those few seconds allowed Kelly to witness from the pod's small viewport, the full extent of the charterist crime. The lifeless bodies of *Maleficent's* crew floated erratically in the vacuum outside a half-dozen open airlocks on each side of the ship.

Seeing the wanton waste of human lives, Kelly felt an emotional wave of guilt descend upon her soul. She had come so near to death but didn't die. If she hadn't gone into the captain's ready room instead of remaining on the bridge, Kelly knew without a doubt she would be one of the dead. How could she go on with her life, without feeling an overpowering sense of guilt for surviving? While wondering if all survivors of tragedies felt as she did.

The pod began to align its flight path for descending into the planet's atmosphere as a movement inside the ship caught Kelly's eyes and her instant attention. A body was being pushed out of an airlock by a figure she knew to be Carter, wearing an environmental suit. When the body was free of the ship, the figure closed the airlock and disappeared from view. She discovered too late, Carter was the charterist agent they were seeking, and it did little to ease her sense of guilt. The information was no longer relevant.

Kelly began weeping for the dead, aware their murderer was alive and for reasons still unknown in sole possession of the ship. It then dawned on her that Cooper was still operational, and Carter was attempting to steal the ship. But how? Kelly asked herself and then knew it was because of Mason. He had successfully discovered a way to subvert the AI's positronic matrix. Leaving the AI's system operational and responsive only to Carter, because the only way to instantly purge a starship is by AI control.

In her gut, Kelly felt Alexander was the instigator of everything that had happened. It became obvious to her Alexander wanted the starship and intended for her to abide by the charter's bylaws and kill Jennifer if his agents failed to complete their mission. She then thought Alexander was no better than the Tyrant because they both regarded everyone as expendable assets.

It shamed her to think Alexander held no respect for human life when it came to achieving his goals. But to murder an entire crew to steal a starship was madness? Alexander enraged her so much that she began to scream and curse his name. Kelly knew Alexander's last day was coming to meet him. She didn't know how or when she'd kill him but swore an oath for her dead crew. "I'm not expendable nor was my crew! Whatever it takes Alexander, my crew and ship will be avenged!"

Inside the main cave, the soft cries of a hungry baby awakened Jennifer from her nap. Reaching for her child lying beside her, she quickly silenced her cries with a swollen breast dripping with milk. Jennifer smiled down at her little girl as she suckled greedily at her breast. "Oh, you're such a pretty girl, Trenna," Jennifer softly whispered, feeling the milk flow from her breast and into her child's mouth with each little swallow.

Jennifer wondered where Taric and Jaxx had disappeared to during her nap. Her mate's uncompromising attitude toward Thomas and the others were beginning to trouble her. The unexpected landing of another escape pod with the Sterling woman inside and her shocking account of the murders committed by an officer only strengthened Taric's low opinion of them.

Jennifer's keen awareness of the complex arena of human politics enabled her to clearly see the whole picture. The hatred of the Tyrant still exists in the hearts of common men and royals wronged by her father so long ago. And yet the human population living on Earth today still desires to inflict revenge against her bloodline.

It saddened her to realize, her chance of escaping him and her past had failed. Her parents did not account for the technological advancement of space travel over the decades they slept inside the *Fulcrum*. With the advancement of the warp drive, her enemies had come to the far reaches of space, seeking to avenge the Tyrant's crimes against humanity with her death.

While Jennifer cradled her child comfortably in her arms, she replayed within her mind, the conversation she had with Taric the previous evening as they lay in their sleeping furs.

"Taric, we can't let them stay out on the plains. Thomas and the others are unprepared and poorly equipped to survive on their own." She dared to say, knowing he'd been pissed off to no end since Trenna's birth. His mood had become so unpredictable that it was like walking on eggshells around him and she was tired of it.

"Did you hear me?" she asked, nudging him with an elbow.

"Ow, stop it! Why should I care about them? The girl wanted to kill you! No!" Taric had angrily answered her, shocked by the request, and then rolled over showing her his backside, which meant without saying anything that their conversation was over.

"Listen, I don't care if your angry, you should be. God knows you have the right. But please listen and trust me once more as you did when we shared our first night under the stars. Remember that night? Please, my love, open your heart and let your spirit guide you," Jennifer softly whispered into his ear letting him hear the pain in her voice.

The tightly held furs slowly loosened and shifted as Taric reluctantly rolled back over to face her. He saw tears welling in the corners of her eyes with a look of a long, sequestered sadness clearly evident on her face. Taric had never seen such sadness in her eyes, and it pained him to think he was the cause of it. "I will listen and think about your words."

She accepted his reply with a kiss and a smile before beginning. "The attempt on my life was not their doing. The agent tried to kill me because of my past and who I was on Earth. I'm the daughter of a monster. My father was the evilest man who has ever lived in human history. At one time, the Earth was home to twelve billion people. My father, who's known as the Tyrant, will forever be vilified within mankind's heart and soul for the atrocities he had committed against his enemies.

"His insane quest for power plunged the Earth into a war that lasted for decades. Over four billion people had already died in his war for dominance when I escaped Earth with my mother.

"My mother was his younger sister, and when she was thirteen, she became pregnant with me. There's no proof of my birthright left on Earth. There were rumors of rape, suspicions of incest, and doubts over the validity of the reports concerning my birth. Most people on Earth believe the Tyrant was my father and that I am long dead.

"But the rumors and suspicions about me were all true. His name has ceased to exist on Earth. The hatred of him and his bloodline still festers in the hearts, minds, and souls of people born years after his death. I've been marked for death by my father's enemies since the day of my birth. My escape from Earth ensures the continuance of his bloodline, which places not only my life but Trenna's life in jeopardy if it ever became known I was alive.

"According to Thomas, the peace is a very fragile accord between the three surviving kingdoms and the American empire. The wounds of the past have not healed, nor have they been forgotten. The Tyrant had to have been a demon born of hell. He infected the human psyche by unleashing an incurable pandemic of hateful distrust into our species. I fear the people of the Earth will never be free of his evil influence.

"Thomas suspects charterists are led and funded worldwide by one or more of the royal families. Taric, you must understand the events happening on the starship right now were planned long before the *Fulcrum* tragedy. Thomas, Kelly, Dr. Mencia, the murdered crew, and I are all victims of a diabolical plot beyond our control. Thomas believes the killing of the *Maleficent*'s crew is the first salvo of an impending war," Jennifer honestly admitted, revealing the truth of her past with the hope he'd understand the why of everything. She began to softly cry, ashamed of the actions perpetrated by zealots who could not let go of their hatred.

Taric's expression had softened as he thought about her explanation. She saw the troubled look in his eyes and knew he was trying to imagine a world where a single individual could initiate an action that could decimate an entire world. He then surprised her when he finally responded, "I do not believe a woman as loving and kind as you can be the child of such an evil man. This Tyrant, as you call him, cannot possibly be your father. It's hard for me to imagine the concepts of your home world. I cannot comprehend the concept of politics in my mind. It makes no sense to me, how one man can rule an entire world and tear it apart? But I will think about what you've told me."

Before last night, she had tried to convince Taric of their good intentions and innocence to no avail. His distrust and strong pride kept him from seeing the truth of her words. She sensed a calming of his mood before he slept. She could only hope his rational mind and natural compassion would eventually change his mind.

Jennifer nudged her child's mouth free by breaking the suction to her nipple with a couple of fingers. She softly guided Trenna's tiny mouth to her other breast to suckle for her milk. While watching Trenna's tiny hands push on her breast for more milk, Jennifer began to hope Taric would accept them back into the cave.

"It's getting too cold, and we can't be confined to a tent all winter. We're exposed, and there's no other cave to take refuge from the elements. Thomas, you need to convince Jennifer and Taric to accept us back into their cave," Kelly said, huddled within her clothing and with a blanket draped over her shoulders.

"If it comes down to freezing to death, I will gain my way inside, even if I have to shoot someone," Dr. Mencia warned as he tried to keep warm by flailing his arms and stomping his feet, trying to generate within his body rapid blood flow and warmth.

"I don't think that's a good idea, Doc. Have you forgotten how protective that doglike animal is? Any sign of aggression and it'll be on you as sure as the sun shines," Kelly added her point to the conversation, then said before the doctor could respond. "You saw how quickly it attacked Tina. Besides, you won't make it past the barricade, Taric's too good a shot with his bow. Do you honestly believe you'd fare much better? Gun or not, you'd be dead as soon as you stepped into the clearing armed with a weapon."

"Burn the barricade then," Mencia shouted angrily back at her, shivering in his thin jacket, unmindful of the commotion he was causing the nearby animals.

"We will not invade the man's home!" Thomas shouted above his two officers, exercising his command as they stood around their small fire, ignorant of the goroc bulls beginning to pace about in reaction to their agitated voices.

"I don't care if your balls freeze and fall off, Doctor! We will do no harm to those people!" Thomas's angry retort momentarily silenced the doctor, allowing him to continue in a quiet but stern voice. "If you try to invade their home, I'll kill you! Got that?"

"Then what are we going to do?" Kelly asked her captain, trusting he would find a way.

"I don't know Kelly. But I do believe groveling and begging forgiveness will be required. I'm betting on Jennifer to change his mind. Until then, we wait here and try to keep warm," Thomas ordered, daring the doctor with a mean glare to say something else.

Taric was watching from the cover of the trees, the three humans standing around their small fire arguing among themselves. He couldn't clearly hear what they were saying over the noise of the nearby herds, but from their flailing arm gestures and repeated stomping of feet, he assumed it was about the cold weather. Taric looked down at Jaxx, sitting calmly beside him with her tail wagging vigorously, her eyes and ears attuned to the rise and fall of their voices drifting over the grass.

He didn't have a reason to be there, except to watch and think about what Jennifer said the night before. As hard as he tried, he couldn't stop the image of the girl threatening the life of his mate and child. Jennifer pointed out, making it clear it was Thomas who gave Jaxx, the few seconds to react in time. She made him see the entire scene play out in his mind. As the fog of his anger cleared from his mind, Taric remembered Thomas placing himself in front of the gun to protect Jennifer and the baby from the assassin's bullet. It was hard for him to accept because he was so upset at the time. He reacted angrily and without thinking when he ejected them from the cave.

A few large goroc bulls guarding the herds nearby kept wary eyes on the noisy strangers. Taric watched as the bulls, who were no more than a stone throw away from their camp, slowly begin to pace side to side in front of the herd. They began bellowing and snorting aggressively toward the source of the loud, angry voices. Ignorant of the animal's behavioral instincts, the three humans stupidly paid no attention to the agitated bulls as they continued to argue inside their camp, believing their fire would deter the animals from attacking.

Anticipating an imminent charge by one or more of the bulls, Taric signaled Jaxx to distract the bull's attention from the humans, using a familiar hunting tactic. Jaxx shot out of the trees howling and barking at the bulls as she ran swiftly at them. She swerved and turned when she neared the beasts, baiting them into chasing her away from the camp.

The massive bulls turned toward the howling lycur as she scampered around them, staying safely out of reach of their horns. She continued urging the bulls to give chase by barking and nipping quickly at their thick legs before darting out of the way. Recognizing the lycur as a threat to the herd, Taric watched as Jaxx successfully baited the bulls into charging after her. Jaxx ran swiftly in the lead, covering the ground with long easy strides, as she lured the bulls down the grass to a safe distance.

Taric then raised his fingers to his lips and whistled loudly over the commotion of the startled herds running away from the guardians and the source of danger. Jaxx responded to the whistle and swiftly turned and darted into the safety of the forest trees, leaving the angry bulls behind her snorting and stomping at the ground with massive feet far from the initial source of the bulls' irritation.

Taric walked out of the trees to stand in the grass, waiting for Jaxx to circle back through the trees and return to his side. Taric started walking to the camp when Jaxx trotted out from nearby thickets. Thomas, startled by the animal's sudden commotion, was the first of the three to see Taric coming toward them. He hadn't seen him for two days since the pod with Sterling inside struck the valley floor.

Thomas walked out into the dry brown grass to meet him halfway. "You seem to have impeccable timing. Always around to save us from our own folly," Thomas said in greeting, admitting he didn't understand the danger they were in until the bulls diverted charge. "Thank you."

Taric swallowed his pride, knowing he'd be no better than them if he allowed the three to die needlessly. So Taric responded by saying, "I had no intention of coming here, but my mind and feet lead me to your camp. Jennifer has tried to explain the social structure and way of life on Earth. I'll never understand the violence of your world, but Jennifer insists most humans prefer to live peaceful lives without ever taking aggressive action against another person."

"Well, Jennifer is right about that," Thomas assured him, not knowing what else to say.

"Bring what you need to the cave. You're too smart for your own good and too stupid to survive the land," he said to him and then, without another word, turned around and walked away. Insulted once again but grateful for the invitation, Thomas smiled as he watched Taric quickly disappear into the shadows of the forest trees.

"Cooper," Carter addressed the AI while sitting in the captain's chair on the *Maleficent*'s bridge. The AI's hologram instantly appeared to stand beside him. "What are your orders?"

"Set our course for a rendezvous with an outbound colonial starship, the *Chameleon*. It's been sailing for Opalla for twenty-two years. Calculate an intercept flight to meet it," Carter ordered, vocalizing the last requirement of his mission. Cooper's ghostly hologram stood quietly for a moment before acknowledging the order. "Course for the intercept is set."

"For the glory of the charter, make it happen," Carter said as the *Maleficent* left its orbital path above Planos in a flash of multicolored light.

CHAPTER 22

Revelation of Intent

It had been an agonizing month for Isabella since receiving the news of her brother's abandonment on Planos. She worried about him constantly and hoped he was faring better there than in the frightening dreams created by her subconscious mind when she slept. Her dreams had become a nightly mixture of chaotic images of Thomas running through dense trees chased by a dark, mysterious beast. Just as the beast attacked, she'd awaken, choking on a silent scream desperately trying to escape her lips. She would then go back to sleep, and with each successive morning, she'd awaken to her reality, never knowing if Thomas escaped the clutches of the beast chasing him in her dream. She knew it was her active imagination overreacting within her subconscious mind, but it was worrisome to her nonetheless.

She was in her office when she received a private hand-delivered dispatch from Admiral Harrington, insisting it was vital they talk privately aboard the starship. Isabella wasted no time in alerting her private security team leader to prepare for an off-planet assignment in the morning.

During the early morning darkness on a cold, rainy night, Isabella secretly boarded her armed shuttlecraft with her security detail, having accepted the admiral's invitation to come aboard the empire's warp drive starship. The new starship had been crewed with trusted officers and cadets personally selected by the admiral as she had requested. The ship was still moored to the construction docks and had been christened as the *Excalibur* in homage to the ancient legend of King Arthur of Camelot.

Admiral Harrington greeted Isabella as she exited her shuttle inside the *Excalibur's* hangar bay. "Welcome aboard the *Excalibur*, Empress Isabella."

"Thank you, Admiral. The ship is an amazing sight to behold. What an exhilarating feeling it was to see it moored to the dock with the moon in the background, it gave me goose bumps as we approached," Isabella happily replied as it was her first-time off-planet.

"I'm happy you enjoyed the flight up to us. If you'd please follow me to the bridge, Captain Stamos has graciously offered to bunk elsewhere on the ship. His ready room and quarters will be your residence aboard ship. My officers will show your men to their quarters," Admiral Harrington responded with an outstretched arm pointing to the hangar bay exit.

"Thank you, Admiral. I appreciate the kind offer from Captain Stamos. As to an extended stay, I'd say it all depends on what we have to discuss privately," Isabella informed him as she walked beside him to the exit and into one of the main corridors of the ship.

"Yes, I see. Empress, what I have to tell you is going to be a story for the ages. I assure you of that! As it is, I can hardly believe it myself," Harrington admitted, if not for the evidence, he'd scoff over the lunacy of it all.

"Really? You're sure the evidence is valid?" Isabella asked him, curious to what he'd soon reveal and wondered if he knew her secret as they stepped into a lift that would take them up to the flight deck where the bridge was located.

"Empress, I'd be a fool to waste your time. I assure you, the information we've discovered is so valid, it could ensnare the empire into another devastating war," he warned her, concern showing in his brown eyes for the continuance of her reign as the lift door opened to the corridor outside the bridge.

"I pray it will not come to that," Isabella responded, then stepped out of the lift, but was unsure of the direction she should go.

"Make a left, the bridge is the first door on the right," Harrington stated, seeing Isabella looking down the corridor to the right then left.

"Thank you. I wasn't sure which way to go," Isabella said with a warm smile, genuinely fond of the tall, lean man.

When she stepped onto the bridge, Captain Terry Stamos stood from his chair and announced. "Empress on the bridge." Instantly every officer and crew member on the bridge stood smartly to attention.

"Please, as you were," Isabella said with a warm smile as she approached the captain.

"Captain Stamos, it's a pleasure to make your acquaintance," Isabella said with curiosity as he appeared to be about the same age as herself. He wore a full head of long sandy-blond hair tied in the back. He had sparkling blue eyes and a finely chiseled chin that supported a boyishly handsome face.

"Empress, the pleasure is mine. Welcome to the *Excalibur*. I hope you enjoy our hospitality while you're with us," Stamos replied, noticing she was a little nervous and out of her depth as she stood on the bridge of a starship.

"Thank you, Captain," she replied to him and then proceeded to meet each member of the bridge crew, shaking their hand and looking them in the eye before moving on. "And you are?" she asked a young man on duty at his station near the view screen.

Flustered by her unexpected attention, a nervous and slightly embarrassed young cadet stammered. "Ah, ah, I'm Cadet Jerald Palmer, ma'am. I mean, Empress."

"Relax, Jerald, I don't bite," Isabella softly said with a kind smile as the bridge crew quietly chuckled over his discomfort.

"Yes, ma'am, Empress," he said seeing her eyebrow arch upward and then stammered. "I can't help it. It's a habit of my mother's upbringing. I'm sorry, I didn't mean any disrespect, because I do." And then he paused in midthought as his mind went suddenly blank. His momentary lapse left a long silence to fill the air between them before he completed his statement in a hurried rush of words. "Respectyouthatis!"

Hearing the bridge suddenly erupt in wild laughter, Jerald knew he had dug himself a hole in which to jump into and disappear. Jerald lowered his head and quietly stared at his console, forcing himself to say no more.

Laughing with him but not at him. Isabella patted his hand in reassurance and responded with a wide smile and kind words to let the poor boy off the hook as he raised his head to look at her. "Jerald, I admire your mother. She's raised a fine son. There's nothing like a little laughter to set a nervous mind at ease in a strange environment. I needed that. Thank you for your humbling gift."

Jerald was then caught by surprise when Isabella leaned in close to whisper into his ear. "Actually, I prefer *ma'am*, titles are cumbersome for me."

Isabella then stood erect as Jerald replied to her in a quiet whisper only she could hear before she moved on. "Yes, ma'am."

She smiled at him and then turned her mind onto the business at hand. She quickly greeted the remainder of the crew and then walked over to where Admiral Harrington patiently stood waiting to escort her inside the ready room. As Isabella passed into the room and took a seat on a very worn but comfortable brown leather couch near a window, she heard Harrington order. "Captain, proceed to our destination."

From inside the ready room, Isabella heard Captain Stamos reply from his chair. "Aye, Admiral."

When Harrington entered, closing the door behind him and saw Isabella reclining on the old couch, he couldn't stop himself from apologizing for the ugly thing. "Umm, sorry about the couch. There was a brand-new couch in here, but apparently this old thing is Terry's favorite. He brought it up from his home and claims it's more comfortable than any bed."

"It's worn but quite comfortable," Isabella replied, leaning back and settling into the plush cushions of the couch. She indicated with a hand for Harrington to share the other end as they talked.

"Stamos is very young to have earned the rank of captain of a starship. Are you sure of him?" Isabella asked Harrington, intrigued by the captain's boyish good looks.

"Don't let his age and vid-star, devil-may-care smirk fool you. He's the smartest man I've ever met, and I've been around the block a few times in my life. Don't ever play chess for credits with him, he'll clean you out," Harrington warned her, having felt his touch into his pocketbook after losing six times in a row.

"Oh? He's that good," Isabella responded and added, "How much did he get you for?

"Empress, I'm a damn good chess player always have been but Stamos. Well, he's different and kinda wicked when he plays. We were having a late dinner in the mess hall and the world chess championship results were being reported on the vids. So I kinda started bragging about my younger days in school, when I bet a hundred credits a game playing chess in my dorm.

"Terry asked if I wanted to play him, and I stupidly replied. Sure, got a hundred credits? So we played. I don't like him much when he plays. He smiles the whole time like the Cheshire cat did to Alice in Wonderland and brilliantly clears the board. I'd bet good credits. He'd win a match against that guy Davis, who just won the world championship and beat the pants off him. Terry is that good at the game. He took six hundred credits from me!" Harrington finally admitted, laughing at his folly, knowing he'd never play for credits against the young man again.

"Wow, six hundred. Thanks for the warning," Isabella responded while wiping tears from her eyes with a tissue from her pocket as she laughed at his story. Putting the tissue aside, she changed the conversation to the purpose of her visit. "So, Admiral, why am I here? You must be sure of the information to sail away from Earth with me aboard, which could be construed by others as an abduction."

Harrington quickly became serious and began to explain, "I'm very sure of myself and of the information. The investigation team is filing charges and presenting the evidence to the courts. Believe me, you won't regret placing your faith in me when this all started."

"You have my undivided attention. Please explain the reasoning for this flight," Isabella countered, warning him of the consequences if he was wrong.

"We started with the Imperial Fleet credentials Cole Mason presented when he boarded the *Maleficent*. Imperial Fleet credentials are only obtained at our Fleet academies. There's only four, one in each kingdom. It was easy to research the various clerks' financial records that worked at the four institutions for discrepancies.

"Our agents ended up arresting a clerk whose elaborate lifestyle exceeded her base salary as a clerk. When pressed, she confessed to supplying three sets of blank credentials to a man without a name. Mason's credentials had been obtained through the African Fleet Academy in Somalia. Her financial records linked her account to a very well-funded private account set up some twenty-five years ago by an anonymous benefactor. This account had provided the tuition funds to three different universities around the world. However, the recipient's identities remained a mystery as the students' names did not match the names on the credentials.

"So we decided to do a facial recognition of the university students over the last ten years to see if any matched the photos of the *Maleficent*'s crew. That's when we hit pay dirt. Cole Mason, Tina Marlowe, and Dan Carter were the only students from those schools, who matched the identification photos on the credentials turned in upon boarding.

"Armed with imperial warrants for crimes against the empire, the agents forced the banking institution that held the account into revealing the benefactor. It turned out to be a shell corporation, which was a subsidiary of another and another and so on until finally the agents were able to give us a name of this mysterious and very generous benefactor." Harrington paused in his narration, anticipating the question that was forthcoming.

"Who's the mystery man behind it?" Isabella quietly asked and waited, already suspecting the identity of the charterist traitor.

"The benefactor is none other than the leper, King Alexander Sterling," Harrington calmly stated and added, "That's only half of the story. As crazy as it seems, there's more, which, when fully told, will bring us to the here and now."

"Well, please go on then," Isabella replied as she watched Harrington rise from the couch and press a button on the console at the captain's desk. "Bring it in," he said to the image on the screen.

"Be there in five minutes, Admiral," they heard the reply over the speakers.

"Bring what in?"

"You'll see. Please be patient, Empress. In the meantime, I'll continue on. The account was set up twenty-five years ago, about the same time the prototype of the warp drive was approved for construction and testing. It's not a coincidence of timing. This conspiracy is one for the ages. it's so farfetched, I didn't believe the agents myself until I met it," Harrington said as the door to the ready room opened to reveal a middle-aged man being slowly escorted into the room. He was shackled and shuffled his feet as he walked beside two burly security men, who appeared to be twins.

"You brought Alexander's impostor aboard the ship!" Isabella exclaimed, immediately recognizing the man who stood quietly in front of her, knowing he'd been infected with an incurable hybrid strain of the leprosy virus after his coronation ceremony twenty-two years earlier.

"How did you know he's not Alexander?" Harrington asked her in shocked disbelief.

"I've known since shortly after his coronation. The real Alexander Sterling has a nervous twitch in his left hand. His ring finger was always nervously tapping his side, when he made appearances and had to stand in front of cameras," Isabella explained, impressing the astonished admiral.

"Impressive, my lady. But if you knew, why didn't you expose him?" Harrington asked her.

"Simple, because I didn't know what he was up too," Isabella answered truthfully.

"So you decided to let a surgically altered impostor, pretend to be Alexander for the last twenty-two years? Were you aware, he's not even sick. It's theatrical makeup," he said, wiping some makeup off the man's face to prove his claim.

"I wasn't sure if he was diseased or not," Isabella responded honestly. "So I kept my distance just in case."

"The infection was part of Alexander's plan to isolate himself from everybody, even you. Incurable leprosy is a very valid excuse to conduct meetings via vid conferences hidden behind a sheer veil curtain with foreign dignitaries and businessmen over the years. It was a perfect cover until now. You can take him back to the brig," Harrington stated with a smug look of satisfaction on his face as the detail led the man out of the room.

"Admiral, I'm convinced. So where do you suspect Alexander is hiding?" Isabella asked Harrington as the ship sped through the darkness of deep space faster than the speed of light to an undisclosed destination.

"To be honest, we're not exactly sure," Harrington admitted, holding a hand up to stall Isabella so he could finish. "But there's strong evidence to support the probability that he's on the colonial starship *Chameleon*, which left Earth twenty-three years ago and is currently sailing to Opalla."

"How did Alexander get onto the starship without anyone the wiser? Why was there no inkling of this operation taking place?" Isabella asked, shocked by the revelation of Alexander's far-reaching conspiracy.

"The same way Kera Collins and her husband got off-planet. It was the Sterling's that helped the Jennifer girl onto the *Fulcrum*. Alexander is not a charterist. He's a royal with balls and ambition. The Sterling family suffered the most under the Tyrant's thumb. Their bitterness has no constraints or boundaries. Alexander's grand-father set up funds through a network of shell corporations to finance charterist cells' militant actions worldwide.

Alexander took advantage and segregated a single cell or a succession of secret cells to eventually infiltrate and steal the first warp drive starship and rendezvous with the *Chameleon*, no matter how long it took to accomplish," Harrington explained, giving her the known facts and probable theory behind the events taking place.

"You said the experts claimed it was impossible to steal a starship without an AI assist. Now, you're saying its possible?" Isabella asked him, knowing he had an answer, she wouldn't like.

"Yes, it's possible. At the time when the Cooper AI became standard systems on our colonial starships, their positronic matrix was considered infallible, but technology advances over time and changes things. When I posed your question to the experts, they immediately replied, 'Impossible.'

"However, a few enterprising engineers decided to give your questions some consideration. They came back and reported that with today's technological advances in the field of positronic engineering, it was very easy to subvert the original AI programming, leave it operational, and allow a single individual to command the ship without a crew," Harrington answered, feeling the pressing weight of time working against them.

Isabella remained silent for a few moments analyzing the information in her mind before speaking. "I take it we're sailing to the *Chameleon* on an intercept course to reclaim the *Maleficent*."

"Your deduction is correct," Harrington assured her then continued. "This ship is armed and very capable of blowing the *Maleficent* out of existence if necessary. If the *Maleficent* is already docked to the colony ship, then it goes as well."

"Oh, I see," Isabella calmly replied but disagreed with the outright destruction of the starships. "Admiral, although I admire the work you've done to unravel the conspiracy, I cannot in good conscience sacrifice innocent lives to stop one man's crazy scheme. There's another way."

"What way? The best tactical action is to ensure his death in a fiery explosion. That's how you end an insurgency!" Harrington angrily replied, confident his action was best.

"Calm yourself, Admiral. Mother always hedged her bets, when cooperating with multiple corporations from the four kingdoms. Each kingdom has contributed to the building of our orbiting infrastructure. The construction docks and starships for the colonization of new worlds were built by a conglomerate of major corporations worldwide. I'm no different than my mother. Alexander may have lost his secrets, but I still have mine," Isabella stated rather calmly for the excitement she was feeling.

"What are you talking about?" Harrington asked, confused by her evasive response.

"The *Maleficent* will not be destroyed. I want the ship back under fleet control. There's another AI installed on our missing starship. It monitors the ship and takes no action until prompted. The AI functions independently and doesn't show up during system diagnostic tests," Isabella revealed her secret and saw a large smile with bright white teeth appear on Harrington's face.

"So what's your plan?" Harrington asked his young empress, amazed by Isabella's foresight to anticipate troublesome scenarios with a backup AI system secretly installed on the starship.

"Since the end of the war, we've been plagued by charterist militants' wasteful attacks against our new way of cooperation between the four kingdoms for advancing human life. Earth is finally showing signs of healing from our predecessor's negligent stewardship of the planet's resources. People are prosperous once more and at peace back home. They don't want another war. They want to live, grow old as their children grow up, and die with their children and grandchildren around them.

"However, the prejudices and hatreds of our past needs to be changed within the minds of our people to avoid a war. We have to isolate charterists and change the thinking of their sympathizers. Inform Earth and all the colonies, King Alexander Sterling has been charged with treason and is a fugitive of the empire. Gather the evidence for the courts and present a chronological order of events to the vids. He's to be portrayed as a criminal and wanted for conspiring to incite another world war for personal gain.

"People will then be convinced Alexander purposefully fed the hate with unlimited credits to fund charterist militants. We will win this war before it has a chance to begin. Our people will not tolerate another Tyrant!" Isabella exclaimed to her admiral, who still looked bewildered and confused.

"So what will the other AI do?" Harrington asked, feeling awkward for asking.

"Get this ship within visual and hailing distance of the *Maleficent*, and I'll take care of the rest," Isabella assured him with a grim smile of satisfaction on her lips.

CHAPTER 23

Thirty-Six Hours

Captain Stamos was in his temporary quarters, sleeping soundly as a bear sprawled over a chair. He was slouched in an awkwardly twisted reclining position, with one leg hanging over an armrest, arms flung wide to the sides, head all the way back and snoring through his mouth when the door of his room opened.

Light from the corridor cut through the darkness of a typical crewman's windowless living space. A ship's steward, holding a tray in his hands with a container of coffee and a cup, announced his presence as he stood in the doorway. "Captain, it's time to wake up. You're expected in the ready room for breakfast with Empress Isabella and Admiral Harrington."

"How long?" Terry said with closed eyes as he twisted in the chair to straighten up, yawning, stretching his body's lean muscles to their fullest extent in order to ease his body out of the chair.

"Thirty minutes, sir," the steward replied as he came in and set the tray on top of a small slide-out table inserted into the wall on the opposite end of the room beside the bunk.

"Not breakfast. How long was I asleep?" Terry asked with his eyes still closed as he relaxed and collapsed back into the plush chair.

"Sorry, sir, I don't know? Ship's time is 0630," the steward answered, informing him of the time. He watched as the captain finally moved to climb out of the embrace of the chair and stand up only to stretch his arms to the ceiling once more before hearing an acknowledgment.

"Ahh, only six hours," Terry grumbled as he accepted a cup of coffee from the young steward and sat down on the bunk. He sipped his coffee, allowing the rich aroma to awaken his senses as the steward retrieved a green-and-gold fleet uniform from a tiny closet in the wall.

"Thanks for the coffee. I'll be ready in ten and be there on time," Terry said with good humor and a smile.

Seeing how the captain slept, the steward couldn't help but ask. "Ah, sir? Did you sleep okay?"

"Slept like a baby. Why?" Terry asked him. "Do I look tired?"

"Ah, no, sir. You look fine," he stammered as a confused expression appeared on his face and asked before leaving. "Is there anything else, sir."

"Naaah, I'm good," the steward heard him say into his cup as he drank the warm liquid. Once the steward was out into the corridor, he quietly whispered to himself while walking away. "Weird."

Terry entered the bridge asking Cooper's hologram persona, who was navigating the starship through space at warp speed. "What's our timeline?"

"I estimate long-range scanners will detect the *Chameleon* in thirty-five hours, forty-seven minutes, and eight seconds," Cooper flatly replied without inflection in its voice.

"Thank you. Carry on," Terry replied as he approached his ready room door. Although the room was part of his quarters aboard ship, Terry buzzed and waited a few seconds for the door to open and ask for permission to enter.

Harrington waved him in when he saw Terry standing in the doorway. Stewards were busy setting tableware and utensils on a table with three chairs around it. Terry noticed his couch was not in the room and figured the stewards had moved it somewhere to make space for the table.

"Have you seen the vids?" Harrington asked as they waited for the empress to join them.

"No. What's going on?" Terry asked, watching the stewards going about their business listening to every word, hoping to hear a tidbit of information not on the vids. And then, share the information while quietly gossiping about it during their mealtime conversations throughout the ship.

"The news of Alexander's impostor has set the European kingdom in a state of complete disarray. The Sterling family has denied having any knowledge of Alexander's plot and has renounced his kingship. The impostor's handlers over the last twenty-odd years have been indicted and arrested for conspiracy to incite a war.

"Charterist sympathizers are renouncing affiliations with militants worldwide. The empire's most wanted charterists are in hiding deeper than they ever were. Security forces within the four kingdoms are dealing with communications networks becoming overloaded with tips on suspect's locations.

"People are protesting in the streets in support of Empress Isabella on Earth as well as in the colonies. With commercial warp drive technology, colonization will be less expensive and will be open to anyone who wants to begin a new life. Imagine, leaving Earth and within a month or two, start a pioneering life discovering a new world and making it your home. People understand the advantages warp drives will bring to human society as we spread out into the galaxy.

"Interstellar trade between the colonies and Earth in real time will boost the empire's economy to levels of prosperity unforeseen in human history. The people are making it clear, they will not tolerate another war," Harrington informed him when Isabella stepped into the room from her quarters.

"Good morning, gentlemen. Sorry to keep you waiting. I've been informed by the courts, Alexander Sterling's personal assets on Earth and Opalla have been impounded or confiscated, until the end of the investigation. It's a standard procedure for any imperial criminal investigation. If convicted, Alexander's fortune will become a dedicated source of funds for financial reparations to the victims of charterist crimes over the last twenty-five years," she said with a smug smile on her face as she took a seat at the table. The stewards left, but one remained in the room and quietly stood beside a cart waiting to serve breakfast.

"Why twenty-five years? Why not all the way back to the end of the war?" Terry asked, surprised by the disclosure but felt the span of time was too short. As he believed the funding of credits to the charterist was begun by Alexander's grandfather and should also include the years of his rule.

"Unfortunately, the law states that reparations are for victims injured or killed during a crime. Alexander's crime is still ongoing," Harrington answered from his place at the table as the steward began serving them.

"The evidence, which has been presented to the courts, allowed the panel of judges to determine the duration of the crime. Alexander's crime of treason against the empire began the day of his coronation twenty-five years ago. The judges have ruled to proceed with the case. Due to the severity of the numerous crimes he has funded over the years, the judges have officially declared Alexander an outlaw of the empire," Isabella added to the conversation.

"Outlaw?" Terry asked, never having heard the term used in modern courts.

"Yes, an outlaw! Beyond the protection of the law as in the ancient middle ages and then in the old Wild West of the 1800s. An outlaw is a fitting designation for a criminal, like him," Harrington declared with contempt, aware the ruling meant dead or alive, giving him an option if things didn't work out as suggested.

"Gentlemen, before I left Earth, I handed my aide Freddie, a message for the vid networks CEOs. He was instructed to demand a vid conference with the CEOs as a group and deliver my request after I left the estate in the shuttle. I gave them access to Mason Cole's file and knowledge of my location in exchange for keeping this starship behind schedule and inside the orbiting construction dock on the vids. The cover story is the ship's progress has had another setback to its expected completion date due to supply chain disruptions of vital components. I promised one more thing to get their cooperation, live real-time coverage of the outcome of this endeavor, whatever it may entail. We will stream our encounter with Alexander back to

Earth, the moment this ship drops out of warp and confronts the *Maleficent*.

"With the evidence presented to the courts and subsequent release to the public, it's apparent they have honored my request for secrecy. I think the Cooper AI on the *Maleficent* is still receiving vids through Earthlink. It's a chance the hijacker of our starship is watching them. He may believe Alexander has won and has all the time in the world to move against us.

"Captain Stamos, what are the odds we reach our destination before the *Maleficent*?" Isabella asked, wondering what the man was thinking.

"Well, since we're following a trail of evidence uncovered after the fleet was notified of Cole Mason's suicide. The odds are we won't. I expect the ship to be in Alexander's control when we drop out of warp," Terry honestly replied and added as a side note. "I think Alexander intends to attack Earth, and by that, I meant you, Empress. Alexander's long-range planning is a brilliant piece of work. However, because of his arrogance, the plan is destined to fail, because it's flawed in more than a few ways, here's a couple of examples.

"Alexander was aware of the extreme cost of building a warp drive starship. He left Earth assuming only a single ship would be built. Stupid, because he failed to imagine the enormous cost advantages of building starships in pairs to quicken our development of a fleet.

"Alexander wanted to taunt the empire while initiating fear and unrest into the population with the theft of our starship. Cole Mason's suicide and false identity were meant to be discovered and expose his secret cell of charterist agents aboard the ship.

"Once the *Maleficent* left Earth, Alexander knew we couldn't prevent the theft of our starship. If Mason hadn't died, we'd still be wondering how the AI's Earthlink failed and be sailing to Planos on a rescue mission. Instead of being here in a position to stop him."

Thomas's relationship with Taric had improved over time, but not without some misgivings, while they adjusted to living together in the cave system. They were given a wide space behind the large firepit inside the water cave in which to reside. Using the ample supply of cured hides, Jennifer had helped them settle in and get used to living in the wild. Thomas found the cavern comforting in the semi-darkness when he laid down to sleep while listening to water falling into the pool and flow down the channel to drop away into a black abyss at the cave's low end. It also allowed him the serenity to think calmly and be at ease with himself.

Dr. Mencia mostly stayed inside the cavern, examining little Trenna, making sure she was getting the nutrients she required from her mother's milk. His curiosity of Trenna being a hybrid child of parents from different worlds became an intriguing obsession of his. Mencia often moaned for not having access to the modern medical equipment within his lab aboard ship. If he was, he'd be able to examine her DNA and see just how the two vastly different strains of the parents' DNA, blended to create the precious life of Jennifer's darling little girl.

Kelly had to admit living as they did, she was more of a rustic homemaker than she had thought. She and Jennifer quickly became good friends, enjoying their time spent in each other's company as Jaxx kept a watchful eye on their surroundings when they foraged.

They'd go outside with Trenna snuggled securely in a sling around Jennifer's shoulder and waist as she learned how to gather the last of the seasonal grains and berries growing nearby. Kelly was amazed by how much Jennifer had learned since she became marooned and fell in love with an amazing man of Planos. Their friendship became a sisterly bond, and Kelly often wondered as she lay down to sleep, if she could easily leave when the rescue ship arrived to take them home.

Kelly had learned to enjoy the hard work it took to live off the land. She was free of the invasive technology and of the constant complications modern society life entails for the first time in her life. Each night as she dozed off to sleep, Kelly found herself wishing to remain behind and never go home.

A strong cold, dry wind blew down from the mountain peaks and into the wide plain at their base as winter finally set in. Thomas stood outside the cave under the nighttime sky wrapped in a runner hide to keep warm, searching the heavens for the telltale signs of a shuttle entering the atmosphere. His vigilance so far was for naught, but he knew it was too soon to expect a rescue.

Thomas looked up at the sky nonetheless with the hope of one day seeing Isabella once again. He missed her more than he had expected when he began this adventure into the far depths of space. The vast distance between them made him feel the pain of her absence within his heart, unaware she was physically closer than she was a month ago when he arrived on Planos.

Thomas heard someone at the barricade's door and turned his head to see Taric, wearing a heavy coat, step outside and stretch before walking over to stand beside him.

"That hide will not keep you warm out here by midwinter, it's too thin. A few goroc hides could provide all of you with winter clothing before it really gets cold. Kelly has agreed to go hunting in the morning, care to join us?"

"Yes, of course. I'd be thrilled to come along," Thomas answered, glad for the opportunity to experience primeval hunting as his human ancestors did. "What's it like?"

"What?"

"Hunting. You know, in the wilds with bows and arrows when taking down large animals," Thomas answered, clarifying his question.

Taric smiled and replied in his simple way. "It's tiring, dangerous, and very exciting to bring down a goroc with lances and arrows because you got to get close. However, because of your long guns, you won't need to get close to them."

"Well, yes, that's true. Our rifles are very effective against long-range targets, but I was hoping to hunt with Jennifer's bow," Thomas answered, wondering if Taric would agree.

"Thomas, gorocs will attack a perceived threat with the intention of goring the attacker or knocking it onto the ground and stomping the animal to death. Goroc hunting requires every hunter in a tribe working together to be successful. If you run, you're dead. It takes a stout heart to control your instincts to run when they charge.

Two or more bulls work together patrolling the outside perimeter of a herd. Rarely are they alone. Separated by a few steps, two hunters face a goroc bull using a heavy pair of strong lances. The tribe stands behind and to the sides of the hunters holding the lances with their bows ready. Placing the butt end of each lance into the ground, the hunters hold them at an angle facing the bull they want.

"The tribe's hunters supporting them begin to scream and make noise to get the animals nervous, agitated, and mad enough to charge. The two hunters aim the tips of their lances to strike at the base of the goroc's neck. The force of their powerful charge allows the lances to penetrate deeply into the chest cavity. Once lanced, the goroc is mostly immobile and can then be killed with an arrow or two through the eyes into the brain," Taric replied to answer him, explaining the tactic used for a successful hunt, letting Thomas know the peril he'd be in without the advantage of their long guns.

"I didn't realize it was so risky. Jennifer told me not to risk my life recklessly. I'm sure that when my people come for us, she doesn't want to tell them I died hunting a dangerous animal. Maybe, I can use a bow on a smaller animal somewhere further down the grass-lands?" he asked with an excited expression clearly evident on his face.

"We can go hunting for small to medium-sized animals another day but not tomorrow. This will be the last chance to hunt a goroc as snow will be coming within the next few days. We need three gorocs to make your winter clothes. Your long guns will be the only chance to get three at once," Taric said and actually looked forward to going hunting with the humans in the morning.

Cooper's AI persona dropped the *Maleficent* out of warp as it reached the estimated rendezvous point in space to encounter the *Chameleon* sailing on its one-hundred-thirty-seven-year voyage toward Opalla. "Sensors have detected the *Chameleon* approaching our position. I'm hailing the ship's AI," the hologram informed Carter, who was sitting behind the computer console in the captain's ready room, watching the vids streaming from the Earth.

"Shit! The whole world is going to crap!" Carter exclaimed angrily, while forcefully pushing the chair back with his legs from the desk. Carter walked onto the bridge to see the *Chameleon* approaching his ship on the view screen.

"I alerted the *Chameleon's* AI, we have an emergency situation aboard ship and intend to dock. It has complied with our request, we are free to dock with it," Cooper's hologram informed him and waited for its next command.

"Proceed with docking," Carter ordered the AI, standing beside the captain's chair, watching the two starships maneuvering into position as they closed the distance between them. With precise movement, the AI's aligned their ships and slowly closed in for a successful docking with the central core of the starship's superstructure.

With a dull thud and slight shake of the floor, Cooper announced, "Docking is complete. The *Chameleon* is now ready to be boarded."

"Maintain ship systems until I'm back from the *Chameleon*," Carter said as he walked out of the bridge into the empty corridor.

Carter rode the lifts connecting the decks throughout the ship and walked through their empty corridors until he finally boarded a lift that carried him down to a narrow corridor leading to a pressurized docking port, which locked the ships securely together. "Open the airlocks," Carter demanded and waited impatiently for the AI to open the doors. "Hurry up!"

Once the doors opened, Carter stepped onto the colonial starship and realized the docking port opened into a featureless gray corridor, centrally located between the starship's forward flight deck and the ship's propulsion systems in the aft. Seeing no markings on the wall indicating forward or aft directions, he began walking briskly down the wide main corridor of the mile-long starship toward two of four hibernation-bay access doors, one on each side of the starship's central core, seeking a door labeled "RA7500-RA10000."

Walking near the end of the wide corridor, Carter approached a door and read it's white-stenciled labeling "RF00001-RF25000" and cursed loudly. "Shit! Just my fucking luck, I go the wrong way! Damn it!" He stood looking back down the corridor to the aft end of the ship's central core and as he began walking back the way he'd come, Carter cursed once more. "Shit!"

Twenty minutes later, he was standing next to the access panel for door RA7500-RA10000. Holding his breath, Carter pressed his hand with an open palm against a print identification screen, aware it would alert the *Chameleon*'s AI. Instantly, the hologram image of the AI's Cooper persona appeared to stand next to him and say. "Access to hibernation bays is restricted to ship's officers only."

Carter ignored what it said and replied, "For the glory of the charter."

Cooper's hologram flickered in the air as the code phrase activated a dormant program hidden within its matrix and severed the AI's loyalty programming. Carter knew he succeeded when the AI spoke. "Captain, what are your orders?"

"Open the door and initiate awakening procedures for hibernation pods RA9823 through RA10000," Carter ordered, walking over to the center as the heavy door began to split open in the center and slowly slide into the walls. When the halves moved wide enough to walk through, Carter stepped into the bay as automatic lights began illuminating the twenty-five hundred hibernation pods aligned in precise rows within the interior.

One hundred seventy-seven hibernation pods suddenly activated as auto docs within the pods began reviving the sleepers within them. Movement caught Carter's attention as the hibernation pods rose to a forty-five-degree angle while the canopy retracted out of the way behind the pod, leaving the sleeper to slowly awaken and step into the future. Carter stood beside pod RA10000 and waited for his king to awaken and reclaim the throne to the empire the usurper Hendricks had stolen from his family. Carter looked at his king's familiar features, ingrained into his mind by staring at photos and vids over the years as he grew up. Alexander hadn't aged as his plan unfolded to create this moment. He was a tall, thin man in his midthirties with short coal-black hair, a narrow, elongated face, and thick bushy eyebrows above his eyes and a short stubby nose. It was clear, Alexander was not a handsome man, but Carter believed, behind the face was the mind of the most creative military tactician alive.

Alexander's eyes opened to see a young man's unfamiliar face looking at him. "Who are you?"

"Carter, a humble servant, my king," Carter answered, in awe of the man who lay in the pod before him. "You have succeeded. I have brought you a gift, the starship *Maleficent*."

Alexander's mind was still groggy from the effects of hibernation but understood him and smiled wickedly as he lay in the pod before replying in a hoarse whisper to the charterist agent, "Well done."

The morning greeted the three hunters as they stood outside the barricade with an overcast sky mixed with hues of pale-white to dark-gray clouds. A gentle mist fell softly around them as they moved through the trees toward the herds. Taric, in the lead, kept them within the trees and abreast of the milling animals, so their scent would not alert the bulls of an unseen presence. Taric squatted to a stop in a gap between thickets of grass and berries. From his position, he could see through the trees, the animals of the grasslands quietly grazing on the last of autumn grass.

"Stay here. I'll be right back. I'm going to see where the bulls are roaming," Taric instructed Thomas and Kelly in a whisper as they crouched, holding their long guns tightly in their hands with nervous anticipation. Taric set the lance he had carried down on the ground and then began to crawl through the shrubs toward the edge of the grasslands.

Thomas watched as Taric crawled over the ground without making a perceptible noise that would alarm the animals and quickly disappeared from sight. Thomas, living the greatest adventure of his life, beamed a wide smile at Kelly and whispered in her ear with a twinge of nervousness in his voice. "The hunt is on!"

CHAPTER 24

Out in the Wilds

Taric moved easily and silently through the forest and down the gentle slope of the valley, always keeping abreast of the milling herds out on the grass. From a distance, he heard the savage roars of a pride of kessras and slowed his pace to a cautious walk as he neared the edge of the grasslands

An enraged goroc bellowing in pain with a broken hind leg was bravely trying to ward off multiple attacks upon its flesh while standing on three wobbly legs streaked with blood and dirt. A coordinated pride of five snarling predators swarmed around the overwhelmed and helpless beast. Watching the grim scene play out, Taric could tell the animal was weakening as its body swayed awkwardly with each vicious attack by the relentless hunters.

Weakened and exhausted from the fight while standing on faltering legs, the bull courageously swiped its thick horns toward a kessra leaping into the air. The bull's horn met the attacker in midleap, goring it deeply into the chest and was instantly flung to the side as the bull turned its head toward the others while trying to recover for the next attack.

The pride ignored their loss, instinctively sensing the bull could not defend itself much longer, and moved in for the kill. A pair of kessras kept their prey's attention by alternating positions in front of the bull. One would pace back and forth, growling and snarling with deadly intent as the other darted in close and then quickly backed away out of range of the bull's horns. The tactic allowed the remaining pair to attack from behind the goroc's head and bury their sharp teeth into the bull's thick leathery neck. Blood seeped out the sides of their clenched teeth as the pair reached out extending their front legs, digging their paws thick long claws deep into their prey's flesh. As a team, the kessras easily forced the suffocating goroc onto the grass. The pair of natural killers held on to their prey until the goroc was dead before releasing their hold and began to feed on its flesh. Once down, the other pair rushed in, sinking their massive claws into the underbellies soft flesh, ripping off large patches of skin and fur to bite into the warm blood-rich meat of their kill.

With an awareness of scavengers and predators would soon be drawn by the scent of fresh blood in the air, Taric slowly backed away into the trees and left the surviving kessras to gorge themselves on the kill. He moved quickly up the slope searching the herds for some gorocs outside the massed herd and close together. Taric was halfway back to where he left Thomas and Kelly when he spotted three adolescents near the outskirts of the herd. Looking back down the plain at the kessras feasting on the kill, he saw large goroc bulls moving toward the feeding pride in an effort to block them from the nearby herds. Having found the objects of his hunt, Taric raced back through the forest trees to rejoin his companions.

Kelly sat comfortably on the ground, leaning her back against a tree, patiently waiting for Taric to return from scouting out the gorocs' location. She was watching Thomas's facial features as he crouched beside a tree ahead of her. He seemed off and she wondered if there was something wrong but held her tongue and said nothing. She continued to watch him and noticed the animal sounds coming off the grasslands was a constant influx of unfamiliar noise to his senses. She could tell the sounds were unnerving him, and then suddenly, Thomas flinched and almost bolted when he heard a loud rustling of dry leaves coming from underneath the limbs of a nearby thicket. A fat, fully grown skike emerged from beneath the thicket of tangled limbs to quickly scurry away into the safety of another thicket of shrubs and prickly berry vines in search of its food.

Thomas turned away in embarrassment as he silently cursed himself for being so skittish. "Settle down, Tom, there's nothing creeping up on you," he quietly whispered as he peered through the trees trying to see something while hearing Kelly's lighthearted chuckles come from behind him. He then wished Jaxx had not stayed behind in the cave with Jennifer and little Trenna. He'd gotten too comfortable with the animal's guarding presence when he was outside the cave's stout barricade. His host had noticed his reliance on Jaxx to keep a watchful lookout. Taric told him that he must learn to use not just his eyes but all his senses if he wanted to stay alive on Planos.

He realized Taric was correct; he could not rely on Jaxx to live in this world; he must learn to guard himself when outside the safety of their cave. Taric had learned to train his eyes and senses since childhood to constantly scan the area around him. Always on the lookout for subtle movements within the thickets under the shade of the forest trees or out on the open grasslands. Any small movement could reveal a predator stalking prey as it followed a scent trail to its source. Thomas flinched slightly with every unfamiliar noise and realized he was out of his element on this world, and as his imagination toyed with his subconscious mind, he grew fearful.

Kelly was the first to see Taric crouched down low, moving swiftly through the trees and thickets. "There he is," she whispered quietly to Thomas with an excited smile while pointing her hand in the direction of his approach.

Thomas let out an audible sigh of relief, trying to calm his jitters as Taric fearlessly moved through narrow gaps between the thickets and trees at a steady pace toward his spot by the tree.

"You need to relax a little," he heard Kelly say while watching Taric quickly close the distance between them. Thomas knew Taric was completely in tune with the natural surroundings of his world, whereas he was not.

Taric came up to rejoin them where they waited. Kelly greeted Taric with an excited smile on her face filled with anticipation for the coming hunt while giving him a warning nod of her head toward Thomas.

Taric looked at Thomas and saw a ghostly paleness to his pink-ish skin as he nervously held a rifle tightly in his grip with white boned knuckles, revealing an obvious attack of nerves and lack of experience in the wilds. Taric looked at them with a calm, reassuring tone of voice and said, "There are no predators around us. Far down the plain, I saw a pride of five kessras attacking a goroc with a broken leg. The bull put up a proud fight and managed to gore one to death before falling to the others. Every scavenger and small predator in the area has smelled the blood in the air by now and is moving down the grasslands to fight and feast over the kessras' leftovers."

"Really?" Thomas cautiously asked while knowing Taric had noticed his uncertainty and nervousness but had the courtesy not to show it.

"Did you see some gorocs?" Kelly asked, wanting to move from the trees and out into the grasslands.

"Yes, three adolescents are grazing not far from here without any large bulls near them. Follow me, keep your eyes alert, and be as quiet as you can as you move through the forest," Taric quietly stated so as not to alert the nearby animals before beginning to lead them in a single file toward the gorocs they were to hunt.

The adolescents had moved up the plain, away from the gath-ering of scavengers drawn by the scent of warm blood. The gorocs stood on the edge of the rust-colored plain, eating long dry grass intermixed within the thickets of thorny vines and berries when the hunters approached, stooped low behind the foliage of a thorny tan-gled thicket of berries and grass.

Taric knelt down on a knee, waving his hand for Thomas and Kelly to join him. When they were all huddled together, Taric began to quietly whisper his instructions. "They've moved closer to us and away from the herd. That's good. Once you fire your guns, the herd will stampede. Do not panic. They'll be confused by the noise but will see the gorocs fall. The herd instinct is to run in the opposite direction of danger.

"Aim for their eyes. Thomas takes the left one, Kelly gets the one on the right, and I'll take the one in the center. We stand as one, and when I let my arrow fly, shoot your guns. Be prepared to back up my arrow, if need be. I'm not sure if it will work. Ready?"

"I'm ready," Kelly whispered with excitement and turned to Thomas.

"Sounds easy enough," Thomas replied nervously but held himself together by showing a slight grin on his flushed face.

Seeing they were ready and prepared, Taric notched his new arrow onto his bow. He hoped the arrow's thicker and stronger shaft would drive a new larger arrowhead deep into the goroc's brain. "Stand, aim and fire when my arrow flies," Taric said and slowly began to stand, guiding them to stand on a firm footing. Standing abreast of each other, Taric pulled his bow back to its fullest extent and concentrated on his target's eye. With the familiarity of a lifetime of practice, Taric held his breath to steady his aim and let his arrow fly.

Taric's arrow was followed a second later by the rifles loud reports as he quickly notched a second arrow to his bow. Taric instantly understood the advantages of a rifle over his bow. The bulls on the left and right were already dead and falling onto the ground when his arrow penetrated the eye socket a fraction of a second later, sinking deep into the brain cavity of his target. Taric had his bow up and ready to release a second arrow, only to relax his grip when he saw his bull crumple to the ground.

"We did it!" Kelly and Thomas yelled out as their targets lay dead on the grass. True to Taric's instructions, they watched the massive herd stampede down the slope in the opposite direction of the danger. The noise was deafening as thousands of animals thundered down the plain, panicked by the sudden blasts of gunfire.

An elated Thomas leaned his rifle to rest against a fallen log. "I'll get the poles for the hides, be back in a minute," he said before quickly disappearing into the trees.

Taric set his bow and quiver of arrows near the rifle Thomas had left behind leaning on the log, unaware the stampede had frightened the kessras away from their kill, scattering them deep within the forest in different directions.

"Now the work begins," he said to Kelly, pulling Jennifer's steel bladed knife from a sheath that was tied to his waist as he walked up to his goroc.

Kelly watched as he plunged his knife into the thick skin of the neck near the base. Slicing cleanly, he pushed the blade all the way around, severing the skin of the neck and head from the rest of the body. He then moved the knife from the neck quickly down the center of the animal's underbelly to the anus, spilling the bloody entrails onto the grass. From the anus, he sliced around the animal's tail before cutting the skin around the base of each leg, just above the massive hooves. Taric then completed the preparation for pulling the skin from the body, by cutting down the underside of each leg to the center.

Panting heavily from its exertions, a kessra rested under a thicket of tangled vines after running up the slope to higher ground, hiding from the wild hooves of the panicked herds. It sniffed the air, smelling the many lingering scents of the area's inhabitants. The kessra's sensitive nostrils detected a scent that was too powerful to ignore, the scent of blood, and it was much closer than the kill it was forced to abandon. Instinct compelled it to investigate the blood-rich scent. The kessra rose on strong muscular legs and began to follow the enticing aroma with its nose leading the way up the slope of the mountain forest. It plodded silently beneath the thickets on tough padded paws as it searched for the source of the enticing smell.

Thomas came out of the forest shade and stood at the tree line with the lances for the travois held firmly in his hands. In his excitement, he foolishly left without a weapon and was forced to be cautious walking back to rejoin Taric and Kelly, after having seen a pair of lycurs darting through the trees ahead of him.

Thomas stood looking around the clearing and didn't see the kessra peering at Taric and Kelly from beneath the cover of tangled vines. Their backs were to the forest as they worked skinning the gorocs. Thomas was about to shout out his return when a slight movement from beneath a thicket nearby caught his eye and stopped his voice cold. He stood transfixed as the deadly animal slowly backed away and disappeared into the cover of the forest and knew it was hunting.

Shaking off his shock, Thomas set the lances softly onto the ground without making any noise and then crept over to the log where his rifle lay. He knew the animal was near and hadn't noticed his presence as its senses were overwhelmed by the strong, pungent odor of fresh blood spilling onto the ground.

He reached for the rifle but only managed to knock it over and fall onto the ground behind the log out of reach, just as the kessra revealed itself once more. "Damn it!" he whispered under his breath while scooting closer to the log, reaching with outstretched hand and fingers for the bow and quiver of arrows. Selecting the new arrow Taric had made for the hunt, Thomas notched it to the bow and pulled it back to the fullest extent of the crude weapon.

Thomas remained quiet, kneeling on one knee while watching the animal intently. Aware it was driven by the smell of blood, he waited for the kessra to charge. It leaped silently out of the thicket with a swift burst of speed as Thomas rose to his feet, tracking the animal as it closed the distance to his friends. Sure of his aim, he let loose the arrow and watched it fly toward his target. The heavy arrow struck the charging kessra through the ribs, which reacted by piercing the air with a loud agonizing roar of pain. It tumbled to the ground in a tangled mass of legs and lay still on the ground with the arrow's tip and tail feathers exposed on both sides of the dead animal.

"Oh my God! That's too close!" Kelly exclaimed, frightened to death once again by one of the fearsome beasts. She then wondered if her luck would run out someday with these creatures if she chose to stay and live in this wild world.

A shocked but intrigued Taric stood staring down at the kessra with one of his new arrows sticking through the animal in utter fascination. He then turned to look back in the direction of the arrow's flight to see Thomas holding his bow forty paces away. It was a humbling experience, and Taric admitted to himself he'd been too harsh and judgmental toward Thomas. Without shame for admitting his wrongs against the man, Taric walked over to Thomas and embraced him within his arms while saying, "I was wrong for blaming you for the girl's action against Jennifer. You and your people will always be welcome to share the fire of my cave."

CHAPTER 25

Alexander

After spending twenty-two years in hibernation, one hundred seventy-seven people awakened to a new reality set in motion by Alexander, their king. Fueled by his vision of their future and the success of his plan, Alexander's devoted vassals boarded the *Maleficent* with the confidence and assurance that they would right the wrongs of the past and, within days, restore lawful order on Earth. As Alexander's vassals dispersed throughout the ship to their duty stations, they claimed the vacant quarters of the former crew without feeling any remorse, accepting their deaths as a necessary detail in the plan.

Alexander allowed the agent to lead the way to the bridge. They were followed by a large burly mute. He walked behind them at a respectful two steps back, which made Carter nervous as they walked down the corridor. Every time he glanced back at the large muscular bodyguard, the man held a bland, emotionless expression on his face. Carter knew he was a killer and kept his nervousness at bay by suggesting, "The captain's ready room and adjacent private quarters have been prepared for your arrival."

"Excellent," Alexander responded while walking beside the agent, barely listening as he droned on and on. While they traversed the corridors, Alexander tried to identify his location within the ship from memories of the design plans to no avail. Distracted by the fool who would not stop talking as they walked. Alexander was about to tell him to shut up so he could hear himself think, when he heard him finally say something of relevance.

"My king, you have succeeded beyond belief. The *Maleficent* is the first of your fleet. The empire decided to build starships in pairs but not to worry. The sister ship to this one is still under construction in space dock due to vital shortages of components necessary for the warp drive. Its completion date has been pushed back to an undetermined date. A third starship is in the initial stages of construction inside the dock vacated by the *Maleficent* and is years away from completion."

"You've done well. Together we will restore my family honor and regain our rightful place in the world. Thank you," Alexander replied and then asked, "What about Jennifer Hendricks? Did you succeed in docking with the *Fulcrum* and kill her inside the hibernation pod?"

"No, my king. The *Fulcrum* was destroyed inside star system WLF1954, around a planet called Planos, eighty-six years into its journey to Opalla. Jennifer Hendricks was the only survivor. The Tyrant's daughter still breathes on Planos, my king. Our agent failed to execute the girl after landing on the planet. She's dead. She was attacked and killed by a vicious animal native to the planet. It's all I was told about her death. However, we have the girl's location recorded in our ship's log. She will not be hard to find as winter is coming soon to her area.

"The *Maleficent*'s former captain is also marooned on the planet with her, along with two members of his crew. A doctor, who's of no importance, and the ship's first officer, Kelly Sterling. I had orders not to take the ship until she was aboard. She's a relation of yours and has betrayed your honor by siding with the empire against you. She was aboard during the purge but somehow managed to get into an escape pod and return to the planet," Carter answered truthfully, knowing he was not responsible for the missed opportunity to kill the Hendricks girl or the lucky escape of his king's betrayer.

"Well, no matter. We have plenty of time to finish up minor details. So tell me, who of the usurper's family is ruling my empire?" Alexander asked him, needing a name to direct his revenge onto.

"Empress Isabella Whitlock rules the empire. She's currently indisposed, recuperating from appendicitis surgery at a family retreat deep in the mountains outside of Seattle," Carter answered with the news reported on the vids of her well-being and whereabouts over the past two weeks.

"Little Izzy, that snot-nosed runt of a girl. She rules the empire?" Alexander scoffed as he remembered her as a homely, dull-witted child without imagination. "How in the hell did she get the throne?"

"She's very intelligent and has grown to be widely accepted by the people. I must confess, my king, she has turned everyone on Earth and in the colonies against you. Your family has disowned and denounced your right to rule the kingdom. They have decided to support Empress Isabella. All your personal assets have been impounded by the court. My king, the imperial court had the audacity to declare you an outlaw of the empire," Carter informed him as they reached the lift to the bridge deck.

"Outlaw!" Alexander exclaimed, laughing loudly at the audacious fool's outlandish label as he stepped into the lift. "Dumbasses, all of them. They declare me an outlaw because they're powerless to stop me. It's nothing more than a final act of a dying regime," Alexander added as the lift's door opened to a corridor curving around the outer rear wall of the bridge.

"This way, my king," Carter said, leading Alexander toward the bridge once more. After walking a short distance down the corridor, they stood at the door. When the door opened, Carter added with a proud smile of accomplishment. "King Alexander, I present to you the *Maleficent.*"

Alexander stepped over the threshold, feeling a euphoric elation over the success of his plan. He walked slowly over to the captain's chair and, without a word, took command of the ship by reclining comfortably in the chair. Carter stood beside Alexander watching him as his eyes gazed around at the empty duty stations and their consoles and spoke into the air. "For the glory of the charter," he said, speaking the charterist phrase, and then added, "Cooper, report."

Instantly, the AI's hologram persona appeared to stand beside Carter as it addressed the chair's new occupant. "What are your orders, Captain?"

Alexander looked back at his bodyguard and nodded slightly as he said to his charterist agent. "You've done very well in accomplishing your mission. I feel you deserve to be rewarded for the outstanding performance of your service."

Carter proudly replied to Alexander's gracious offer, "My king, service to you is enough. I don't deserve the gifts you wish to honor me with. I'm simply your servant. With you ruling the empire, my charterist brothers and sisters will finally hold our place within the empire."

"Oh, I agree. However, service and dedication to duty must be rewarded for this amazing accomplishment. You shall be the first to embrace the future of your brothers and sisters. Your service, my friend, must be rewarded!" Alexander exclaimed, keeping Carter's attention focused on him as his man quietly moved to stand closer and behind the charterist agent.

Alexander feigned a smile of genuine gratitude on his face and offered the charterist his hand to shake. Carter, feeling proud and honored by the gesture, stood tall beside his king and willingly clasped his hand into Alexander's open palm.

Suddenly, he felt Alexander's hand tighten unexpectedly hard around his wrist, crushing it in his grip, and before he could react, he was pulled off-balance to fall over both armrests of the chair. Looking into Alexander's eyes he knew, he'd been betrayed and was nothing more than an expendable pawn in his grand game. He felt the bodyguard's weight pressing down heavily onto his back as Alexander laughed wickedly seeing the fear of death forming on the man's face as his bodyguard quickly plunged a knife up into the base of the agent's skull.

Alexander let the body drop onto the floor and laughingly smiled in approval to his mute bodyguard. "My father taught me to never trust a charterist zealot when using their services. Use 'em and lose 'em, he'd always say. Today, I have honored his teachings and his memory by claiming this amazing starship."

Alexander glanced down at the body with indifference as it slowly bled out onto the floor in a congealing puddle of dark-red blood and ordered his mute in a calm, casual voice, "Take the body to an airlock and release it into the void. But before you return. Find someone to clean up this mess."

The hologram of the ship's AI stood motionless and silent until Alexander asked it. "What's the status of the ship?

"The *Maleficent* is fully operational, all systems are functioning within design parameters," the AI responded in its flat monotone voice.

"Anything on long-range scanners?" Alexander inquired as he began thinking about the next objective that was blocking him from reclaiming the empire, Isabella Whitlock.

"Long-range scanners are clear."

Alexander heard the AI's monotone response and then proceeded to give the cold, lifeless AI instructions. "Continue monitoring long-range scanners and keep us docked to the *Chameleon*. The airlock must remain available for passage between ships as there are some supplies in the *Chameleon's* holds I require.

"Inform the cafeteria staff to begin cooking meals for the crew if they haven't already done so. Have them send a steward to serve me in the captain's quarters when the food is ready. Inform all section leaders to get their people acquainted with the ship and settled in. I expect everyone to be ready for duty in twenty-four hours. Now, put the vids on the screen and leave me."

"Yes, Captain," the AI responded before fading away as the view screen on the bridge became alive with the images and sounds of Earth's resurging animal life back home.

After finishing his meal in his quarters and tired of watching the vids, Alexander went into the sleeping quarters, climbed on the soft bed, and let the solid food's vitamins begin replenishing the meager intravenous nourishment provided to his body during hibernation and went to sleep.

Alexander didn't know how long he slept when the AI's voice filled his bedchamber. "Captain, a starship is approaching our position."

At the same time, the science officer aboard the *Excalibur*, Ensign Sara Nichols informed sitting behind her station's console on the bridge. "Captain, our long-range scanners have picked up the *Chameleon* and the *Maleficent*."

"Drop us out of warp and come to a stop, Cooper," Captain Stamos ordered the AI piloting the ship.

"Shutting down warp drive and switching to impulse power. Manual control is restored," Cooper replied as the view screen lit up, showing a multitude of faraway stars shining brightly in the darkness of space.

"Red alert! Let's get a fix on their position. Magnify the view and begin live transmission of our cameras to Earth," Stamos ordered calmly from his chair. Red lights illuminated the ship's corridors as alarm klaxons sounded throughout, alerting the crew to their stations.

The magnified image on the view screen revealed the colonial starship *Chameleon* docked with the *Maleficent* as Isabella walked out of the ready room to the front of the bridge and faced the screen.

"Are we within hailing range?" she asked, turning to look at Captain Stamos sitting in his chair as Admiral Harrington stepped onto the bridge and walked up to the front and stood beside her.

"Open a channel," Stamos ordered his communication officer, who he saw had instantly obeyed. "Empress Isabella, the bridge is yours to command."

With a nod in acknowledgment, Isabella spoke with the confidence of experience that contradicted her young age. "Attention, *Maleficent* hijackers, stand down and surrender to the imperial starship *Excalibur*. Do so and your lives will be spared."

"Incoming transmission," a nervous communication cadet announced in a wavering voice.

Stamos turned toward the young girl at her console and calmly suggested with a reassuring smile. "On screen, please."

Alexander was alone on the *Maleficent*'s empty bridge sitting in the captain's chair, glaring at her. His hair hung down his head in a tangled mess and appeared as if he'd just awakened from sleep. Isabella smiled politely into the angry eyes staring back at her and asked, "I hope this isn't a bad time to meet?"

Alexander laughed and replied with a vain smirk. "Now or later, it matters naught to me. Little Izzy, you've grown up since the last time we met. I regret to say, time and growth have not been kind to you."

"Your insults are nothing more than a spoiled boy's weak attempt to intimidate. Please," Isabella drawled. "Spare me the privilege of listening to your warped wit and surrender the *Maleficent*. Do so, and I'll spare the lives of your followers."

"Oh, how magnanimous of you. But I think not Izzy. I'll tell you what. When I have something of importance to say, I'll give you a call," Alexander responded and then severed the connection between the ships.

"Cooper, uncouple from the *Chameleon* and slip behind it. Once were in position, lock all weapons on the *Chameleon* and hail the *Excalibur*," Alexander ordered the ghostly image of the AI.

On their view screen, Captain Stamos was the first to see the docking port uncouple and calmly remarked. "He's moving."

"What's he doing?" Admiral Harrington asked and then realized the *Maleficent* was positioning itself behind the colonial starship and shouted in alarm. "He's using the *Chameleon* as a shield!"

"Well, it looks like the mouse wants to play," Stamos remarked while sitting up straight in his chair, amused by the brash would-be emperor's antics.

"Captain, this is not the time for wisecracks," Isabella chided as the *Maleficent* disappeared behind the mile-long starship.

"I apologize, Empress. Sometimes, my thoughts just come out," Stamos replied, with a slightly contrite look of penance to his face.

"He's back," the communication cadet warningly announced. "Putting him on screen."

The view screen changed to see the *Maleficent*'s bridge occupied with Alexander's followers sitting or standing at their station's consoles, behind Alexander. But before he could say anything, Isabella cut him off. "Answer me this question. Where's the charterist, Lieutenant Carter?"

Alexander laughed hysterically after hearing the unexpected question and replied with gleeful abandon. "Why, he suffered an accident. Somehow, he found a knife stuck in the back of his skull."

"I see. Very well, as I've mentioned before, surrender the *Maleficent*, and I'll guarantee your lives and a fair trial with the best legal representation available. There's nothing to gain by continuing this madness."

"Madness! Madness!" Alexander loudly exclaimed. "This is not madness! It's revenge! Revenge for the pain and suffering my kingdom endured during the war. The Tyrant may have won the day and stole the throne, but the war is far from over."

"Why? It's history, a horrible part of our past. It's not my fault your great-grandfather was jealous of the Tyrant's father and his growing popularity within the kingdoms and had him assassinated. But it was a mistake because he was unaware of a family secret regarding the king's young son. The truth is, it was his action that propelled a schizophrenic psychopath with homicidal tendencies to the American throne! A political mistake, which cost the lives of over seven billion people worldwide. But the Tyrant is long dead. He no longer matters. We've moved on," Isabella informed Alexander, allowing the empire to know the real facts behind the event that started the war. After the Tyrant died, an agreement was made with the surviving Sterling family to ensure the signing of the treaty and the continuation of the Sterling royal bloodline.

"Oh, no! It matters a great deal, Izzy. I'll not be denied our revenge against the Tyrant's bloodline. I know Jennifer Hendricks is alive! You didn't think I knew that, did you?" Alexander sneered at her and added in his rage. "When we're done here, I'm going to kill her and end the bastard's bloodline forever."

"She's been dead for over ninety years in the hearts and minds of everyone in the empire," Isabella exclaimed and went on. "What does it matter if Jennifer Hendricks is alive? She has no relevance within the empire of today. She escaped her terrible father to begin a new life on Opalla as a pioneering girl. If the *Fulcrum* had been able to complete its flight to Opalla, her name would've been known upon arrival as Jennifer Collins."

"History is always written by the victorious. I'm sure you believe the words you say, but you're wrong because it's a lie." Alexander scoffed and then tired of the banting of words between them and declared with bravado. "Surrender to me now, Izzy. Or I'll kill everyone onboard the *Chameleon*."

"A moment please," Isabella begged, then turned her back to him and conferred with Harrington and Stamos in a hushed intense conversation. "Do either of you have any doubts about his willingness to destroy the ship?" Isabella asked the pair of men, whose judgment she had grown to value.

"None whatsoever! His hatred and need for revenge have consumed his soul," Harrington adamantly exclaimed. Having had come to the conclusion, Alexander was as crazy as the long-dead Tyrant.

"If we move, he'll blast the *Chameleon* apart. We can't let that happen! Empress, whatever it is you've got hidden up your sleeve, it's time to use it," Captain Stamos admitted, knowing he was powerless to stop Alexander's threat with a starship filled to capacity with innocent people in between them.

"Follow my lead," Isabella whispered and then turned back around and faced Alexander's leering, smug look of satisfaction on his face, believing he'd won. "Well, What's your answer, Izzy? Or should I make an example of the *Chameleon* for your continued defiance."

"No, please wait. There's no need for that." Isabella pleaded and then calmly stated to throw him off. "I chose the name *Excalibur* for this starship. I hoped the ancient name would inspire the brave knights chosen to fly this marvelous starship to conduct themselves worthy of King Arthur's legend. Warriors against our enemies and saviors of our weak and downtrodden people. I just wish Merlin was here to help me."

Instantly, from the *Excalibur*'s bridge, they saw the lights on the *Maleficent*'s bridge flicker, dim, and then brighten back to normal illumination. Alexander looked around the bridge with a confused look on his face and said in a high-pitched voice that cracked when he saw the Cooper AI's projection disappear.

"What the hell was that? Cooper! Report!" Alexander screamed, but nothing happened, and in the background, they could see Alexander's followers looking worriedly at one another.

"Allow me to introduce you to a little surprise I thought up. My wizard Merlin, reveal yourself," Isabella calmly stated as a holographic image in the likeness of the Tyrant appeared to stand next to Alexander. Isabella chuckled as she watched him leap out of the chair in sudden fright from the hologram.

"What the hell!" Alexander angrily yelled at her and then loudly ordered the Cooper AI. "Fire all weapons!" Nothing happened. The chameleon was still between the ships as long seconds passed until Alexander angrily ordered, "Switch to manual control and fire!"

Isabella calmly watched as Alexander, pushed his follower aside at the weapons station, and repeatedly pounded his fist on the console, trying to force the relay into firing.

"Merlin, instruct the AI on the *Chameleon* to proceed with its flight," Isabella ordered as Alexander continued to scream at his followers as the *Chameleon* powered up and began to sail away, leaving the *Maleficent* exposed to the *Excalibur's* weapons.

"You've no option but to surrender. Merlin has control of the ship. It's over, you've lost. For the lives of your people, I beg of you, surrender the *Maleficent* peacefully," Isabella implored, not wishing to sacrifice the lives of his followers.

"Get this ship back under our control!" he ordered his people on the bridge.

"The AI has locked us out. We can't get Cooper to respond," one of his men replied. Without hesitation, Alexander pulled a phaser and fired. Watching the faces on the bridge cringe away as he screamed. "Do what I ordered! Get the AI working!" All the while, waving the phaser erratically around the bridge, refusing to believe his perfect plan for revenge was slipping away.

Isabella knew she had to end this before Alexander killed another of his people on the live transmission being sent back to Earth. She underestimated his father's disturbing lifelong conditioning of Alexander's hatred for her family. When they saw on their screen, a warrior kneeling on one knee and say, "My king, the AI was to fly and fight this ship. We're soldiers, sworn to fight your battles on land. But we can't fix something we know nothing about. You must surrender."

Within a heartbeat, Alexander pointed his phaser and shot the brave man in the head as Isabella screamed, "Nooo!"

Alexander then turned around with wild eyes and looked at Isabella's shocked face and said, "You want me? Well then, come and get me, bitch!"

Tears streamed down Isabella's round plain face for what she must do. She slowly regained her composure, while wiping her eyes softly with a tissue handed to her by Admiral Harrington. Straightening her back, she faced the monster still glaring and taunting her on the screen.

"Alexander Sterling, you have been declared an outlaw of the empire. You're hereby charged with providing credits to fund charterist militant crimes for the last twenty-five years with the intent to spread civil unrest within the kingdoms of Earth. The number of crimes is still being tallied by the imperial court. You're also charged for treason against the empire for murder and stealing an imperial starship with the intention of inciting a war. How do you wish to answer these charges?" Isabella formally stated and waited for Alexander's reply.

Alexander's people fled after the killing leaving him alone on the bridge. His hands shook with rage as he stared at Isabella calmly waiting for his answer. Her smug face and honest remorse for the dead was infuriating to his senses. "As I said, come and get me, bitch!"

Isabella let the insult dissipate in the air as she refused to lose her composure and replied, "Surrender now or face the consequences of your actions."

On the screen, Alexander held out his hand, holding it stiffly out with a clenched fist and slowly raised his middle finger pointing it straight up and loudly screamed, "*Fuck you!*"

"Very well," Isabella calmly said before turning her back to him and looked at Admiral Harrington standing beside her. She grasped his hand for support and asked him to switch to an outside view by saying, "A faraway view will be less graphic for young viewers whose parents may have them watching."

With a heaviness clearly heard in her voice, Isabella turned around and faced the screen once more. She then declared, "Alexander Sterling, I hereby sentence you to death. May God have mercy on your eternal soul. Merlin, purge the *Maleficent*."

Instantly, every door and airlock built into the ship opened to the vacuum of space. On the screen, bodies rocketed out of the ship as the vacuum sucked them out into the void.

"End transmission," Captain Stamos sadly stated as Isabella crumpled in Harrington's strong arms. He lowered her slowly onto the floor as she cried for the lives of Alexander's people she was forced to take.

"Captain Stamos, take some cadets over to the *Maleficent* in the shuttle. Take whomever you need to fly our starship home," Harrington quietly requested of his young friend as Isabella sobbed mournfully in his arms.

Captain Stamos respectfully rose from his command chair and replied to his mentor and friend, "*Excalibur* is yours, sir." Then walked off the bridge with the intention of asking Isabella to go out on a date with him when she returned home.

"Cooper," Harrington called to the AI. "When the shuttle returns, set a course for Planos." He then gently lifted Isabella into his arms and carried her to the bedchamber for some needed rest.

CHAPTER 26

Home

Winter snows covered half of the northern hemisphere of Planos when the *Excalibur* entered orbit around the planet. Admiral Harrington stood beside Isabella sitting comfortably in the captain's chair, a privilege Harrington insisted upon whenever she walked onto the bridge. "It's beautiful," Isabella remarked as the ship orbited the planet, taking in the planet's rich hues of vibrant color with awestruck eyes.

"According to the records transferred over from the *Maleficent*, it's the middle of the night at the location we have for your brother. The location is a high grassland at the base of a mountain range. It's wintertime down there. Snow parkas and boots have been loaded onto the shuttle," Harrington informed her, knowing she was anxious to see her brother, Thomas.

"Have we performed a geological survey of the area?" Isabella asked, wanting to know if there was an active volcano near her brother's location.

"A full scan of the surface will be completed by the time we leave orbit," Harrington answered and then asked, "Why the interest in the survey?

"Simple curiosity is all," Isabella replied with a simple smile on her face as she looked up at her tall friend. "Thank you, Admiral."

"For what?" Harrington asked, thrown off guard by her thanks.

"You've been very kind to me during this entire ordeal. I can't thank you enough for your faith and support. What can I do to show my appreciation for your service?" Isabella asked him as he stood beside her, looking at the world below them.

"Empress, I've been in your family's service my entire adult life. Since you're asking, I'd like to retire from active duty. But! I don't want to retire and disappear into obscurity. I'd like to do something worthwhile with the remaining years of my life. I'd like to be head-master of Fleet Academy," Harrington replied with a gentle smile for the young woman he'd grown to love and respect.

"Granted," Isabella happily replied while squeezing his hand fondly. "You'll make a splendid headmaster."

The sun's rays had barely cleared the mountain peaks when Jaxx raised her head off the sleeping furs and growled low in her throat while staring at the heavy hide pegged to the cave wall. Jennifer awoke to hear Jaxx's low growl and, in the dim light of the fire, flashed her a hand signal to be quiet. Jaxx obeyed but continued to stare at the hide, listening. Jennifer sat upright in the furs, leaned forward, held her breath, and listened intently to the muted sounds of the land's nocturnal activity. Above it all, Jennifer heard from beyond the heavy goroc hide and the barricade the faint voice of someone speaking.

"Did you hear that?" Isabella said, standing in a snow-covered clearing outside a barricade of poles lashed together with wide strips of tough leather.

"I didn't hear anything," Harrington replied and then asked, "What did you hear?"

"It sounded like an animal's deep low growl, but I don't hear a thing now," Isabella answered while looking at the stout and effective barrier built to deter predators.

Jennifer jumped up from their sleeping furs, flinging them off Taric sleeping soundly on their bed of soft, warm furs. She giggled and smiled as he flinched with the sudden chill of cold air on his naked body. Jennifer leaned over him as he awakened, shivering and frantically searching with a waving hand for a fur to cover himself with when he heard Jennifer say in an intense whisper, "Taric, get dressed! I think there are people outside the barricade."

Before Taric could react to what Jennifer had whispered, from outside they heard an unfamiliar female voice say, "Hello? Is anyone home?"

"Jaxx, go get Thomas," Jennifer instructed the attentive lycur and watched her companion slip through the hide hanging over the opening to the storage cave and disappear.

Dressing quickly, Jennifer checked on Trenna sleeping comfortably within her fur-lined basket and decided to let her sleep until she wakes normally. Once dressed, Taric showed no signs of having just awakened from sleep; instead, he appeared to have been awake for hours, whereas she did not.

Jaxx bounded into the cave, followed by a sleepy and agitated Thomas, who entered the cave struggling to get his shirt on. He watched Taric smiling as he unpegged the goroc hide and let it slip to hang to the side of the entrance when he clearly heard his sister's voice. "Hello, can you hear me?"

"Izzy?" Thomas quietly asked, dumbstruck and astonished his sister would travel so far to find him as he rushed to the barricaded door yelling her name. "Izzy!"

Isabella and Harrington instantly recognized Thomas's familiar voice from inside the barricade as a flicker of light could be seen between the cracks of the logs and a figure moving quickly to the door. Isabella recognized her brother between the cracks as the door was flung open and she looked into the eyes of her bearded brother's face and cried with joy. "Oh, thank you, God! Thomas, you're alive. I was so worried. Oh my God! You're alive and safe."

He wasn't listening as he wrapped his arms around Izzy and held her tightly to his chest and cried with her. By then, everyone had dressed and begun to file out of the barricade and greet the arrivals. The shock of seeing Empress Isabella and an admiral of the Imperial Fleet standing outside the cave brought Dr. Mencia and Commander Sterling to stand at attention and salute the powerful dignitaries.

Jennifer, with Jaxx at her side, stood leaning against a smooth boulder, holding in her arms, snuggled warmly in a fur, little Trenna, who had awakened with Thomas's shout. Taric stood on the opposite side of her with an arm wrapped around Jennifer's waist in a protective stance, when he heard Jennifer whisper, "Taric, my love, relax. I'm in no danger."

Hearing Jennifer behind him, Thomas broke his embrace with his sister and said with an expression of great joy, "Taric and Jennifer, I'd like to introduce Empress Isabella Whitlock and Admiral Harrington."

The entire time she held on to Thomas, Isabella was looking at Jennifer, beaming her a smile of gratitude and joy. "Please, no titles. Call me Izzy. We're family after all," she said happily holding on to her brother's hand, afraid to let go, lest he disappear once again.

Isabella slowly approached the young couple, nodding toward the fleet officers as she crossed the short distance.

Jennifer remembered Thomas saying that his sister was plain looking, but she disagreed as she looked at her smiling face so filled with joy, she thought Izzy was beautiful. Then unexpectedly, Izzy stepped up and kissed her on the cheek and whispered in Jennifer's ear. "Thank you so much."

Taric relaxed, seeing the mood of the strangers, and suggested in perfect English, "Why don't we move inside, where it's warmer."

"Yes, please come inside," Jennifer said a bit flustered by the unexpected kiss and led the way through the barricade's door with Jaxx walking at her side.

Harrington waited for everyone to enter but noticed Taric curiously staring at him, never having seen a man with skin the color of night. Then he surprisingly asked, "Are you from Earth or another world like mine?"

Harrington flashed a wide smile and kindly replied, "I'm from the Earth. Our home has a variety of skin tones of people from many cultures. My name is Steven."

"Taric," he replied, holding out his hand as human custom dictated.

Steven clasped his dark hands over Taric's copper-hued skin and gave it a friendly shake. "It's a pleasure to meet you."

"Please, come inside," Taric said with a warm smile, instantly liking the tall dark man.

During the journey to Planos, Isabella imagined the harsh conditions and danger her brother would endure marooned on a primitive world, but it was not the case as she looked around the interior of the cave. She didn't expect to see her brother wearing warm fur clothing and in good health. The cave was not what she expected. Soft furs covered the entire area except around the central firepit, and a huge supply of firewood stacked neatly against the back wall. It was obvious they could not all sleep in this cozy little cave and asked, "You don't all sleep in here? Do you?"

Thomas laughed and looking to Jennifer, he asked, "Mind if I give her a tour of your home?"

"Go ahead. Kelly and I will get something warming in the fire for breakfast," Jennifer answered with a warm smile.

"No, I haven't met everyone yet. I can't be so rude to take a tour of someone's home without meeting this cute little darling," Izzy said with a warm, gentle smile as she knelt to her knees, ignoring the large black animal lying on its side with legs curled protectively around the child wrapped in warm fur.

Taric could tell the women wanted to be alone and suggested to Steven and Thomas to follow. "Let me show you around. I think you'll be amazed," Taric said and pulled the tall man through the hide into the storage cave.

Jennifer beamed with pride for her baby as Isabella saw her cousin flash a hand signal to the animal as the men left. Without hesitation, Jaxx rose and went to her sleeping furs and lay down.

"Impressive training. What's is it?" Izzy asked as she knelt beside the baby with Jennifer kneeling on the other side of the soft bundle.

"Izzy, meet our daughter Trenna. Jaxx is known as a lycur, this world's version of a wolf," Jennifer answered as she removed her baby's fur wrap to show her off.

"Oh, you're so beautiful, just like your mother," Izzy cooed, although surprised by Jennifer's choice of a name for her baby. Looking down on her newest relation, Izzy softly asked, "Can I hold her? It's been years since I held a baby in my arms."

Jennifer happily handed her daughter over to Izzy's waiting arms. Izzy instantly began to sway from side to side, rocking little Trenna in her arms. "Trenna is an interesting choice of name. Please don't misunderstand me, Trenna is a beautiful name for her but an intriguing choice coming from you with your background," Isabella inquired in a casual tone expressing her interest without judging her.

Jennifer answered as she assisted Kelly at the fire with their morning meal. "She's named after Queen Trenna Sterling of the European kingdom. She was my Aunt Ella's secret lover long before her marriage. It was a political union she could not avoid. She never loved her husband. In her eyes, he was as bad as the Tyrant. Trenna was the one who provided Ella with the documents for my parents' change of identity and mine as well. I'd be dead if not for her. It's the least I can do to honor her memory."

"I thought as much," Izzy sadly replied, knowing she didn't know of the consequences Queen Trenna Sterling suffered after committing treason against her husband.

Jennifer saw the look in her eyes and understood the sudden sadness reflected in her voice. "She was killed, wasn't she?"

"Yes, before the Tyrant's death, which was roughly twenty years after the *Fulcrum* left Earth. Your aunt Ella and the Tyrant had a really intense fight. She was so angry and bitter at him for ruining the family, she confessed to planning your escape." Isabella paused, not sure if she should go on as she saw the emotional impact her narration was having on her. "You can imagine the rest," Isabella sadly added, scorning herself for ruining this happy moment.

"No, please. Tell me, I've been hiding all my life, I can't hide any longer. I need to know the truth of what happened," Jennifer softly pleaded to her, knowing there may never be another chance to speak privately.

"Very well. After beating Ella until she confessed every detail of your escape, the Tyrant, out of pure hatred and spite, informed his rival of his wife's betrayal before taking a sword and removing Ella's head as if he were a samurai warlord.

"Trenna's husband wasn't as gracious in granting a quick death. Trenna Sterling's death was broadcast throughout his kingdom. Out in the center of the palace lawn, she was stripped naked and lashed repeatedly with a whip until her body was nothing but torn bloody flesh. She was then tied to a stake and was set ablaze. Her husband laughed and made crude jokes the entire time of her torment, hearing her agonizing screams with an expression of great joy on his face during the entire ordeal. I'm truly sorry, Jennifer," Isabella cried as the emotional impact hit her in the telling as it did for her innocent cousin.

"So many people have died because of me. It would've been better if I was never born," Jennifer cried, feeling an overwhelming sense of guilt descend upon her as if she were an accomplice to the killings.

"No! No, never say that! Your life matters more than you know. Believe it or not, because of you. The last lingering vestiges of the great war is going away. Jennifer, your life exposed a conspiracy of manipulating the vids and kept our society on edge by using the charterist militants' hatred after the Tyrant's death to keep the peace on fragile ground. Alexander was hoping to engulf us in another useless war. People on Earth and the colonies are rejecting the concept of war as a united species for the first time in our recorded history. They're rejoicing Alexander failed and are truly happy you're alive," Isabella responded, letting her determine within her soul how to move forward with her life.

Little Trenna began to squirm in Izzy's arms. She handed her over to Jennifer so she could feed her baby and said kindly, "I envy you. I so want to have a child someday."

"You will. I'm sure of it," Jennifer said as she guided Trenna to a heavy breast.

"Between us," Jennifer confided, letting Izzy and Kelly in on an observation she had about Thomas. "Although Thomas loves you and missed you during his time here. I think he's reluctant to leave."

"What's he been doing while here?" Izzy asked, wanting to know how he spent his time.

She was instantly answered by Kelly's enthusiastic reply. "He's been cataloging the various animals living around here in his mind. Every evening, he taps into Taric's enormous wealth of knowledge to learn the habitats and instinctual characteristics of the animals, in order to determine if a similar animal exists on Earth. He has an impressive list already, but to do the job right, he needs a lab."

"And you?" Isabella asked her, aware by Kelly's enthusiastic answer and suggestion that she was attracted to her brother. "What do you want?"

"Thomas has been studying this world's animals and the ecosystem that supports them in the wild. A few simple conveniences would improve things a great deal. But for the most part, this is a life free of the complexities of modern living. I'd stay and help Thomas achieve his dream if he didn't feel so obligated to his duty to you," Kelly bluntly answered, knowing she hit the truth of their relationship.

"I see your point, and I'm aware of his passion all too well. But I need and trust his judgment. I don't know if I can let him go. Thomas keeps me humble," Isabella honestly admitted, knowing she relied too much on her brother and, by doing so, sidelined his scientific ambition. She then decided to make amends by telling him to go and live the life of his choice.

"Well, that's enough girl talk," Jennifer said softly after getting a big burp from Trenna before putting her down in her fur-lined bedding. "Now, let me show you around my home," she said with her openly delightful smile. Isabella then heard Jennifer say with an infectious laugh. "I like to call my home's decor, Neanderthal chic."

ABOUT THE AUTHOR

Mr. Frame lives a quiet retired life in Mt. Vernon, Washington, with his wife, Elynne. Only the story matters! As an author, he writes only to share his imagination, while hoping the readers can lose themselves within the story and bond with the characters while the story unfolds. When he's not writing, he spends his time walking wooded trails with his dog, working in his garden, or fishing the local lakes and rivers.

CPSIA information can be obtained
at www.ICGtesting.com
Printed in the USA
FSHW012227100321
79363FS